Jacksonville JUDAS

outskirts
press

Jacksonville JUDAS

A Novel

SUE ANDREWS

outskirts
press

Outskirts Press, Inc.
http://www.outskirtspress.com

ISBN: 978-1-9772-3518-3

Library of Congress Control Number: 2020920357

Outskirts Press and the "OP" logo are trademarks belonging to Outskirts Press, Inc.

PRINTED IN THE UNITED STATES OF AMERICA

To all my friends in the South,
especially the late Tina Sheree Baisden

TABLE OF CONTENTS

ACKNOWLEDGMENTS

I'd like to acknowledge the California Writers Club, especially the Inland Empire Branch, without whose assistance I would never have become a writer.

I'd also like to thank my Tuesday night critique group, consisting of Libby, Judy, Jim G., Drew, Jim K., Millie, and Susan. These were the special authors who helped me in my journey to becoming more than a writer but a published author.

To Libby and Kathryn, who agreed to be my beta readers. I'd also like to thank Neil Nevills, CPA, Kathleen Flannery, attorney at law and Randal Hannah, attorney at law, with whom I had the pleasure of discussing portions of my novel. They generously gave of their time to assist in the trial chapters with their legal expertise.

Finally, to my husband, Ken, who has supported me daily on my journey to create dreams bigger than myself.

Judas
Traitor: One who betrays under the guise of friendship

Chapter One

THE LETTER

*M*egan Briscoe arrived at the municipal building in downtown Manhattan with her stomach in a knot. Several attempts to reach her father had gone straight to voicemail. The routine of conversation before work had bonded their father-daughter relationship since her mother's death. It was after she'd moved from Florida to New York to practice law. His calls always brought her solace.

Where is Dad? Something's wrong. When she reached her desk at the DA's office, she dialed again with the same results. Not knowing what else to do, she called her good friend, Brittney, her childhood friend in Jacksonville, the daughter of her dad's business partner.

"Brittney?" Megan said. "I can't reach Dad. He's not picking up at the house."

"Oh?" Brittney paused. "The police haven't contacted you yet?"

"The police? No. Why?"

"Are you sitting down?"

"Brittney." Megan's stomach churned again, and she raised her voice. "What's happening?"

"I hate to be the one to tell you, but Dad found your father slumped over his desk this morning."

"What?" Megan found it hard to form the words. "He's all right, isn't he?"

"Sorry, hon," her best friend said. "Your father must have died late last night. At least that's what the police told Dad."

"Oh my God!" Megan felt like she'd been kicked in the gut. She couldn't catch her breath, and her throat closed.

"Megan? Megan!"

"Can't talk. Give me a minute."

"Of course. Call me back when you are able."

Megan's dad, Michael Briscoe, had been her biggest supporter her whole life. She thought about how hard he'd worked to put her through law school at Columbia. Now she felt as if she'd abandoned him. She called Brittney back.

"I don't understand," Megan said. "My father was in excellent health."

"I know," Brittney said. "I just saw him the other day when I popped in their office. Everyone here is in a state of shock." She paused. "Hey, want me to check out some flights for you? You can stay with us if you don't want to stay at your dad's, and—"

"This is insane," Megan interrupted, not hearing a word of Brittney's other offers. "Sorry, hon. What did you say?"

Brittney repeated. "I'll get some flight options for you. And think about staying here if you'd like."

"Thanks for the offer, Brittie," Megan said through her tears. "That's sweet of you. You can check into those airline schedules, if you'd like, but right now I need to get off the phone."

"Sure thing," her friend said.

"My mind is spinning," Megan said. "Let me get a hold of Erick and think this through. Thanks, Brittie. I'll get back to you."

As soon as Megan hung up, the phone rang again. She knew it would be the police. The pain in her stomach had moved up toward her neck and head. Her migraines came at stressful moments, and she felt one coming. She rubbed her temples with her thumbs to try and soothe the ache away. But her attempts to fight the migraine weren't working.

The police told her what she already knew plus the fact her father's body had been taken to autopsy.

She got off the phone, finding it difficult to control herself. Memories of her mom's death and now her father's passing made her want to throw up. She walked from her desk and closed her office door. She sat in her chair, turned it around, and tried to call Erick. She didn't want anyone to see her cry. When he didn't answer, she grabbed some tissues and let go the flood of tears. She imagined herself turning into a giant bird soaring out her office window, flying down to rescue her dad in Jacksonville.

She tried phoning her fiancé, Erick, one more time, but his line went straight to voicemail. Not being able to contact him upset her more. She needed his warmth and touch. After a few minutes, she pulled herself together. She needed to tell her boss but felt compelled to stop at the ladies' room first. She felt a wreck and must look it.

She looked in the ladies' room mirror. Her face had become a black mask of uncontrolled mascara. Her eyes needed washing, her nose needed powdering, and her lips a touch of color. She rehearsed in the mirror what to tell her boss. It would take her a few minutes to get to his second-floor office.

When she got there, the door was open. "Mr. Marchman?" Megan said as she knocked. "May I come in?" She saw him lift his head from his desk and wave. She walked over to his desk.

"I just received a call from Florida. My father has died. I need to leave for Jacksonville as soon as possible."

"I'm sorry for your loss, Ms. Briscoe," he said. "I think you have some vacation time coming, don't you? Take what you need. I'm sure Erick and the others can cover for you."

"Thanks, Mr. Marchman," she said as she turned around to leave. She thought Mr. Marchman took her bereavement request well and was glad he didn't ask a lot of questions.

It took her the rest of the morning to put her business affairs in order. While taking care of some calls, she remembered something odd her father had once told her. "Should anything happen to me, please call my friend, Wade Nevlin."

She called Brittney again.

"Hey, Brittie," Megan said. "I just remembered something Dad told me. For the past year, all he ever talked about was his new friend, Mr. Wade Nevlin. They'd become fishing buddies. Dad always talked with excitement whenever he went out on Nevlin's boat. Could you please get his phone number for me and call me back?"

"No problem," Brittney said. "How're ya holding up?"

"I guess you could say, I'm taking it in baby steps. I feel like I'm sleepwalking, and this is all a dream."

"Take care, kiddo. Here's the flight options you asked for.

I'll call you back later."

Megan hung up and went back to the second floor looking for Erick. When she couldn't find him, she put a note on his desk and left the building midday. She took a cab home like usual, only alone. Passing Central Park from Midtown to their apartment on the Upper West Side made her cry. She and Dad always jogged there whenever he visited. She didn't want to think about it and closed her eyes.

Megan didn't know when she would return, so she booked a flight for the next morning with an open-ended return ticket. Spending one last night with Erick would at least be comforting, she thought. Erick, her college sweetheart, and she had recently gotten engaged. They'd achieved the careers they wanted, had some serious talks about marriage, but never got around to a confirmed date.

When Megan arrived at the apartment, she opened the door hoping to find Amelia, her cat, waiting for her. Megan had come home earlier than usual, so she had to look for her.

"Amelia?" Megan said, in a singsong voice. "Where are you? I need a hug."

After finding the cat, she grabbed her off the floor, held her close to her heart, and gave her a comforting belly rub. The phone rang.

"Glad I caught you," Brittney said. "I have that number you wanted."

"Thanks, Brittie. You're a lifesaver." She put down the cat and grabbed the pen and notepad on the sideboard. "What is it?"

After Brittney gave her the number, she said. "Hey! Did you know your dad's friend was an attorney?"

"No, Dad never mentioned that. However, I'll be arriving

5

in Jacksonville late morning. Hope to see you then and Mr. Nevlin too."

"Okay. See you then. Hugs."

After hanging up, Megan walked into the bedroom and slipped into some casual clothes. She went back into the den and poured herself a glass of Châteauneuf-du-Pape. She looked at the number written on the pad of paper and dialed.

"Hello," the woman said. "Wade Nevlin's office. Sally speaking."

"My name is Megan Briscoe. May I speak to Mr. Nevlin, please?"

"Hold on. I'll put you through."

"Wade Nevlin speaking," the attorney said.

"This is Megan Briscoe. My father—"

"Say no more, Miss Briscoe," he said. "I've been expecting your call. It's been all over the news. So sorry for your loss. Your dad was a great guy."

"Thanks. Dad spoke highly of you too. He so enjoyed your fishing trips, although he never mentioned you were an attorney."

"Yes, I wrote up two trusts for your dad," he said. "Since this is your first time hearing about this, I think it best you read these documents before coming down. I can overnight them. There's also a private letter from your dad. Where would you like me to send them?"

"Mail them to my office. It'll get there faster. I can swing by for them on my way to the airport. Thanks, Mr. Nevlin."

"Please call me when you get into town, whenever it's convenient."

"I will," she said. "Thanks again."

The news of Michael's death had spread around the NY DA offices and Erick had found Megan's note. On his way home, he picked up Chinese takeout from their favorite restaurant around the corner. He thought the food surprise might ease her pain.

"Hi, honey!" Erick said as he opened the front door. "I brought egg rolls and moo shu pork."

Before Erick came home, Megan had been thinking about the future she had lost with her dad. Even her favorite dish from Mr. Chen's couldn't cheer her.

"Poor Daddy," Megan sobbed. "How could this have happened?" She ran to Erick and threw her arms around his waist. She buried her head into his chest while he held the bagged food. She looked up into his comforting eyes. Megan always thought of him as irresistible. She loved his slight twist of curl that often fell on his forehead when he bent to kiss her. "Now Daddy will never be able to walk me down the aisle."

"Oh, hon," Erick said, as he put the food on the dining room table. With hands free, he gave her a tighter embrace. "We'll get to our wedding soon. I promise. What would you like me to do? Go with you?"

"No, sweetheart," she said. "Not sure if Mr. Marchman would allow it, anyway. I'm sure I can take care of myself. You're needed here in New York. We'll see what happens. I'm sure if everything's in order; like Dad once told me, it'll be quick and easy. I'm the only child. Everything will be left to me."

"Okay. But if you change your mind, you know I'll be on the next flight down."

She wiped away a tear. "I know. Now, let's eat. Thanks for bringing me the moo shu."

7

After dinner and finishing off the wine, Megan dozed in her fiancé's arms. Amelia curled in a ball on her lap. They all fell asleep on the sofa. The next morning, Megan woke up in their bed, grateful Erick had moved and undressed her from the night before.

She took a shower, had a quick bite to eat, and packed a suitcase. She stopped by the office and retrieved the certified envelope as planned. In the taxi, she opened the overnight package and found four items. A professional letter from Mr. Nevlin with two trusts and a standard white envelope marked, "For Your Eyes Only." She recognized Dad's handwriting and opened it.

If you are reading this, my darling, it can only mean one thing. Someone has succeeded in killing me. For the last several months, I thought I was sick due to something I ate. My pains were intermittent. The doctor checked me out and said everything was fine. Later I lost the stamina for my daily run. I couldn't figure out why I started to lose weight. At first, I was able to keep my food down but then couldn't eat much. Recently, I've suspected it must be someone with access to the refrigerator in the executives' office, because the pains would stop when I didn't eat lunch there. When I did, the pains continued.

Megan put the letter down and stopped reading. She didn't know what to think about her dad's words. Was it just due to poor refrigeration in the office lounge or something the doctor missed? Why hadn't Dad mentioned this to her before?

She couldn't believe she'd lost her dad so close after her mother's passing. He had been her rock. It was fall of 1987, and she hadn't seen her dad since Christmas when she flew home. Last June, her father made an excuse to not visit her in New York and he didn't want her to fly home. He said it was due to business and didn't reschedule.

Could his suspicions be true? Did someone try to kill him and succeed? Everybody loved him. Could it have been a heart attack? Jim Fixx, the famous long-distance runner, had died of a heart attack in his fifties. Could the same thing have happened to her father? It wasn't like Dad to think someone might harm him.

While waiting to board at the airport, she had time to think about everything Brittney had offered. She called her.

"Brittie, I decided to get a rental car," Megan said. "It's no problem. As for staying with you, Steve, and the kids, I don't want to impose. Don't worry about me staying alone at the house. I'll be fine."

"Okay," Brittney said, explaining she would be happy with whatever decisions Megan made. "But let me know if you change your mind."

"Sure thing," Megan said, and added, "Hugs," their special way to say good-bye.

The three-hour flight to Jacksonville International landed on time. She was thankful the young man sitting next to her slept the whole way. It avoided small talk. After picking up her rental car, she drove downtown and stopped at Briscoe-Elmore and Associates located in the Arlington area. She walked into the two-story Victorian house that had been converted into the brokerage firm owned by her father and Bryce Elmore.

As soon as Bryce saw her, he stood from his desk and rushed to give her a hug.

"Hey, Meggie," the distinguished man said. Addressing her as Meggie, the nickname he and her father called her, made her feel at home. "I'm so sorry."

Bryce looked much different than she remembered. He'd lost weight and shaved his beard, and gray sprinkled his temples. Since Christmas, his whole appearance had changed, making him look younger, more striking. *What's up with that?*

Megan couldn't hold back tears any longer. She loved Bryce. He'd been her dad's best friend and partner since before she was born. Megan put away any negative thoughts and looked up into Bryce's concerned blue eyes. His tender action of pushing her hair from her forehead made her think. *He couldn't have hurt Dad. Our families have been best friends forever.*

"I need to see Dad's office." She broke away from the hug.

"I wouldn't go in there if I were you," Bryce said, following her.

"I have no choice." She walked over, turned the knob, and looked inside. She started shaking and felt like fainting. Papers, boxes, and files scattered everywhere. Dirt and dust covered the cluttered landscape.

"Would you like me to join you?"

"No. I'm okay. Was Dad's office like this when you found him?"

"I'm afraid it was. Been that way for almost a year."

They stood in the doorway staring inside. She waited until Bryce left and walked away. She entered the room, closed the door, and locked it. *Why would Bryce lie to her?* She'd been here less than nine months ago. Dad's office didn't look like this. She sat at his desk between piles of papers. She shuffled through some of them. One sheet looked as if he'd spilled red wine on it. Not unusual. Her father often enjoyed a glass in his office at the end of the day with a colleague.

She pulled the overnight package from her purse, then leaned back in the chair to reread the trusts from Nevlin. She needed to read her dad's letter again first and Nevlin's letter. His last sentence was, "Please contact me when you get into town."

She picked up the phone. "Mr. Nevlin," she said. "I'm here at my dad's office."

"Great," he said. "I'll be right over."

Chapter Two

THE DAY OF THE INCIDENT

*W*ade Nevlin, Esquire, arrived at his penthouse suite in the Independent Life Building. He knew he'd be alone for several hours as, Sally, his secretary, had to take the morning off. He liked the solitude of these times when he could work alone without any interruptions.

He picked up the *Florida Times-Union* newspaper outside his door and brought it inside. He always read it cover to cover before getting to his files. When he turned to the business section, he didn't expect to read its headline.

"Michael Briscoe, Age 59, of Briscoe-Elmore and Associates Found Dead in His Arlington Brokerage Office."

"Christ!" he said aloud. He took his feet off his mahogany desk, stood by a photo of his friend, and threw the paper on the marble floor. *Why did this have to happen?* He stomped on the paper and paced the room. *We were just together last night...*

Before he had any more time to think about his good friend, a knock at the front door startled him. Nevlin walked out of his office and through the lobby past Sally's desk, wondering who was on the other side. He wasn't expecting anyone.

"Mr. Nevlin?" the short, bald man said. "Detective David Alvarez from the Jacksonville Police Department. We're looking into the death of Michael Briscoe."

"What?" Nevlin said, taken aback. "What did you say your name was?"

"Alvarez," the man said, standing in the hallway.

"Oh yes, now I remember." Nevlin thought he'd seen a ghost looking like a younger version of someone else. "Knew your father. Fine police captain."

The young detective seemed at a loss for words and mumbled something. "Ah, um, thank you."

Nevlin noticed beads of sweat trickling down the back of the officer's neck. "Come on in. It's cooler in here than it is out there."

"Thank you," Alvarez said. He followed Nevlin to his back office and took one of the leather chairs. He pulled out a scheduler from his casual sport jacket. "I have Mr. Briscoe's daily planner. It looks like you were his last client yesterday."

"Yes," Nevlin said. "I suppose I was."

"Well?"

"Well, I wouldn't call myself a client," Nevlin said as he walked around the room and sat facing the detective from behind his desk. "It was the other way around. Michael came to me over a year ago to write some legal documents. We became friends and fishing buddies." He pointed to the large blue marlin mounted on the rear wall.

Alvarez didn't turn around and ignored the gesture, getting straight to the point. "Why was your name in his planner for 6:00 p.m. last evening?"

"As I was saying, we were fishing buddies. Michael had

never been to the Keys. We planned to leave next weekend for a trip down the Intracoastal."

"Oh. Planning a trip. How did Michael seem when you last saw him?"

"Happy. Excited. Looking forward to our vacation."

"What time did you leave?"

"I left around 6:30, 6:45."

"Did you see anyone else or notice anyone coming as you left?" said Alvarez.

"No. Everyone in the office had gone home for the evening."

Nevlin knew where this was headed. Years of working in the DA's office had taught him. The last person to see someone alive was the prime suspect. "I went home...alone."

"One more thing. Can you think of anyone who would want to hurt Michael?"

"No. Damn it! Everyone loved the guy. He was a pillar of our community."

"I'll be in touch. Don't leave town. We might have further questions." Alvarez closed the planner with his notes and got up to leave. They shook hands and said good-bye.

Nevlin stood at the door and watched Alvarez scurry down the long corridor of law offices before catching the elevator.

—∞—

The next day Megan called Nevlin from her dad's office. He had said he'd be right there, but she couldn't figure out what was causing him to be late. Downtown was not far from Arlington.

She had waited in her dad's office long enough. Looking at the mess was starting to give her the creeps. It saddened her. The thought of her dad breathing his last breath gave her goose bumps.

She took a walk over to Bryce's larger office but could see him talking on the phone. She also saw Christy, the head secretary, engaged in a conversation too, and she dared not interrupt. She looked around the office. *Life went on even with Dad gone.*

She walked to the lounge and poured herself a cup of coffee. Many associates at Briscoe-Elmore had known her since childhood. She appreciated every hug and condolence they gave, but she wanted to get out of there. She headed back to the foyer of the Victorian-home-turned-offices with her coffee when she saw the front door open.

The man waved at her with a smile. She set her coffee on a nearby table and walked toward him.

"Miss Briscoe?" he said. "I'm Wade Nevlin. Sorry I'm late. Nice to finally meet you, albeit not under these circumstances."

"Hello, Mr. Nevlin," Megan said and shook his hand. "Glad to meet you too."

"Is there somewhere where we could talk privately?"

"Sorry, Dad's office is unavailable. I'm afraid the company has no conference rooms. Everyone uses their own room for their business dealings."

"Well, it's getting close to lunch," Nevlin said. "How about we get something to eat? I know a place called Harry's I think you'll like."

"Sounds good to me," Megan said.

"It's not far. The restaurant is located within a new mall called the Landing on the waterfront. I can drive as well as treat. All right?"

"Wonderful. Just give me a minute to tell Bryce I'm

leaving."

As Megan said good-bye to her father's partner, he said, "Let me know if there is anything Laura and I can do for you. Stop by the house or call if you need anything, promise?"

"Okay, Bryce," Megan said. "I will."

Mr. Nevlin drove her over the Matthews Bridge to the Landing. After parking in the lower garage, they walked up the stairs to Harry's Bar and Grill.

"This is the hippest place in town," Nevlin said. "It's where the city workers congregate for lunch."

She'd never met Mr. Nevlin before but willingly accepted a ride with him. After all, he'd become one of her dad's closest friends besides Bryce. The secret letter from her father started to haunt her. She wondered if she could trust him. Whom *could* she trust in her hometown? Most of her childhood friends had scattered since college—apart from Brittney Elmore, Bryce's daughter. She felt she could rely on her.

Mr. Nevlin pointed out a place by the window where they could be seated with some privacy.

"I hope you like burgers and fries, because that's their specialty," he said. "They make both in a variety of ways."

"I'm not fond of beef," she said, "but if they have something with fish or shrimp, I'm in. I sure miss Florida seafood."

"I'm sure they do."

She looked out the floor-to-ceiling glass panes. She'd almost forgotten the breathtaking view of downtown Jax, as the locals called it. When the waitress came to take their orders, Megan spoke first.

"I'll have the po' boy shrimp sandwich with french fries and some sweet tea, please."

After Nevlin finished ordering his jalapeño burger with onion rings and a Coke, the waitress disappeared. There was a short uneasy silence until Megan spoke again.

"Mr. Nevlin, how did you get to become executor of my father's estate? I don't quite understand."

"Let me explain. As you read in the documents, I am not the executor of his personal estate. You are. But your father wanted me to handle the business part of his company. I take it you weren't aware of this?"

"No," Megan said. "Not until I read the paperwork you overnighted to me. Thanks for sending them."

"About a year ago, I received a call from your dad. A mutual friend had referred him. Your dad and I had several things in common and hit it off. He shared the whole history of the Briscoe-Elmore relationship from beginning to end. Did you know they had a recent falling out?"

"No, I didn't."

"Well, before your father met me, he found out Bryce had been having an affair. He kept it a secret from your dad, but soon your father suspected it, and things happened."

"Things? What kinds of things?"

"Well, your dad confronted him. Bryce denied it at first, but then a week later, they went out for drinks, and Bryce admitted it. Your father basically told him to quit his office fling. The argument ended in a sticky mess, and your father called me."

"What?" Megan frowned. She didn't know what to say and thought it not the right time to divulge the contents of her dad's letter. "Mr. Nevlin, why did my father feel he needed someone like yourself? I mean, I am a lawyer and his sole heir,

17

right? Why was Dad so concerned? And what do you mean by 'sticky mess'?"

"It would have been cut and dry if Bryce hadn't gotten his own attorney with a contract for you to sign. It states in the event of your father's death, Michael's half of the company would be turned over to Bryce due to some past unfair dealings. That's why your dad hired me."

"Dad's unfair dealings?" Megan said and took in a deep breath. "My dad never made an unfair deal in his life. And why does Bryce think I would sign over my half? Are you kidding me?"

Just as their food arrived, Megan noticed two police officers standing by the hostess podium. The shorter uniformed man wore his sunglasses backward on top of his shaven head. The sun reflected off his sunglasses and flashed as he walked. The two men were seated at a nearby table.

"I suppose not only the office set come here to eat but the police detail as well," she said.

"Yes, their main office is just around the corner on Bay Street," Nevlin said. "As for the shorter man. Name's Detective Alvarez. He's the one investigating your father's death."

Chapter Three

THE RESTAURANT

*N*evlin dropped Megan off at her dad's office, and she drove the rental car home. She found the extra key in the same family hiding place and opened the front door.

Oh no! This day is getting worse by the minute. What the hell happened here? The house her mom had prided herself in keeping immaculate no longer existed. It looked like the chaos in Dad's office. Megan sat on the living room couch filled with rumpled clothes and started to cry. Seemed like she had been breaking down with every crazy happening. *Get a grip, Megan!*

Within minutes, she composed herself to stumble through the maze of boxes in the four-bedroom home. Thank goodness the kitchen telephone remained in the same spot on the wall, or she wouldn't have been able to find it.

She called her best friend in New York. "Veronica, I need you," Megan said. "You've got to come here right away."

"Hold on there, sweetie," she said. "Where the hell are you anyway? Catch your breath. What's wrong?"

Megan explained why she had left without saying good-bye.

She shared the contents of the letters and told her friend of the disarray everywhere. Her dad's office looked like nothing had been filed for months and his home looked like he'd been hoarding. Now she'd found out his partner had planned to have her sign over her portion of the company.

"Geez, Megan," Veronica said. "As much as I love and support you, you're not thinking clearly. I can't leave work, drop everything, and fly down there. I'd love to, but I have my boutique to run. Remember? It's only me here. Call Erick."

"I know. I know," Megan said as she wiped her tears. "I just haven't been able to reach him since arriving, and since I couldn't reach you last night, I needed to hear your voice. But you're right. Erick will know what to do."

"Okay. Now call him. I know it's hard to ask a favor. But isn't that why you're together? To be there for each other. You know he will."

"Yeah. I understand," she said. She walked to the sink with the long-corded phone for a glass of water. She hoped it would help her stop crying.

"You haven't called Brittney yet, have you?" Veronica said.

"No, I figured I'd wait for her to call me. I have a wake, funeral, and memorial to plan."

"Well, call me anytime. I mean it—day or night."

"Thanks, Veronica."

Megan hung up and called Erick at work. She hoped he might be at his desk getting ready for the next day's case. They had talked before she'd left in the morning. He knew where to find her. Her parents' phone number hadn't changed since they had attended Jacksonville Episcopal High School. "Call me later" was all she said when his phone went to voicemail.

She looked around at the home she once shared with her mom and dad. What a disaster. She walked into her bedroom hoping to see it free of litter, but it looked the same as all the other rooms. Her room had been used to store her dad's jazz albums. His music collection had grown since her mother had passed. She cleared the bed to put clean sheets on and finished unpacking. She needed a nap.

She slept for a few hours, until the doorbell woke her. She wondered who it could be. She wasn't expecting anyone. To her surprise, Brittney stood on the front porch with half her brood surrounding her. Ten years out of high school, and she looked the same. Without makeup and after giving birth to four kids, Brittney somehow maintained her sleek figure and smooth complexion. Meagan wondered how she did it.

Brittney had one of her twins attached to her hip and held the hand of the other toddler standing next to her. The three of them wore matching University of Florida T-shirts and cutoff jean shorts. The towheads looked like an advertisement for her husband, Steve's, alma mater.

"Oh, Brittie," Megan said as she walked onto the front porch. She flung her arms around her childhood friend and the twins. The women cried as the two-year-old twins looked around not knowing what to make of the flow of emotions.

"Oh, Meggie," Brittney said. "I'm so sorry, honey. Thought I'd stop by while the other boys were in school."

Brittney continued. "Dad called and said you were in the office, then left with a Mr. Nevlin? Who is he? When I couldn't reach you, I decided to give you a while before popping over to see if there was anything I could do."

"Come on in," Megan said as she opened the front door.

21

"Holy shit! I mean shoot!" Brittney corrected herself for the children's sake. "What on earth happened here?"

"That was my reaction. Look at this place! Have you ever seen anything so messy? What happened to my dad?"

"I'm really sorry, hon. I had no idea. Is there any place we can sit down?"

"Follow me to the back porch. It seems to have been left alone."

Brittney followed Megan through the maze from the hallway to the den and back porch. They sat on the patio furniture with the kids. Other than being surprised by the disorder in the house, Brittney acted the same as usual. She talked nonstop about her family and asked a few questions of Meggie, without giving her time to answer. Megan marveled at Brittney's patience whenever she had to stop and discipline her children. But that never interrupted her chatter.

"Do you think we could get a bite to eat later?" Megan said, changing the subject to food. "Just the two of us?"

"Hungry?" Brittney said. "Sorry. That was rude of me to go on and on. I bet you haven't had a thing to eat since you landed."

"That's okay. I did have lunch with Mr. Nevlin around noon. But the fridge here is empty, and I'm getting famished."

"Hey, why don't I go home and freshen up? As soon as Steve arrives from work, he can take over with the kids. Give me some time to change. I must look a mess in these clothes. How about I pick you up around six?"

"Sounds good. The plans for the services can wait until morning anyway. Thanks, Brittie."

"Great! I think a nice long chat over dinner is in order."

22

Megan thought about Brittney's cheerfulness. *Perhaps she feigned a happy face for my benefit?* She hoped the evening alone together might bring forth more information.

Brittney picked up Megan right on time in her new Cadillac filled with infant car seats and toys scattered everywhere. The back seat looked as if she had thrown whatever had been in the passenger seat over her head. Megan smelled the faint odor of baby wipes. She didn't mind and smiled to herself, happy it wasn't her life.

In that moment, she was glad to be back in her hometown with a good friend. She wanted her stay in Jax to be short so she could get back to her life in New York. Did Brittney know anything about their dads' quarrel? Or anything about the business? Megan planned to play dumb and let Brittney do all the talking.

"Are you up for pizza?" Brittney said.

"Sure! I'm always up for Luigi's, if that's what you mean." Megan smiled as they drove north on San Jose Boulevard to downtown San Marco.

They parked across the street from the restaurant near the fountain and walked back to Luigi's.

"Hey, where's Nick?" Megan said as she walked to the counter.

A young man answered her. "Where've you been? Luigi's son, Nick, retired over a year ago. But we're keeping the old man's name. I'm the new owner."

The women smiled at each other. Luigi's had been the most popular place in town for more than twenty years. Luigi Baldessare, an immigrant from Italy, started it from scratch. It'd become the hangout for teenagers and the favorite of locals

23

since it started.

"Well, I hope you haven't changed any of his recipes. Nick and his dad always had the best pizzas in town."

"No, ma'am," he said. "What will you ladies have?"

They ordered their usual, a Papa Special with an antipasto salad to split and two glasses of merlot. The women took their drinks and looked around. The diner still had the same Chicago-style feeling with chrome tables and chairs. Though the red plastic cushions looked replaced, they'd been arranged in the same way. Chicago skyline and landmark photos decorated the walls. Megan and Brittney sat at a booth in the back. They popped in some coins to play tunes on the tabletop jukebox.

"So, what's up?" Megan started, sipping her wine. "What's been happening since I went back to New York? It sounded like you have a lot to tell me."

"There is, and there isn't," Brittney said. "Steve, the kids, and I are fine. It's Dad. Things had been running smoothly at the company for years. That was until Dad decided to have his midlife crisis fling. You know Christy, the head secretary? 'Big Boobs Christy'? Business and morale dropped to a staggering low after Christmas when the word got out."

When Megan saw the anguish in her friend's eyes, she realized Brittney's bubbly attitude had not been just for Megan's benefit but for her own too.

"Do you know how the affair started?" Megan said. "How long had this been going on? When Erick and I were here for the Christmas party, I never suspected a thing."

"Well, no one really knows for sure, but I think it started before that. They were able to hide it until then. Didn't you notice the flirtatious fawning Christy laid on my dad?"

"I guess a little." Megan shrugged her shoulders. "But I thought she did that to every man."

"They may have fooled you, but they didn't fool me. After the new year, things got worse at home. Dad would be called back to the office at all hours of the night, or he'd stay later than usual. Mom told me she suspected Christy."

Megan saw the pain her questioning caused and thought it best not to comment further. She didn't want to talk about Brittney's dad anymore. Their conversation was going nowhere with Brittney making it all one-sided, dwelling on the affair and how she hated Christy.

Megan tried to change to a lighter subject like Brittney's kids, but her friend interrupted.

"None of us knew he was sick," she said. "Did you?"

Megan couldn't hold back her emotion any longer. As her tears flowed, all she could do was stutter, "No." The two women hugged, cried, and sipped their wine for a few silent moments.

"Excuse me a minute," Megan said, needing some fresh air. "I'm going to try Erick again. I haven't been able to reach him." She hurried out of the restaurant and down the street to the corner phone booth. She got in and closed the door for privacy. When she heard his voice, she briefly summarized the circumstances surrounding her father's death and the secret contract Bryce had written. Everything had upset her. She ended the conversation with "I'll tell you the details later. I need you, babe." As soon as Erick heard that, he promised he'd be on the next plane out of JFK to JAX.

By the time Megan came back to the table, their pizza had arrived. Neither woman wanted to continue the previous conversation. Megan changed the topic by showing Brittney the ring on her finger again. She hadn't had a chance to tell her the details of her recent engagement.

After two bottles of wine, Megan felt like old times when the two of them were young, single, going out, and having a good time. Megan's plan to get Brittney high boomeranged, however. They both got more relaxed before the night was over, and the alcohol became the conduit that guided their conversation back to the dads.

The next morning, Megan made the arrangements for the wake and funeral for the following weekend. She called Mr. Nevlin and told him of the arrangements. She hoped he could make it.

"Of course, Megan, I'll be there," he said.

"Thanks, Mr. Nevlin. I'd appreciate it. We can postpone our appointment to discuss the trusts after it's over. My fiancé, Erick, will be joining us."

"Of course, not a problem," he said. "I'll look forward to meeting him."

That afternoon Megan drove I-95 to the airport. Its barren landscape with vacant grassy flatlands and scattered palm trees comforted Megan. Her childhood memories of family picnics and fishing with her dad on the shores calmed her nerves. The landscape drew a contradictory parallel from the city of New York with its concrete and tall buildings. She felt peaceful knowing she'd soon be with Erick.

She parked at Jacksonville International and went inside. When she saw him disembark from the plane, she ran to him, gave him a hug, and kissed him in the middle of the seating area. They walked to the car and got in, and Megan started driving.

"Sorry, hon," she said. "I guess the wine got the best of me last night. My plan backfired. I did all the talking instead of Brittney. I'm feeling hungover."

"That's okay, sweetheart," Erick said. "You deserve to get a little tipsy every now and then. Especially now."

"Hey," Megan said, as she drove closer to town. "I just thought of something. Want to grab an early lunch? Mr. Nevlin showed me this neat bar at the Landing called Harry's. It's on the river. I think you'll like it."

"Sure, honey," he said. "Whatever you'd like. Sounds terrific."

The Landing, halfway between the airport and the Briscoe's residence, made for a convenient stop. Megan parked in the underground garage, and they walked up the stairs to the waterfront bar and grill.

Erick was impressed. "Gosh, I wish they'd had something like this when we were growing up. That would've been fun."

The hostess seated them at the same table where she and Nevlin had been the day before.

"I had forgotten how beautiful Jacksonville was," she said.

"I guess you've forgotten why you left," he said and winked at her with a smile. "To follow your heart. Right?"

The couple laughed at their inside joke. Erick had been the first to pass his bar exam in New York. After Megan passed hers, he got her a job in the same office. Sitting by the water brought back memories.

"Remember when we used to water ski on the St. John's River?" she said.

"Do you miss this?" he said as he grabbed her hand across the table.

"It was fun growing up here. But I wouldn't trade anything for my life with you in New York." They ordered their food after watching some of the luxury boats and yachts cruise by.

"Okay," Megan said. "Down to business. Dad's friend, Mr. Nevlin. Turns out he's a lawyer too. In fact, he'll be executor of the business."

"What? Your dad hired an attorney while he had a daughter and almost son-in-law who are attorneys?"

"Well, we're not exactly estate or business attorneys, right? And we don't practice in the state of Florida."

"Guess you're right. Now what were you saying about Mr. Nevlin?"

"I was going to say there's something about him I can't figure out."

"What do you mean?"

"Mmm. That's just it. If I could describe him, I would say he's *too* nice."

"That doesn't make sense, Megan."

"Maybe not, but you'll see. We'll soon be working with him, and you'll meet him at Dad's service."

"Okay," Erick said.

"And there's something else. While we were eating yesterday, the policeman who's investigating Dad's death happened to be sitting at the table right over there." Megan pointed to the one closest to the bar. "Nevlin and one of them exchanged strange looks."

"Now, that's weird," he said.

"I'm wondering why Dad didn't share his private thoughts with him. I mean, if they were so close, why the 'For Your Eyes Only' letter? Something's not adding up."

"You have a good point," Erick said. "I'm glad you faxed those papers to me. Do you really think someone killed your father?"

"I'm not sure. Too early to tell. Besides the letter, the disheveled house and office, and Bryce and Nevlin acting odd, everything else seems normal."

"Normal? What's Bryce been doing? Having an affair and writing up a contract for you to sign. Nothing sounds normal to me."

"You're right. I just don't know whom to trust. As for Bryce, not only has his appearance changed, but his actions seem insincere too. Maybe he's feigning confidence? I think he's up to something. It could be the contract or perhaps maybe a guilty conscience?"

"Shit, Megan! Who does this guy think he is? Why would he think you'd sign such a deal? Someone or something must be behind it, and we need to find out who or what. Do you think it could be Nevlin?"

"I hope not," she said as they finished and paid the bill. "He seemed more genuine about losing my dad."

"Last night I never got Brittney to divulge anything," Megan said as they drove home. "Either she really doesn't know anything about the situation between our dads or she just isn't talking. She just went on and on about how her dad destroyed their family and how mean he'd been to her mother. I'm not sure if the affair is over or ongoing."

"Oh my," Erick said. "No wonder Brittney was so upset."

"That's not all. Laura confirmed her suspicions when she checked Bryce's pockets before sending a suit to the cleaners. The fool left a receipt for a bed-and-breakfast in Fernandina

Beach where she'd never been. She confronted him; he said it was a one-night fling and would never do it again. But Brittney doesn't believe it."

"Does Bryce know you are aware of the contract plan he has for you?" Erick said, changing the subject.

"Not to my knowledge. My father got a copy without Bryce knowing. Dad photocopied it for Nevlin. The two of them kept it a secret. Nevlin is the only other person knowledgeable of it."

"I think the only way we are going to get more information is to ask Bryce directly. We'll have to confront him in court anyway if you contest it. You *are* going to contest it, aren't you?"

"Of course I am."

Right before they got to the house, Megan prepared Erick for the disorder inside. They parked in the driveway and walked inside. Erick scoped out the living room and other parts of the house he barely recognized.

He looked at her. "Oh, babe," he said. "We'll get through this," and reassured her with a hug.

Chapter Four

THE FUNERAL FIASCO

*M*egan spruced up every room in the house getting ready for her guests. She thought it looked almost as good as Mother once left it, with fresh flowers in every room. Close family and friends would be invited back to the house after the Atlantic Beach service. She felt content Erick had been there to help her.

The coroner's office called.

"Ms. Briscoe?" the woman said. "I'm calling you with the medical examiner's results. Your father died of a heart attack."

"Thank you," Megan said. "Will you be sending my father over to Harding's funeral home?"

"No," she said. "Harding's will be picking up your dad any minute now."

"Well, I guess Daddy was wrong," Megan said as she put down the receiver. "There was no homicide, Erick. They confirmed my dad died of a heart attack."

"One mystery solved," he said and gave her a hug. "Now we can move on to Bryce's mysterious contract and the Christy

31

involvement. What's the deal behind his takeover? What the hell is going on between those two?"

"Please, Erick. Not now. I just want to get the funeral over. Bryce can wait with his damn contract. I'm not signing anything."

They got ready for the wake and drove to the small funeral home in Atlantic Beach. Her father always loved the beach and wanted to be buried next to his wife in the quaint cemetery behind the chapel where they'd been married. The funeral parlor was not like Megan had remembered. It held enough people for her mother a few years ago, but today there was standing room only. Police officers, firemen, and others in uniform exchanged places with one another to get a close view and pay their respects. Her philanthropic father had been well known in both the city and beach communities, donating time and money to many charities, but she had never realized how many lives he touched.

Megan busied herself talking to relatives she hardly knew. Michael Briscoe's family had once been huge. Michael had been the baby of the family, and through the years, many of the siblings had moved away or died. Those who came from out of town came to see a brother they barely knew.

"So sorry for your loss," Megan heard over and over. The only people in the funeral parlor she knew were Erick, the Elmores, and Mr. Nevlin, and she really didn't know him that well. She wanted and needed to get to know the attorney better. She had her concerns about Bryce too and what he had been up to over the past week.

Megan felt she had no close family now. The relatives lived so scattered, and no one seemed to care to get together except for funerals. Family reunions in the Midwest were only a faded memory now. She could rely only on Erick and her two girlfriends, Brittney and Veronica.

By the end of the wake, many of the locals had left. Then a wave of office people rolled in like a Jacksonville Beach high tide to pay their respects. Christy was at the end of it. Megan's heart raced, and her head started to pound the minute she saw her.

"Oh no," Megan whispered to Erick. "Here comes trouble. She…"

Before she could finish her sentence, Christy had rushed over to the casket. People's eyebrows raised as Christy threw her arms around the corpse, kissing the man's face and sobbing. She kept blurting the same words.

"I'm so sorry!" Christy said. "I'm so sorry! What have I done? Michael, forgive me!"

Everyone sucked in a deep breath. Nevlin hurried over to Christy to pry her off the casket.

"No!" Christy screamed. "Get your hands off me. Let me go!"

"Make sure Nevlin takes her out of here," Megan said to Erick.

"Sure thing, hon," he said and walked over to help Nevlin, who had whispered something in Christy's ear.

Megan overheard Nevlin say to Erick, "It's okay. I'll take care of this." Christy finally had backed away, and everyone watched in silence as Nevlin escorted the secretary out of the building.

Erick whispered in Megan's ear. "Don't worry, babe. It'll be all right." He handed her his handkerchief as she watched everyone stare at Nevlin and Christy leaving together.

Nevlin walked back into the funeral parlor alone. "I told her if she showed her face at tomorrow's funeral, we'd call the police," he said.

"I can't believe anyone would do that," Megan said. "Erick, please tell everyone to leave. I can't take this anymore." She continued dabbing her wet face with her fiancé's hankie.

"Okay," Erick said and turned to the crowd. "Show's over. It's best everyone leaves."

Megan watched as the last few people grabbed their jackets and purses. As soon as everyone had gone, she said. "Please take me home, Erick; I'm starting to get another one of my migraines."

Megan got into the car. "What more could go wrong?" she said. "Did you see those police officers talking? I heard one of them say, 'What is *he* doing with that woman?' I can't believe Christy would do such a thing. What do you think she meant? And why were the police checking out Nevlin? I can't seem to get this whole scenario out of my head."

"I don't understand any of it," he said. "Try to forget about it tonight, babe. You need some sleep. I promise you one thing. We won't leave Jacksonville until we find out."

—⚏—

The following day the torrential rain kept many people away. It was a quiet funeral with mourners dressed in black holding matching umbrellas at the gravesite. Megan was glad it was only the relatives and a few close friends. When it was over, she invited everyone to the house.

Once inside, the people talked in whispers. Megan could

only make out a few mumbled words when she walked by. Were they just being polite, or did it have anything to do with yesterday's incident? Who could forget Christy's grand exit at Harding's?

Megan felt her head would explode after several hours of small talk. How many times would she have to affirm how great her father was? She agreed with friends on several occasions what a lovely job the catering service had done but grew tired of answering questions about her life in New York. The chitchat got on her nerves. She never enjoyed repeating herself. Her eyes started burning from the constant rubbing, and she wanted more than anything to go to bed.

One by one people donned their raincoats and grabbed their umbrellas.

"Don't worry, hon," Erick said after the last guest left. "I'll call the office in the morning. I'm sure the boss will give us an extended leave of absence."

"Thanks, and don't forget our appointment on Monday with Mr. Nevlin. I'd like to know how he will help us. I don't care what the coroner said. I'm not letting go of father's letter. I think there might be some connection to it, especially after Christy's performance at the funeral home."

"We should see Christy as soon as possible," Erick said. "I'm curious as to what she meant. I'm sure she has something to share and would tell us if we showed her some empathy."

"Good idea. Let's see what Nelvin says once we've shown him the contents of the letter. Then maybe he could enlighten us."

—〰—

On Sunday Megan and Erick welcomed the party invitation to the Elmores'. It wasn't really a party. It was more like a gathering between the Briscoe and Elmore families. They hadn't had time to be alone together without a multitude of guests who'd come to pay their respects. Megan was happy Laura had set up this occasion as a celebration of her dad's life.

Megan called Laura. "Would it be okay if I invite Mr. Nevlin? He told me he doesn't have any family here, and I'd like to get to know him better."

"Sure," Laura said. "I'm sure Bryce wouldn't mind. He knows your dad and he were friends."

"Thanks, Laura," Megan said.

The weather changed into a beautiful, cloudless day after the gloom of the rainfall dissipated. The barbeque seemed like any ordinary one in suburban Jacksonville with Bryce at the grill. The women drank wine while preparing side dishes in the kitchen. Steve and Nevlin played ball with the boys in the backyard. Erick mingled between the groups, trying to learn what he could from the family and friends closest to the late Michael Briscoe.

"Hey, Meggie," Bryce yelled through the kitchen window from the patio. "Can you give me a hand and get the meat from the fridge? I'm already done with the burgers and hot dogs for the kids."

"Sure thing," she replied as she walked to the fridge and grabbed the platter of steaks and chicken breasts. Outside, after handing the platter to Bryce, she heard the family's phone ring. Bryce put the platter down beside the grill and ran to their outdoor line.

"Hello?" he answered. Megan noticed a once happy face turn dour.

"Sorry, Meggie," he said, as he put his hand over the receiver. "I have to take this call in my office. Could you hold this for me for a sec?" He handed the receiver to Megan.

"No problem," Megan replied. "Want Erick to start the chicken?"

"That would be great," Bryce said as he hurried into the house. He closed the window blinds overlooking the backyard as soon as he picked up the receiver.

"Okay," said Bryce, letting her know she could hang up. When Megan heard a woman's voice, she hung up and waved Erick to come over. She had wanted to give Bryce the benefit of the doubt, but the voice sounded familiar.

"Honey, could you start the chicken breasts? Bryce had to take that call in the house."

Erick smiled and walked over to put the meat on the grill. He waved Nevlin over for some company and assistance.

"It sounded like Christy's voice," she whispered to Erick. "I've got to see what he's up to. He said it was work, but from the look on his face, I don't think so. I'm going to the restroom to see if I can find out anything."

"Okay, sweetie. Be careful."

With wine in hand, Megan left smiling and laughing, acting as if things were normal. She walked into the house and stopped in front of Bryce's closed office door. She made out a few sentences. "Don't forget our little secret" and "You better keep that to yourself."

Then Bryce shouted, "Why, you little bitch!" She heard him pound his fist on his desk. "Don't you ever call me at home again. We're through!"

Megan had heard enough. She hurried to the restroom,

locked herself in, and flushed an empty toilet. She ran some water and waited. She surmised Christy might have given him an ultimatum. *Guess Bryce and Christy are still seeing each other.* By the time Megan washed and dried her hands, she heard Bryce's convertible revving up in the driveway.

"Sorry, Laura," she heard Bryce yell. "Something important has come up. Gotta go to the office. Don't wait up for me!" Megan walked outside to the grill. Bryce had escaped the family gathering before it even started. Everyone heard Bryce's announcement. She looked at Steve and saw him shrug his shoulders as if it that was typical behavior, Erick shook his head and rolled his eyes, and Brittney comforted her mother as she began to cry.

Nevlin asked Megan. "Want me to follow him?"

"Yes," Megan said. "If you don't mind."

Nevlin made excuses to the hostess that he had to leave.

"Oh no," Laura said. "You too?"

"Sorry, Mrs. Elmore," Nevlin said. "I forgot something at home. I'll be right back."

"Okay, see you later, then?"

"Yes, for sure." Nevlin said his good-byes.

Laura turned to Brittney in tears. "And I thought your father's damn affair was over," she said as she hugged her daughter. Then she turned to Megan. "I'm so sorry, sweetie. I wanted our get-together to be a pleasant evening of sharing remembrances of Michael."

"Laura, this *is* a nice gathering," Megan said and hugged her. "We won't let Bryce ruin it for us. We'll have our party without him. The food is ready, so let's eat. I'm sure Mr. Nevlin will join us later."

Megan was glad Mr. Nevlin was there to follow Bryce. She couldn't have asked Erick to leave as they all needed to be there to support Laura. The rest of the evening was more somber, but Megan was pleased to hear the shared memories of her father. When Nevlin returned, he brought flowers for Laura and the ingredients to make himself and others some dirty martinis. While making drinks, he told Megan and Erick that he saw Bryce go into his office and Christy's sports car was outside.

At the night's end, Erick and Megan drove home from the Elmore house and discussed possible scenarios about Bryce. He'd never come back to the party. Why did Bryce lie to Laura about the affair being over? What hold did Christy have on Bryce? What little secret were they hiding?

The whole weekend's fiasco had Megan's head whirling. She felt another migraine coming.

Chapter Five

THE BURGLARY

Megan's migraine kept her from getting a good night's rest. She didn't feel like fighting rush hour traffic, so she slept in. She awoke to find Erick had prepared a great breakfast for the two of them. She felt blessed he supported and stayed with her.

She drove to Briscoe-Elmore and Associates while listening to oldies on the radio. She hoped to get in a better mood. She wondered if Bryce's demeanor would have changed from the barbeque the night before. Once she got to the office, his Sunday shenanigans became the least of her worries.

Megan saw Bryce from across the room as soon as she walked in the front door. He wasn't alone. His office and her father's were on opposite sides of what was once the living room of the old house. Small desks for the secretaries nestled in the middle of the large central area. The door to Bryce's office stood wide open. He looked dumbfounded standing by his desk with a policeman standing next to him. Bryce gave her a blank look. His office looked worse than Dad's did the week before.

It looked as if someone had torn it apart looking for something. Desk drawers had been pulled out and papers thrown all over the place. File cabinets had been turned over and everything on the top of his desk swept to the floor. Whoever it was knew the safe had been hidden behind the large oil painting of the Sea Turtle Inn behind his desk. *Who could have known that? I sure didn't.* The oil painting had been left opened with the emptied safe door ajar. She saw other police officers dusting for fingerprints.

"I know who must have done this," Megan overheard Bryce tell the detective as she walked closer. "It had to have been Christy Fields, my old secretary."

"Why do you say that?" the detective asked.

"Well, I fired her last night, and she wasn't too happy about it."

When Megan reached the two men, Bryce waved her away. Although the other man never turned around, she recognized Alvarez from the back. Who could forget his stocky build and bald head with his mirrored sunglasses on top reversed?

Megan turned and walked back to her dad's office. She sat down and started to plan what to do next. The same disorganized mess remained as she'd left it. *Where do I start?* A few minutes later, there was a knock, and the door opened.

"Hi, Bryce," she said. "What's going on?"

The detective was hidden behind Bryce's large frame as they entered.

"I'd like to introduce you to Officer Alvarez," he said as he stepped aside. "Looks like someone broke in last night and stole money out of the safe."

Lieutenant Alvarez and Megan shook hands.

41

"Nice to meet you."

"Likewise," he said. "Going to be here for a while?"

"Yes, if it's okay with you," she said. "I just buried my father this past week—Mr. Elmore's partner, Michael Briscoe. If his office is not a part of the crime scene, I'd like to work here and clear out his things."

"That would be all right," Alvarez said. "Sorry for your loss, Ms. Briscoe. We've determined the perp hit only Mr. Elmore's office and safe. You may pack up your dad's things. But I may need to ask you some questions later. Don't leave town just yet."

"Okay. Thank you, Detective Alvarez."

"Please. Call me Alvarez."

"Oh my God, Bryce," Megan said, pretending that she hadn't heard anything earlier. "Who in the—?"

Bryce held up his hand and interrupted her. "I was just telling the detective I thought Christy was behind this."

"Really?" Megan said. "Why would she have done this?"

"I fired her ass last night, that's why. When you have a disgruntled employee, anything can happen!"

"Let's not talk about that right now," Alvarez said to Bryce, pointing back across the room. "Over in your office."

As they walked away, Megan heard Bryce say, "She was trying to blackmail me. I saw her leave with her personal belongings. But she must have come back to do all this."

Megan couldn't wait to call Erick.

"Erick!" she said. "You won't believe what happened. Someone broke into the company last night, pillaged Bryce's office, and stole whatever was in his safe. Bryce is accusing Christy. He's furious."

"Oh my God! Do you really think she did it?"

"I don't know," she said. "But Alvarez is on the case. You know, the same one Nevlin said was investigating Dad's death. As for Christy, I don't think she would know the combination to the safe and doubt that little thing would have the strength to pull over those file cabinets."

"Oh, for Christ's sake," Erick said. "This Bryce guy is a piece of work. I don't trust him. Take care of yourself around there and don't forget to call me with Christy's home number, if you can find it, okay?"

"I won't. I hope we can get some answers from her before the police do."

"That's what I was thinking," Erick said. He started to explain his plan, but Megan stopped him.

"The police are still here," Megan said in a lower voice. "This can wait until I get home. We'll discuss it then."

"Agreed," he said. "See you later. Bye."

Megan worked for a couple more hours tidying up the office. After thinking further about what Erick had said, she knew he was right. Talking to Christy couldn't wait. She found her home number on her dad's Rolodex and called Erick back.

"Here you go, honey. I think it best you ring her up. Invite her to join us at the Conch House in St. Augustine tonight for dinner. See if she'd be interested in talking to us about what she said and why at the funeral parlor."

The Conch House, a favorite place of the Jacksonville and St. Augustine locals, sat on the Intracoastal Waterway. Since it was located forty-five minutes south of Jacksonville, Megan knew it was the perfect place to talk in private. The famous seafood restaurant hid behind the main highway in a residential area filled with ranch homes and palm trees. The noise of the motorboats outside the restaurant and visitors talking on the pier would drown out any conversation. If they arrived early, they might be able to acquire one of the intimate cabanas for dining.

Megan poured herself a cup of already made coffee from the machine in the break room while the cops still swarmed the place. She was glad they paid no attention to her. Bryce continued to have a glazed-over look as if trying to make sense of it all.

She called Erick again, hoping he had gotten hold of Christy.

"Any luck? Talked to her yet?" she said.

"No, but I'll keep trying," he said.

"Okay," Megan said. "Were you able to leave a message on an answering machine? Maybe she'll just show up."

"I wasn't able to," he said. "I don't think she had one."

"Just keep trying," Megan said and hung up.

Now that the office was in more order, she could box her dad's family photos and awards first. Michael had won Broker of the Year and City Volunteer of the Year many times for Jacksonville and the surrounding beach cities. He had also run a few marathons whose dusty trophies sat displayed on his shelves. Megan wasn't sure what to do with any of these but decided to box them anyway.

She combed the office, looking through the files for any little scrap of paper that could be a lead. *Please let there be something that points to a cover-up of lost funds or any suits brought against Dad, anything suspicious.* If she could find leverage to prove Bryce was wrong, she wouldn't have to sign over the business.

She was sure her dad would never do anything illegal. There was a knock on the door

"Megan! Open up!"

"Hey, Brittie." Megan opened the door, and Brittney looked upset.

"Whoa! What's wrong, darlin'?" Megan gave her friend a hug.

"My dad is not talking to me. I came down here to ask him to lunch. He just kept pointing to the mess in his office, saying, 'Not today, hon. Not today,' and shooed me away."

"His office was burglarized last night, and everything in his safe was stolen. I heard him accuse Christy of doing it when I arrived this morning."

"Oh no!"

"And there's something else," said Megan. "The reason why he accused her was that he fired her last night. Besides a messy office, everything from her desk was gone. I guess that made her a logical suspect."

"Well, that explains it," Brittney said. "Since he won't go to lunch with me, how about you taking a break? The kids are at school. The twins are in daycare. I was hoping to get Dad to tell me what happened last night when he ran off from the party. But it looks like that isn't his top priority now. Please say you have time for lunch."

Megan saw the desperation in Brittney's eyes. Her dad's office work could wait until this afternoon.

"Sure," Megan said. "Let's go. My treat. Let me call Erick first."

Megan called her fiancé and told him about her lunch plans with Brittney. She'd see him later, in time for their appointment with Mr. Nevlin.

"Any luck with that call?" Megan tried to be vague in front of Brittney. Erick's answer was negative. "Okay. See ya later. Love ya."

Megan and Brittney enjoyed their lunch at Bennigan's on Baymeadows Road. During their hour-long visit, Megan asked Brittney several questions about Christy and what she knew about her. Did she know anything about the secretary's firing? If she left town, where would she have gone? Did she have any idea what Christy was talking about at the funeral home? Brittney swore she knew none of the answers to her questions. Megan believed her.

When the girls went back to the office, the police were still there.

"I need to get home," Brittney said. "The kids should be getting out of school soon, and I need to run a few errands before picking them up."

"No problem," Megan said. "I have plenty to do here before my appointment this afternoon."

She walked into her father's office and locked the door for privacy. She sat on the floor emptying out the first file cabinet. A few minutes later, she heard another knock at the door. She thought maybe Brittney had spoken to her dad and had come to tell her something new.

"Brittney! I'll be right there." She opened the door only to find Detective Alvarez standing there.

"Ms. Briscoe," he said. "Got time for a few questions?"

"Of course, Officer," she said, then corrected herself. "Hm…I mean, Alvarez. And please call me Megan. Have a seat." She removed papers from a chair to make room for him.

"Well, we had the opportunity to check out the address Mr. Elmore gave us for Ms. Fields. She wasn't answering her phone, so we had the landlord let us in. Looked like she'd packed a few suitcases and left town. No one has seen her. Her car, keys, and purse were gone. Nothing else seemed amiss. We've put out a police alert, Be on the Lookout, a BOLO. We're trying to gather more information. Could you please tell me the last time you saw her?"

"How could I forget? The last time was at my father's wake. She made quite a spectacle of herself and was asked to leave."

"She made a spectacle at your father's wake. How?"

The sheer thought of the incident made Megan's eyes tear.

"I'm sorry, ma'am, but I have to ask."

"Oh, it's all right," she said and grabbed some tissues. "I understand."

"What did Ms. Fields do at the wake? How well did you know her?"

Megan explained what had happened and the incoherent phrases Christy yelled as she hugged Michael's body in the casket. Alvarez took notes.

"I really didn't know her well other than the fact she was the head secretary here for the past several years. I just found out that Bryce and her... They had begun to get, mm...close. I moved to New York City a short time after she was promoted. I didn't really know her except for the occasional times I popped into the office or attended office parties. That wasn't very often. Mom died three years ago, and the last time I was here was at the office Christmas party.

"Were you on social terms with her?"

"Oh, God, no. Since moving to New York, my only friend

47

left in Jacksonville is Brittney, Bryce's daughter. We grew up together, though I can't say we're that close anymore. It's only our childhood memories and families that have kept us friends."

"Thanks for the information, Ms. Briscoe. If you happen to hear from Christy, or see her, please tell her the police are looking for her. We need to ask her some questions."

"I doubt that will happen. We're not on the best of terms. However, if I do, I'll be sure to tell her."

"Thanks again, Ms. Briscoe," Alvarez said as he left.

She stood by the window and watched him drive away. His unexpected questioning made her late. She called Mr. Nevlin.

"Mr. Nevlin," Megan said. "I'm sorry. Erick and I will have to cancel for this afternoon."

"I'm sorry to hear that," he said. "Everything okay?"

"Well, yes, with me, that is," she said. "I just got paid a visit from Officer Alvarez."

"Really?" said Nevlin "What did he want?"

"Briscoe-Elmore was burglarized over the weekend, and the cops have been here all day. Bryce told the police Christy did it. Detective Alvarez wanted to know how much I knew about Ms. Fields, which wasn't much."

"Oh," Nevlin said. "As for the appointment we can make it any day you'd like."

"I'm sorry this has taken up more time that I thought it would. I've gotten nothing done in the way of packing up Dad's things. How about day after tomorrow?"

Nevlin agreed to a Wednesday afternoon appointment, and they set a time. Megan was relieved. As soon as she hung up, she called Erick to tell him she had rescheduled.

"Did you ever reach Christy?" she said.

"No. The phone just rang and rang like before. Why?"

"Well, the police just left a while ago and told me they have a BOLO alert out on her. They've already searched her apartment. Her purse, some clothes, her car, and her keys are missing."

"The police! Damn! I guess we'll never find out what secrets she took with her."

"Maybe she'll come back," Megan said. "You never know."

Chapter Six

THE FUGITIVE

Christy packed up her desk while Bryce continued his rant after firing her. She left while he was still raging and walked out the door with one box of personal belongings. She drove the long way home across the Buckman Bridge to Orange Park. She always liked to drive across one of the many bridges in Jacksonville when she needed time to think and compose herself. *What had happened? How could Bryce have said all those awful things?*

The more she thought about the names he called her, the angrier she got. Once he was her lover and future husband. Now just a memory. She wasn't sure what had gone wrong. Bryce had promised her the world. She realized they were all lies. His tall tales about getting a divorce, becoming a rich man, and marrying her faded. On top of everything, his accusation of her killing Michael hurt her the worst. *How could he think that?*

She remembered the day she'd seen him putting something in Michael's coffee creamer. Michael was the only one in the office who took cream. Everyone else drank theirs black or chose tea or soda. She recalled their conversation.

"Bryce," she said, "what are you doing with Michael's creamer?"

He turned to her and smiled. "Oh, ah. Nothing. You know how Michael's been acting sluggish lately? I asked him if he wouldn't mind me adding some of my energy drink to his creamer. You know, to see if it would help. He agreed. Don't you think he's looking better?"

Surprised, Christy didn't know what to say. She shrugged her shoulders.

"Hey, you could help me out," he said. "Let me show you. Add the powder from this tube to every pint of creamer he brings in. That would help me, and Michael too. But let's keep this our little secret, okay? You know how touchy he is about his health. And we wouldn't want the whole office getting in on this."

"Okay," Christy said and agreed to do it.

Christy didn't question any of it at the time until the day of Michael's funeral. But she wondered. *Have I really been an accessory to murder?*

After last night's huge argument, Bryce had threatened to kill her. He said things he'd never said before. She didn't know what had gotten into him. He had changed from a loving person to a hateful one.

Bryce had yelled, "Your career is over—just like your life here in Jacksonville. I hate you! I don't know why I ever loved you! You're the one who killed Michael, and no one will think otherwise. They'll believe me over you." His last words burned into her soul. Just when she thought things couldn't have gotten

51

worse, he yelled as she went out the door:

"If you don't keep your mouth shut, I'll kill you too!"

The only thing Christy could think about was how far and how fast she could get away. She didn't know where but getting out of Jacksonville was the only option. The police would look in town first. If she ran to her mother's in Savannah, that city could be next. *Think, Christy!*

When she got to her apartment, she pulled out one suitcase and an overnight bag from her closet top shelf. "I can't stay here," she cried while packing a week's full of clothes. She got in her car with only some clothing and a few personal necessities.

She headed west on I-10. It was the only route out of the state without going to her mother's in Georgia. The cream story was so incredible the police would never believe her. But maybe it wasn't the creamer. Maybe Bryce was just making things up.

After driving several miles on the freeway, she remembered her cousin Denise in Baton Rouge. Denise was her good friend she called Cuz. She'd call her after she crossed the state line.

Christy drove all night through the Florida Panhandle. She had forgotten how flat the interstate was until she got closer to Tallahassee. She loved seeing the rolling hills pop up in the distance with the thick, piney woods. She reminisced about the time she left Texas to move to Jacksonville. Once over the Florida state line, she found a quaint, little diner in a charming, small town called Daphne, Alabama. A pay phone was outside. She parked and walked into the restaurant.

"I'd like some scrambled eggs and cheese with grits, please," she said. "And some black coffee too."

With her torn denim hot pants and her low-cut white shirt tied under her bosom, she slipped onto the bar stool looking more like Daisy Duke than Christy Fields. All the men looked her way, but she gave them nothing but a big smile and some slight cleavage back. She had a friendly conversation with the waitress before she asked her question.

"Do you know where I could get a fair trade-in on my car?" she asked. "I'm headed for California and need some extra cash. I'd like to trade it in for something less expensive." She pointed to her car out the window. She knew the police would be looking for her new Toyota Supra. Bryce had given it to her as a gift, though nobody but the two of them knew it. She wanted to get rid of all memories of her horrible ex. She wasn't sure if she would go as far as California, but it sounded feasible, should anybody ask.

"Oh, you need to see Sam," the woman behind the counter said. "He's just a few miles ahead on the south side of the freeway. Sits back a piece off the road, but he'll give you a fair deal."

"Thanks, ma'am," Christy said as she left money with a tip for her check on the counter. "I'll tell him you sent me."

Great! If they are looking for me, it will be difficult to find me in a different vehicle.

She moved her car between the outside of the ladies' room and phone booth. Inside the restroom, she took out a bag full of supplies: a bottle of shampoo, a pair of scissors, some rubber gloves, and a box of brown hair dye. She had also purchased a head scarf and some dark sunglasses. She put on a fresh set of clothes. A different look would guarantee a fresh start.

A half hour later, she walked out of the restroom a new person. She didn't feel like Christy anymore. She no longer had long, blond hair, and in a few minutes, she wouldn't have a Supra either.

She found Sam's place easily.

"Can I he'p ya?" the older man said.

"Got any convertibles for sale?" Christy said.

"Yes, ma'am," Sam said with excitement in his Southern drawl. "Got a few! Any particular color you got in mind?"

"Nope. Just give me your best one with the lowest mileage. I'm heading for California."

They walked around his yard for a few minutes before he took her to the farthest area on the lot.

"Let's have a look over yonder. Might have a blue one, though not in the best of shape."

When Christy saw it, she knew it had to be hers. *Wow! Blue. My favorite color. How perfect—not too fancy or old. That should fit the bill.*

"How much ya askin' for it?" Christy said, laying her old Texan drawl on thick.

"I'll give yer $15,000 for your car. You can have the blue one for $10,000, okay? I've got the cash for the trade too. Never made it to the bank yesterday. Deal?" Sam stuck out his hand.

Christy ignored him and walked around the car, kicking the tires a few times. She pretended to know what she was doing. Then she stuck out her hand and said, "Sold!" They shook on it. Sam got the money from his safe, and they exchanged keys.

After getting her bags from the car, Christy divided her profit and gave half to Sam.

"What's this for?" he said with a puzzled look on his face.

"Let's just call it insurance," she said.

"Insurance? I ain't selling no insurance."

Christy laughed. "Oh, that's not what I meant. It's for a favor." Christy looked at him, smiled, and fluttered her eyelashes.

"What's that?" Sam said, still not understanding.

"Let's just say I gave you the $2,500 as a gift. You can keep that money for our little secret." Christy winked. "Promise me, darlin', you'll never describe me to any man who comes snooping around here or tell him what you sold me."

"Yes, ma'am," Sam said. "Will do." He stood a little taller, puffed out his chest, and added. "I can't remember already. Mum's the word."

"Great! I knew I could count on you," she said, continuing to use her most charming accent. She batted her eyelashes again and gave him a quick kiss on each cheek. Starting the old convertible, she stifled her chuckles at the thought of practically *giving* the car away. Sam could get more for it. Looking in the rearview mirror, she let out a belly laugh. There stood Sam with one hand on his hip, the other scratching his head and a toothless grin as broad as the rearview mirror.

Christy drove away feeling Sam would keep his promise. Men couldn't resist her smile, her baby blues, and her 36 DDDs, which she often used to get whatever she wanted. She'd insinuated that some awful man was chasing her. She noticed how Sam acted all defender-like. He'd just have to keep his mouth shut. *No one will find me now.*

She made it to Baton Rouge a couple of hours later, arriving at her cousin's place by ten that morning. It had been a long, tiring, all-night drive with only stops to purchase gas and her hair supplies. She had had a lot of time thinking about the big argument with Bryce, the threats he'd made, and believing it was over between them. She convinced herself she deserved better. As for Michael, she couldn't stop thinking about him, either. If Bryce did kill him or, God forbid, if *she* unknowingly

55

did, she could never return to Jacksonville. *I'll go back later and get the rest of my things one day. Or maybe not.* All she thought about was starting a new life, somewhere, somehow. She wanted to forget about Jacksonville *and* men.

Her cousin hardly recognized her when Christy drove up in the top-down convertible with short brown hair, big black sunglasses, and a scarf on her head. The Alabama plates must have confused her too, Christy thought.

Denise ran out into the driveway to see who it was. "Christy? Is that you?"

Christy took off her sunglasses.

"Yes, it's me, Cuz!"

"What brings you to Baton Rouge, honey?"

"I tried calling you on my way here, but your line was busy," Christy said. "I'm so sorry for barging in on you without any notice. What brings me here? You wouldn't believe it if I told you. Long story."

"Well, today's your lucky day! The salon gave me the next few days off. I've got all the time in the world. Your story sounds interesting. Come on in and tell me all about it."

The girls went inside and sat on the sofa. Christy explained some of what had happened over the past year but omitted the reason that prompted her quick departure.

"I wondered why I hadn't heard from you in so long. Your Christmas card sounded hopeful and promising. I thought you'd be driving that cool sports car Bryce gave you. Did he leave his wife? My Lord, I thought the two of you would be married by now and havin' babies!"

"Well, Denise, I thought the same thing. Things didn't happen the way I'd planned, and here I am. I traded that shiny sports car for the one outside." She sighed. "But I have a favor to ask."

"You name it. Anything. What is it?"

"From now on, I'd like for you to call me by a different abbreviation of my given name, okay? Please call me Tina."

"Sure. That's easy enough. How come?"

"You know. Fresh start. New name."

"It might be hard getting used to, but I'll try my best!"

"Thanks, sweetheart."

The cousins talked for a few hours and decided it wasn't too early to have a Bloody Mary and celebrate Christy's—rather, Tina's—new life.

"So. Whatcha going to do now?" Denise asked as they walked into the kitchen. She gathered the ingredients for the cocktails and started to mix them.

"I dunno. Find a new job, for one thing. I was thinking about driving to California, but I'm not sure yet. I'll think of something. First, we need to have our celebratory drink, right? A toast to old times and new."

Denise made their favorite Bloodies with celery, olives, jalapeños, and lots of cumin, just the way they liked it—hot and spicy. It was beginning to feel like old times again. The girls laughed, drank, and ate the snacks Denise had put on the kitchen bar. They'd grown up together when their families were neighbors back in Texas. Each girl called the other's parents "aunt" and "uncle" attached to their first names. That's how they thought of themselves as "cousins."

Later Denise watched Tina unpack the few things she had thrown together and helped her get settled in the guest bedroom.

"I think I need a nap after the all-night drive," Tina said. "I'm tired."

"Help yourself. Mi casa es su casa."

Tina was grateful she had a best friend like Denise. After a two-hour nap in her new room, she awoke refreshed. Denise took her for a drive around Baton Rouge and later stopped at a local seafood hangout. The more Tina saw of Denise's neighborhood and hometown, the more she liked it. She'd never been to Baton Rouge before. She put California out of her mind. Maybe Denise wouldn't mind her staying a little longer.

Chapter Seven

NEVLIN'S NEW CASE

$\mathcal{M}$egan and Eric drove to downtown Jax to speak with Mr. Nevlin. They agreed to hold back the contents of her dad's secret letter until the end. They wanted to listen first to what the attorney had to say. Their plan was to glean as much as they could before they would divulge anything more.

When they arrived at the Independent Life Building, they checked his office number on the lobby marquee.

"Wow!" Megan said. "He's on the thirty-fifth floor. That's the penthouse. He must have an amazing view of the St. John's River."

"I bet he has a fee to match," Erick said.

As they got off the elevator, they walked down the long hallway to find Nevlin's office at the end. Nevlin's wealth had made him lucky. He had been able to lease the posh corner suite. His office lobby inside had several leather seats, but Erick and Megan chose to remain standing to admire the view. They marveled at the incredible skyline of Jacksonville they'd never seen from this vantage point before. It took their breath away.

Just as Sally, Nevlin's secretary, offered them a seat, Mr. Nevlin walked out of his double office doors.

"Hey, Megan, Erick. How you two been doing? Please come in. Follow me."

Megan looked around. She could see how Dad had taken an instant liking to this guy. Similar honorary awards adorned his office walls and a few Florida State trophies for basketball. *They were both FSU alumni, and who could miss seeing the large blue marlin.*

"Have a seat," Nevlin said as he pointed to the chairs. He buzzed his secretary. "Sally, please bring me the Briscoe file."

Within a minute, Sally brought in a slim folder and handed it to him. She stood for a second, waiting for him to speak.

"Thanks, Sally. That will be all."

She turned, smiled at the couple, and walked out.

"Let's see," Nevlin said. "My notes show the timeline of events. Your father called me a little over a year ago. We set up an appointment. The day he came to my office, we discussed the two trusts he wanted written. One would be the personal one for you and the other for his business. Within a couple weeks, he sent me the required paperwork, and the trusts were written. One was a revocable trust for you, Megan, being the sole heir to his estate, including the house, its contents, the cars, and the bank accounts. The other trust would be for the business. It would be handled by me because of its complexity and having to deal with his business associate, Mr. Bryce Elmore."

"Mr. Elmore?" Megan said. "Excuse me, Mr. Nevlin, but what's the complexity? Since the business was owned fifty-fifty, I don't quite understand the problem."

"It's an irrevocable trust, isn't it?" Erick chimed in. "How on earth could it be rescinded? Didn't you tell Megan earlier that something else was in a contract Bryce wanted her to sign?"

"Let's back up," Nevlin said. "I'd like to go over the chain of events systematically, if you don't mind."

"Excuse me," Erick said. "Sorry."

Mr. Nevlin continued, "That's what happened on this date." He turned the file around and showed the couple the timeline as he pointed to each date.

"The trusts were signed and notarized here. I gave one copy of the two trusts to your father, and I kept another set for myself. Those were the copies I sent you."

"Go on," Megan said.

"About a month later, Mr. Briscoe—excuse me, your father—came back to my office with new documents. Let me pause for a minute and explain. By this time, your dad and I had become good friends. We started fishing together after we realized we were both widowers and had many other things in common.

"Anyway, those new documents had him upset. Prior to having the trusts written, Mr. Elmore had expressed an interest to buy your father's half of the business. Your dad declined. Behind his back, Bryce got an attorney, who drew up this other contract. That's the one I had explained regarding Bryce inheriting the company due to your father's debts."

"So that's the sticky business you told me about," Megan said.

"Yes, that's right. Have you been able to find anything in your father's papers yet?"

"No," Megan said. "Not yet. We're still looking. I had

hoped to sign whatever papers I needed to today, so Erick and I could be on the next flight out of Jacksonville. We're anxious to return home and back to work as soon as possible."

"Well, that *could* have happened had Mr. Elmore not put a lien on the business," Nevlin said.

"What did you say?" Megan said.

"What the hell?" Erick said. "I thought irrevocable trusts were just that—irrevocable—and that they had the strongest asset protection. Isn't that true in the state of Florida?"

"Yes and no," Nevlin said. "They are if they are set up properly and no provisions are made against the people wanting to contest it."

"Does that mean he's suing me?" Megan said.

"Not exactly," Nevlin said. "Mr. Elmore knew about the trust and considered any loopholes he might use. To transfer business assets on a trust, there must be a legitimate sale, an exchange, or a transfer. He's not going to challenge, of course, the house, cars, etc., just the business. That's not the whole issue. Because of the lien and Mr. Elmore owning the other half, your father's half must go up for sale."

"Oh, for heaven's sake," Megan said. "I never thought Bryce would become a traitor. I suppose he wants me to sell it to him for next to nothing. He knows I'm not interested in Dad's business."

Megan needed time to think. She walked over behind Nevlin's desk close to the floor-to-ceiling windows. She stared at the river. *Should I tell Nevlin about Dad's secret letter? Why has Bryce, our closest family friend, turned against me?* She jumped back into reality when she heard the muffled sound of a tugboat horn, which startled her.

"Megan," Erick said. "Please come back and listen to what Mr. Nevlin has to say. I don't think he's finished."

Megan walked back and sat in the same warm spot she'd left. "I'm sorry. Please go on."

"Your dad came back another time with more papers. See that on the timeline? This is the real problem."

"Now what?" Erick said. "What else does this guy have up his sleeve?"

Mr. Nevlin looked straight into Megan's eyes, ignoring Erick's outburst.

"These were the documents stating your father's side of the business had been losing money over the past couple of years. It proves that if the debt is not cleared up before your father's death, you owe Mr. Elmore this amount." He pointed to the figure.

Megan cried out. "That's six figures!"

"More like a quarter of a million dollars," Erick agreed. "That's probably *more* than half of what the business is worth. What a snake."

Megan pressed her palms against her temples. "Oh, dear God! What am I supposed to do now?" She started to cry.

"There, there," Nevlin said as he handed her a box of tissues from his drawer. "Here are the options as I see it. Option one: Get the financial facts from all your father's files. Let me look at them. Try and talk some sense into Mr. Elmore without getting more lawyers or judges involved. Settle this between yourselves. Option two: If that doesn't work, we'll get to a judge first and see if there can be a mediation agreement without a trial. Lastly, which in my opinion is the worst option, get yourself the best trial/estate attorney and fight the son of a bitch."

"If this had happened in New York, Megan and I would have no trouble finding the best lawyers around." Erick said. "But we don't have ties to the legal community here, and I feel the 'good ol' boy' system is still in business. You've got to help us find the right person."

"I'll be glad to take over this case, if I can," Nevlin said. "I'm sorry it's come to this. I feel partially responsible. If I had had any idea there would have been a lien or you'd get sued over the company, the trust could have been written differently. I'm sorry I didn't set it up with more protection."

"You couldn't have foreseen the future," Megan said. "Erick and I will talk this over and let you know our decision."

"Does Mr. Elmore have any idea we know about this?" Erick said.

"Not to my knowledge," Nevlin said.

Megan nodded "Good. Then let's keep it that way. Looks like we'll be staying in town an extra week to tie up the loose ends of the estate and hopefully take care of this too."

"Yes, please keep in touch," Nevlin said.

"Oh, by the way," Megan said. "Did you read the letter from Dad that was in the envelope with the trusts?"

"No. Of course, not. Your father told me it was specifically meant for you."

"Well, I brought you a copy," Megan said and handed him the letter. "I think you should read it before our next meeting."

"Okay, I will," Nevlin said. His intercom buzzed. "Excuse me a minute."

"There's an Officer Alvarez here to see you," Sally said.

"Just a minute," Nevlin said to her. "I'll be right there. Let me show these folks out."

As Officer Alvarez stood in the lobby, Megan and Erick walked past. The three of them exchanged nods with short words of greeting.

As soon as Megan and Erick arrived at the express elevator, Megan said, "I wonder what that could be about."

"Oh, come on, honey." Erick said. "You know lawyers and cops. They *always* have things to talk about. Jacksonville is a big city. It might not be about us. I wouldn't give it a second thought."

—⁓—

Megan and Erick made another appointment with Nevlin. They had been diligent when looking for the financial papers the attorney needed. They brought a box over for him to examine.

"I found these documents I think you'd like to inspect," she said.

"Sure, I'll be glad to. What are they?"

"I remembered something my father had mentioned to me a while back. He thought Bryce might have been doing some shady dealings, but he had no proof. Perhaps that was when Bryce wanted Daddy to sell and he didn't. Anyway, Daddy never shared anything specific with me. The two of them kept their work dealings separate. However, Christy did the bookkeeping for the whole company.

"After my dad declined to sell to his partner, looks like he kept his own copies of whatever he turned in to Christy, and might have kept it private. I found these papers hidden underneath his desk in a secret drawer. They are his financial dealings over the past couple of years." She stopped talking and waited.

"What do you think?" Erick asked, trying to be more polite this time.

"It's definitely something I'll have to read and look into," Nevlin said. "It may take some time to compare it with the rest of the paperwork you found."

"Did you get a chance to read the letter?" Megan said.

"Do you seriously think your father thought someone was trying to kill him?" Nevlin asked.

"Well, the coroner's office determined the cause of death was probable heart attack," Erick said. "That's what was on the report. It's only the doctor's opinion, but we're starting not to believe it."

"My father was the sweetest person in the world," Megan said. "He wouldn't hurt a fly. Since I've returned, many weird things have happened. Up until this past year, my dad was in the best of health. We used to jog whenever we got together. This letter was a shock to me."

"If the letter *is* true," Erick said, "I'm wondering who had a motive to kill my father-in-law, or did he know something that got him killed?"

"Mr. Nevlin," Megan said, "I can't ignore these strange things. When I got into town last week, I found out Christy, Bryce's secretary, had been having an affair with him over this past year. Then she throws her arms around my father in the casket, as you witnessed, during the wake, shouting, 'I'm sorry. I'm so sorry.' Next Bryce's office was turned upside down and all the money in the safe stolen. Bryce blamed Christy, and now she's nowhere to be found."

"Yes, I see," said Nevlin. "Those are plenty of facts to consider. Has Bryce or his lawyer approached you about the contract he wants you to sign?"

"Not a word," Megan said. "And you? I suppose now he has bigger things on his mind."

"No, he hasn't. And I suppose he has."

"Mr. Nevlin," Erick said. "We'll pay you whatever it takes to solve the mystery of Mr. Briscoe's death. Megan has been sick over this."

Erick continued talking as Megan tuned him out and walked over to the large windows like she'd done at their first meeting. She was fascinated with the perspective of Jacksonville's St. John's from the penthouse view. She heard the tugboats sounding as they brought in the large merchant marine ships to Jacksonville's port. The city seemed so full of life and activity. *How could this be happening to me? Why did Daddy die so young? And why did he leave me in this predicament?*

"We don't know what to do," Erick said. "Is it possible for you to take over for us, so we could leave Jacksonville? We've been here long enough. It's time to get back to New York."

Nevlin cleared his throat. "Megan, how do want me to handle this? Would you like to sell the business?"

"I'm sorry," Megan said. She turned around and walked back to the comfortable leather chair. "What did you say? Oh yes. The business. I've thought about it. For its fair market value, of course. But Bryce's documents claim it's in the hole and I owe *him* money. That's a farce. There's something fishy going on. I believe Dad found something he shouldn't have, and someone killed him. I just don't know who."

"Have you talked to the police about any of this?" Nevlin said.

"The police have nothing to go on," Megan said. "It's just

speculation at this point."

"We don't even know if the police are in any way involved," Erick interrupted.

Nevlin gave him a funny look but didn't dignify Erick's response.

"Besides," she said, "the coroner's office says it's a heart attack—cut and dry. The burglary has a prime suspect of Christy. Both in the same office but the police have no evidence any of this is connected."

"Perhaps there's something in these documents that could lead them there," Nevlin said. "If you get the okay from the police, why don't you kids go back to New York? I'm sure I can take care of the business end. We can keep in contact by phone. I'll look into the questions you have about the death of your father and keep you posted."

"Thanks for your help," Megan said. The three of them stood and shook hands.

"I have a friend who's a private investigator. Name's Fred Jackson. I worked with him when I was in the DA's office. I'll see what he can do. He's retired now but owes me a favor. I'll let you know as soon as either of us find out anything. That is, if you agree we can put him on the job."

"Sounds good to me," Megan said. "I would appreciate whatever your friend can do to help us."

Chapter Eight

A NEW SLEUTH

A few days later, Nevlin got an intercom call from Sally. Alvarez had returned and was in the front office requesting to see him again. Nevlin told her to buzz him in.

"Been a long time since you and my dad worked together in the DA's office, huh?" Alvarez said, making a comment rather than saying a usual greeting. "Thanks for seeing me on short notice."

"Not a problem," Nevlin said. "How may I help you?"

"As you know, we have the autopsy report on Michael Briscoe. It stated probable heart attack, but I'd like some more information."

"Of course," Nevlin said. "What would you like to know?"

"How long were you in Michael's office the night of his death?"

"Twenty, thirty minutes tops, until we got interrupted by a phone call."

"A call? From whom? You didn't mention this the other day."

"Oh, I must have forgotten. I remember after he hung up, he told me he was going to meet someone. We had to postpone our plans until the next day."

"I see," Alvarez said. "Did he ever discuss his health with you?"

"No. Never did. Although I had noticed he had lost some weight."

"Well, that's all for now," the detective said. "And if you think of anything else you might have forgotten, call me."

—⁓—

A week passed, and Nevlin hadn't gotten any further along with the Briscoe case. He hadn't heard anything from the police either. He decided to call Detective Alvarez and see what he could find out.

"Alvarez," Nevlin said, after they got connected. "How's it going with the Briscoe-Elmore case?"

"Still ongoing," Alvarez said. "No leads, I'm afraid. Christy's red Supra hasn't turned up, and neither has she. Why? What's up?"

"Since I'm the executor of Michael Briscoe's half of the company, I'm calling on behalf of my client Megan Briscoe. Would it be all right if Megan and Erick head back home to New York? They want to return while they still have their jobs waiting for them. They've already dealt with Mr. Briscoe's personal estate business. I'll be dealing with Mr. Elmore from now on and arranging an agreement regarding the trust."

"So," Alvarez said, "you're the executor of half the Briscoe-Elmore company? Well, I'll be dammed. Guess I'll be dealing with you should anything more come up."

70

"That's right," Nevlin said. "May my clients fly home now?"

"Yes. That'll be fine."

"Thank you. Call me anytime."

"Don't worry, I will," the detective said.

What Alvarez didn't tell Nevlin was the police had gotten an anonymous tip. Someone called the JPD and told them to check into Bryce's financials. The person also said the police should investigate Nevlin's dealings too. The phone call came from a pay phone and the caller didn't stay on long enough to trace. The only lead Alvarez had was that the voice belonged to a woman.

As soon as Nevlin got off the phone with Alvarez, he called his old pal, Fred Jackson. Fred was a Jacksonville Police Department detective who'd retired from the force. He went into freelance private investigating at the same time Nevlin left the DA's office to go into business for himself. They had remained friends but didn't see each other often. Fred had recommended Michael to Nevlin.

"Hey, I missed you at the funeral of our old pal, Michael. Where were you?"

"Yeah," Fred said. "I'm sorry I missed it. The missus and I were on vacation. St. Simon's. To visit my wife's, Lucy's, folks."

"Hope you had a good time in Georgia. Have things been crazy around here. I got some important news and perhaps a job for you. When did you get back?"

"Yesterday."

"I was wondering if you had time for a drink. Could you meet me after work today?"

"Excuse me?" Fred said. "A drink? Didn't you know I quit

the stuff? Yep. Gave it all up right after I left the force. Lucy gave me an ultimatum—it was either her or the bottle."

"Sorry, Fred," Nevlin said. "But good for you. Okay, let's meet for an early dinner at the Chart House. My treat. Sorry this is last minute, but can you make it?"

"Sure. Can't wait to hear what you've got to say."

Nevlin buzzed in Sally. After she walked in, he gave her a set of instructions.

"Something's come up. I'm taking the rest of the day off and tomorrow as well. Please clear my calendar and reschedule my clients for next week. Thanks, Sally."

Nevlin took the elevator to the garage and picked up his 500-Class Mercedes-Benz. He looked forward to seeing Fred and reminiscing about when they used to work together on homicide cases. They always had a great working relationship.

The drive to the Chart House over the Main Street Bridge was short. It was a popular hangout for undercover law enforcement. He walked into the upscale restaurant and asked the hostess for a private table for two at 5:00 p.m. With an hour to himself, he stopped at the bar and ordered a dirty martini. This was a habit he'd started when his wife became sick with cancer. He never broke the routine after she died. It had become an ingrained pattern.

After finishing his drink, he approached the hostess again. "Is there any way my friend and I could sit next to the waterfall by the window?"

"Sure. Not a problem," she said. "Would you like to be seated now?"

"That would be great!" Nevlin followed the waitress to the last empty table next to the waterfall and sat with his back to the window.

Almost as soon as Nevlin was seated, Fred walked in. Nevlin liked that about the man. He had many admirable qualities like conscientiousness, punctuality, and dependability. All the traits one needed to be a good cop.

Nevlin stood up to greet him. They shook hands. Fred, an African American man, and Nevlin, the white former DA, had been friends for years even before the civil rights bill was passed. They always worked on the right side of the law and never let race get in the way of their friendship.

"Hey, Fred," Nevlin said. "How's it going?"

"Not too bad," Fred said. "Lucy and I needed a vacation. Even if it was with her folks. Business is looking up. I like being my own boss. It's fantastic. How about you, and what's so important?"

"Well, a new case has become complicated. What was once a simple irrevocable trust has turned into a possible murder."

"Murder? How could that be?"

"I'm sorry to tell you," Nevlin said, "but it's about our mutual friend Michael."

"What? Michael? Dear Lord!"

They ordered their food, and Nevlin told the story to Fred over appetizers and dinner. He explained the letter Michael had written his daughter, the strange gesture Christy, the head secretary, made at the funeral parlor, the affair Bryce Elmore had been having with her, and the break-in at Bryce's office at the Briscoe-Elmore and Associates company.

Nevlin added, "There's one more thing. Remember the story of Captain Eliseo Alvarez? You know, the cop who was murdered in his home with his wife and young son. The 1970s burglary that went wrong."

Fred had a strange look on his face. The kind showing memory loss.

"It was the case where the older brother was away at college when it happened. No matter if you've forgotten. Anyway, that college son is now grown and on the Jacksonville police force. Name's David Alvarez. He's the one who is on the break-in case and investigating Michael's death. You remember Bryce Elmore, don't you?"

"I'm confused. That's a lot of information to digest. But what's the complicated part? Nothing sounded complex to me. As for Bryce, I just remember him as a jerk."

"Well, for some reason young Alvarez has been on *my* case. Because I was the last person to see Michael alive, he won't leave me alone. I think the police believe I have something to do with all this. I was the one who drew up the trusts. I was at the funeral and pulled Christy away. They've seen me several times with the family. I guess that's reason enough for Alvarez to be suspicious. I admit not putting enough safety features into the trust in case of a death, but I didn't think Michael would be dying anytime soon."

"You've still not told me your plan," Fred said. "Why am I here?"

"Ah, yes, the favor," Nevlin said. "This is what I wanted to ask. I'm not sure if you or Lucy are going to like it. The job's out of town."

"Where is it?"

"New York City."

"New York City?" Fred said. "What the heck?"

"Calm down, Fred," Nevlin said. "I'll pay you well."

"First, you better tell me what it is you want me to do.

74

Then I'll decide."

The server came by to ask if they needed anything.

"Two dirty martinis," Nevlin said.

"Nev, I told you I don't drink," Fred said, calling him by his nickname. "I just got my second-year chip."

"Sorry, pal," Nelvin said. "They're both for me. I'm going to need them to explain my plan." He turned to the waitress and added. "Please give this man whatever he wants to drink."

— ⬬ —

Megan and Erick had flown on the red eye bound for JFK International. They wanted to sleep in and spend one more leisurely day in their home and routine before going back to the office. They noticed the leaves had turned colors, and the cool autumn breeze flushed their cheeks. The view from their high-rise on the seventeenth floor on the Upper East Side overlooked Schurz Park. They loved where they lived because it gave them the opportunity to jog every morning between Schurz and Central Park before leaving for work. Because of the late-evening flight, they skipped their usual run for a warmer experience—a long and slow love-making session in the bedroom.

After the final cuddling, they looked out over the water towers on the shorter buildings' rooftops. They compared Jacksonville to New York. Although Jacksonville did have its ocean, river, and Intracoastal, they would never trade their new city for any place else in the world. They loved its cosmopolitan vibe, museums, shopping, and culture. It made them feel more alive. With their salaries, they could afford to do the things they enjoyed the most, including the symphony and ballet.

"Want to grab something to eat?" Megan said. "Then we could take a stroll in the park on the way home. I'd really like that. I'm famished. I'd love to smell more of that fresh, crisp air mixed with the street vendors' food."

"Okay, hon," Erick said. "Let's take a shower first. Then I'll run down and get a newspaper while you finish getting ready."

"Sounds wonderful," Megan said. She gave Erick a kiss good-bye like one he would never forget.

After getting dressed, Megan and Erick ate at one of the local delis and started to meander through Central Park. They didn't notice a man who had been following them since he'd eaten at the deli too. The man made sure he stayed far enough behind not be noticed.

Because of all the people in the park, it was easy enough for the disguised man to blend in among the walkers, joggers, cyclists, and Rollerbladers. Children laughed everywhere throughout the park. It was a typical Sunday with everyone enjoying themselves, except perhaps for the mothers and nannies who pushed crying babies in their carriages.

Too much in love to be bothered by anyone, Erick and Megan clung close and never noticed the old Black man with white hair, black coat, and hat with a cane. They hugged and kissed every time they stopped to look at something. Now the old man approached and passed them, walking with a small limp. In one of their many embraces, the lovebirds didn't notice him.

When they arrived home, Erick threw down the keys to their apartment in the bowl on the sideboard.

"What shall we do for the rest of the day?" Erick said. "I don't want to think about work."

"How about a museum? We haven't been to one in quite some time. Maybe the Met? Whaddya think? We could go there and maybe the Rock for dinner? I'd love that."

"Yeah, that sounds relaxing," Erick said. "I'm in. But how about another little nap first?"

"Sure, hon," she said. Megan knew exactly what his code word meant by the smile on his face. He hadn't had enough of her in Florida. They'd been too busy.

Later, they dressed for a night out. They wandered through the Met, taking their time enjoying the regular exhibits of artwork as well as those on special consignment. They took a taxi to the Rock and enjoyed their dinner and drinks in Rockefeller Center's pricey restaurant.

The evening ended up being luxurious for Megan. Just what she needed. She wanted to be as close to Erick as she could get. She knew their predictable everyday work in the law office would begin again in the morning. But she couldn't take her eyes off the man sitting at a table far away from the couple. He looked like a wealthy Texas tycoon with a Stetson hat, handlebar mustache, and respectable suit. She thought the African American man looked familiar. *I must be seeing things.*

—⟋⟍—

In the morning, Fred called Nevlin, his friend and now employer.

"I don't know how long you want me to stay up here, Nev," Fred said. "Nothing seems out of the ordinary between those two young lawyers. They ate, they slept, and they went to dinner. They went for a walk in the park, visited the Met, and ate at the Rock. Now, that was expensive. You gonna get a big bill for that one. They never knew I was following them."

"Well, for crying out loud, Fred. It's not really them you need to be concerned about. It's anyone else who might be following them. Don't you remember? With Michael Briscoe dead, Christy missing, and God only knows…possibly dead too, the only thing preventing Bryce from owning the whole business is Megan's death. You see to it nothing happens to that young lady. Understand?"

"Yes, Nev," Fred said. "I understand. I'll stay put for now. You are paying me well."

"Damn straight I am. Until I find out who's behind this paper trail, you're their guardian angel."

"Are you sure you don't want me to call the police while I'm here?"

"And tell them what? That there *may* be someone who *may* want to kill them? We don't even know that yet. Hell, I haven't even told the Jacksonville PD."

"Sure, boss," Fred said, as he caught himself because Nevlin told him never to call him that. "I mean, Nevlin. I'll see it through."

"Thanks, Fred."

—⟋⟍—

On day three, Fred got up and went downstairs to grab a quick snack from one of the vending machines in his hotel lobby. He wasn't sure when the "kids," as Nevlin insisted they be called, would be leaving for work. Fred had a hunch he might catch them hailing a cab from across the street if he woke up early enough. His timing paid off. As soon as he saw them enter a taxi, he hailed another.

"Follow that Yellow Cab," he told his driver. The kids had left in a hurry, and he didn't want to lose them. His driver knew just how to finagle his vehicle in between the other cars down Broadway and Eighth near the East Village. Fred was happy his cabbie wasn't in the mood for idle chitchat and thankful the drive was short from the Upper East Side down Broadway.

When he saw Megan and Erick—the kids, as he now called them—exit the cab in front of him, he told the driver to drive one more block where he would get out and walk. He paid the driver, exited the cab, and strolled across the street. He'd noticed a coffeeshop opposite the law firm with a good view. He walked inside, ordered a large coffee with cream and sugar and an almond croissant.

He was lucky to find a window seat available. He sat and spread the *Times* and *Wall Street Journal* he'd purchased on the table. He'd sit there all day until someone kicked him out of his booth, he thought. Tomorrow he'd bring his steno pad notebook and wear a different disguise. He packed several to be prepared.

Midmorning, Fred grew tired of reading the papers and decided to take a walk to the Village and look around. It had a younger feel with its artsy shops and Bohemian-style restaurants. It was Fred's first time in New York City. He felt awkward listening to people talk. He felt like a stranger in a strange land. He tried to eliminate his Southern accent and blend in.

Chapter Nine
THE CONFESSIONS

With only a partial fingerprint on the picture frame, Alvarez's team couldn't find any match in their system. The only prints they found were Bryce's and an unknown partial. Alvarez deduced it must have been a professional job or an inside one. Who else could have known about the safe hidden behind the beautiful scene of the Sea Turtle Inn on the beach? Lucky for Alvarez, the suspect became sloppy and accidently touched the side of the frame to close it. The detective paid another visit to Briscoe-Elmore and Associates.

"Like to ask you some more questions, Mr. Elmore," Alvarez said as he came into his office. He looked around and noticed that the company looked as if nothing had happened the week before. Everything was back in place. "Got a few minutes?"

"Sure," Bryce said. "Have a seat. Happy to help. Find Christy yet?"

"Well, no. That's one of the problems. Can you think of anyone else who would want to steal from your company?"

"Hell, no!" Bryce said. "Like I told you guys. No one could

have done this but Christy. She's the only one with a motive."

"Her apartment looked fine," Alvarez said. "Nothing out of place. Her furniture's still there, with lots of clothes in the closet. Doesn't look like foul play, but no one has seen her. Do you have any ideas where she might have gone?"

"Her mother lives in Savannah," Bryce said. "All other relatives live in Chicago. That's all I know. I haven't any knowledge as far as friends are concerned. She had a best friend in California, but her pal, Susan, died about a year ago. I took Christy to her funeral."

"I see," Alvarez said. "You haven't seen or heard from her since the break-in, right?"

"Right," Bryce said. "Like I told you. I fired that bitch's ass the night of the robbery. Told her I never wanted to see her again. I just want my money back."

"Money? What money?" Alvarez looked surprised. He pulled off his sunglasses and turned them around. "May I call you Bryce? I don't understand. You fly across the continent with this woman for her friend's funeral—a person you don't even know. Now you say she owes *you* money. There's something you're not saying. Get straight with me."

Alvarez noticed Bryce's hands became sweaty and his neck turned red.

"Christy started working for the company several years ago. She always was a looker. Know what I mean? That sweet Southern accent of hers kept tempting me. We kept it professional until a few years ago. Things changed after that."

"Yeah, I saw her once," Alvarez said. "I wouldn't have kicked her out of my bed. Go on."

"Christy was upset she couldn't afford to fly to California

for her friend's funeral. So, I offered to take her. I'd do a little business out there and then support her by accompanying her to the service.

"It happened the evening after it was over. We had adjoining rooms at the hotel, and Christy knocked on my door crying in the middle of the night. I comforted her, and then, well, before you knew it, we became more than friends."

"What happened next?"

Bryce thought he saw Alvarez falling into his empathetic trap.

"After a year of messing around," Bryce said, "we tried our best to keep it from everyone here. I confessed I loved her. I promised to divorce my wife and we'd live happily ever after. But months later, everything became twisted."

"How do you mean?"

"Christy changed," Bryce said. "She felt like she owned me. Started bossing me around, calling me at home and demanding I come back to the office. She said we needed to do some work. But not really *work*, ya know?"

"Go on," Alvarez said.

"She became increasingly dependent and needy," Bryce said and loosened his tie. "I couldn't stand it. I'd been trying to call it off for months, but she wasn't having any of it. If she weren't at home, she'd call me from a motel begging me to meet her. The final straw was when she called me at home during a barbeque and asked for another meeting. I came here, we argued, and the same night I fired her. The same night as the break-in when she took everything from her desk."

"You said you wanted your money back? What money?"

"When things were hot between us, I started giving her

money. I couldn't give her a ring, so I gave her money for our little love nest. She kept it inside her bedroom mattress."

"Why didn't you tell me this before? How much did you give her?"

Bryce started to pace the floor. He looked like he didn't want to talk about it any further and ignored Alvarez's questions.

"I was embarrassed," Bryce said, changing the subject. "It was an affair, and now it's over. When Christy left, the safe was intact. I might have told her one night during a moment of passion. But I don't remember giving her the code. She must have found out somehow. The money she owes me is the nest egg we shared for our future together. All of it was mine. She robbed me of that too!"

"I think you can kiss that money good-bye," Alvarez said. "Think of it like you said, an old engagement ring. Que será, será. Who else knew about the combination to the safe?"

"Only Michael and he's deceased now," Bryce said. "Think she had an accomplice?"

"Not sure," Alvarez said. "I'll keep in touch." The detective left and went down to his office at the Jacksonville PD headquarters. He had a hunch Bryce wasn't telling the whole truth. He tried to think of who else might have a motive. If Bryce held back information about Christy and their affair, what else was he holding back?

He needed to find Christy and hold her for questioning. She could be the only one who could shed light on the crime. He wasn't buying the story of Christy doing the burglary. The tossed furniture would have been too heavy for her, and she already had cash in the mattress. Why was Bryce blaming her? What was he up to?

Alvarez made several calls that afternoon. Bryce had given him a slip of paper, which he assumed was Christy's mother's phone number. The detective tried the number but it had been disconnected. Alvarez's search came up empty. No one had seen the girl with the long blond hair in the red Supra. All efforts to find her car had been futile. What was Bryce not telling him? What was Nevlin hiding? What were they up to? He had to do something quick. He asked his team to put surveillance on them both.

—⟋⟍—

Laura Elmore walked into the Basilica of the Immaculate Conception on Duval Street in Jacksonville. Although she was going to confession, she thought it better not to confess in her home church. She had been a devout Catholic her whole life and grew up in a bilingual home. She had been baptized, confirmed, and married in the basilica but hadn't been back except for the occasional marriages or baptisms of family or friends.

Her strong belief taught her sins could only be absolved by a priest. However, it didn't matter what Catholic church or what priest. She didn't want to confess to Father Pat at her home church. She was sure if she confessed to him, he would corner her later and tell her to seek counseling. She wanted nothing to do with that.

Going to the basilica made more sense. She would go when the priest on duty would be a Spanish speaker. Admitting her sins in Spanish to a priest she hardly knew seemed brilliant. She had to tell a priest and get her sins off her chest. It had been a month, and she couldn't live with herself any longer. It felt strange as she walked in. She put her hand in the baptismal font with holy water and crossed herself. With her rosary in her hand, she walked down the same aisle she had walked as a bride thirty years ago. Now she was going to confess something she never thought she would.

She continued to walk toward the sanctuary and turned left. Many votive candles were glowing, and some had been left waiting for more lighting of prayers and supplications. She knelt, lit a candle, held her rosary with a grip of life, and asked for strength for what she was about to do.

After praying, she rose and strolled over to the confessional booth. When inside, she closed the door. She knew what had to be done but wasn't in a hurry. *Priests are always patient,* she thought. *He'll wait for me.*

"Perdóname Padre, porque he pecado," Laura started. *Forgive me Father, for I have sinned.* "Han pasado años desde mi ultima confesion." *It has been years since my last confession.*

After Laura's penance, contrition, and absolution were given, the priest blessed her and freed her of her sins. Well, not all of them. Laura only admitted the venial ones. She'd planned to confess the mortal ones, too, but backed out at the last minute. She had plenty of time to confess those. She thought she was smart to confess in Spanish at the basilica. But now she felt stupid. What the hell was she doing? Different priest, different church, and different language? How silly.

She walked out of the basilica and into the parking lot. Her mind was wrapped up in her confession and didn't notice the black Mercedes parked several spots away. That was until the tall man standing next to a car close to hers called her over.

"Hey, Mrs. Elmore? Is that you?" Nevlin said.

"Excuse me?" Laura said, not recognizing the attorney until he walked closer. "Oh, Mr. Nevlin, I'm sorry. How are you?"

"Just fine," he said. "Fancy meeting you here. Everything all right?"

"Yes, I was just dropping off a donation. Bryce and I were married here and still do what we can to keep the church going. You?"

"Father Garcia and I have some business to take care of," he said.

"Oh," Laura said. "I'm sorry. Can't be late for work. See you later."

Laura jumped in her car and drove off. She thought it a strange coincidence Nevlin was there to see the same priest she'd sat across from in the confessional. But didn't dwell on it.

She drove to Baptist Medical Center. She knew her colleagues and patients would give her the lift she needed. Her job in obstetrics had encompassed her whole nursing career. Working with mothers and their babies brought her joy. Her career was her passion, and she rarely missed work. The only time she ever missed was during her marriage to Bryce and when she'd asked for extended leave after Brittney's birth.

When Brittney became older and was in school full-time, Laura changed to a part-time position in the evenings. Bryce told her she didn't have to work, but if she really wanted to, and it didn't interfere with their daughter's school or extracurricular activities, he'd let her continue. Her part-time status as nurse continued even after Brittney married and had kids. Laura was able to set her own hours, so she could spend more time with the grandkids, pursue her tennis at the country club, and be involved with the women's club at church.

The more she got involved with church, the closer she became to Kathy, Michael Briscoe's wife. The family already had a close friendship because of the men being business partners. Kathy and Laura had their children within months of each other, and as the two daughters grew up, the families began vacationing together.

They attended the same church too. Laura and Kathy served on several boards and charitable organizations at Assumption Catholic Church. It all ended when Kathy became sick with breast cancer. Kathy suffered a long time, and Laura did all she could to help her friend, including bringing homecooked meals over to the Briscoes'.

After working a four-hour shift, she passed by the empty Briscoe house on her way home. She stopped and parked in front, staring at the "For Sale" sign. She thought about happier times when the families would get together for barbeques and vacations.

"I miss you, Kathy. I miss you too, Michael," she said out loud to herself. She silently prayed again for forgiveness using her rosary before taking off.

It was a short drive down San Jose Boulevard to her daughter's house. The road, lined with palm trees mixed with firs, gave her a sense of serenity. She parked in front and walked to the side. She loved the neighborhood where they all lived. She could hear sounds coming from the backyard and followed the voices of her grandchildren. The door to the garage was unlocked, so she walked through.

"Hey!" she called outside the kitchen window. "Anybody home?"

"We're out here by the pool, Mom," her daughter yelled. "Want to swim with us?"

"That's okay," Laura said. "I didn't bring my suit. Wasn't I supposed to babysit today? Did you forget your doctor's appointment?"

"Mom, I think you're the one who's forgotten. That's tomorrow."

"Oh, shoot," Laura said. "Guess I was somewhat distracted today."

"Well, as long as you are here, how about a glass wine or a margarita? Come sit with me. We can watch the kids together until our husbands get home."

"Don't mind if I do," Laura said. "I didn't have anything important today anyway."

Chapter Ten

NEW YORK CITY TAILS

Fred thought he would enjoy himself in the big city. But within a few weeks, the days became monotonous. He found some touristy things to do but had never ridden the tour bus. Trying it today might give him ideas to pursue while Megan and Erick were at work. He wanted to spend his time more productively. He knew he'd be up north for a while longer.

The kids' situations had become routine but also were a problem. He never knew when they would clock off, and it was difficult to follow them. It was a crapshoot as to when they would leave work and hail a cab for God knows where. There were endless possibilities in the city and outskirts as to where he would have to follow them in the evenings.

Fred was determined to find a better way to spy on them. If only he could bug their phone, he thought, he'd have better luck. He had no connections in New York, and he needed help.

He read the newspaper at the local deli and walked back to his hotel room. He called Nevlin and described his frustrations.

"Nev," Fred said. "This job has become tiresome. The exact same thing happens every day. I'm not having any success, and I'm running low on cash."

"Are you sure you're watching the environment around the kids, like I told you?" Nevlin asked.

"Of course! But this is ridiculous. They eat; they sleep. They go to work, come home. That's what I'm about ready to do too. Come home!"

"Whoa, buddy!" Nevlin said. "Why do you think I am paying you for this job, plus all your expenses? I'll send you some extra. Haven't you seen anyone?"

"That's what I am trying to tell you. It sure would help if I could find a way to bug their conversations. Sometimes they leave, and I have no idea where they're going or for how long. Sometimes my cabbie loses them too. It's been futile."

"But everything seems normal there?"

"As normal as New York can be," Fred said with a snort. "This is a crazy place. Don't you have someone else who could switch places with me? Maybe getting those bugs would make me a happy camper. Then I'd know in advance where they're headed and for how long."

"Let me see what I can do," Nevlin said. "Sorry, Fred. I really thought something would have happened by now. I'll call you later."

"Okay. Hey! What about Christy? Jacksonville PD find her yet?"

"Nope. In fact, Bryce hasn't made his move to collect any money from Megan, and she hasn't budged to sell her half of the company. I think she's waiting for him to make his move first. So, we're at a stalemate for whatever reason."

"That's strange. Don't you think there's got to be something more?"

Nevlin agreed. "Yep. Got that right. Until they find Christy or Bryce talks, which I doubt will happen, the police have a cold case."

"Geesh," Fred said. "I wish somebody would do something, so I could come back home."

"Come on, Fred. I told you this might take some time. Remember what I'm paying you? I transferred money into your account yesterday, so you're good for the rest of this month and a couple more."

"Months. Oh, shit."

"Admit it, Fred. You weren't making *that* much money in Florida. Think of it as part of your pension. I paid you for this month and several in advance. There's more if you need it. You can do what you want during the day. It's when Megan and Erick are on the move in the evening that I'm most concerned about."

"Okay, okay," Fred said. "See what you can do to help me get me those bugs. I need them to do my job. Hurry up, and maybe I'll learn something."

"Promise I will," Nevlin said. "Talk to you soon."

In Jacksonville, Nevlin made a few phone calls to his old cop buddies still on the force. He only called those he knew he could trust. He didn't want anyone, especially Alvarez to know what he was doing. Some cops owed him favors, and he didn't think this would be too much to ask. When Nevlin told his friends still on the force that he thought a young woman's life was in danger, the officers were ready to help.

Nevlin called Fred that afternoon. "Hey, Fred. I got what you were asking for."

"Great!" Fred said. "Can you overnight them to me? I'd like to get this job working as soon as possible. I also need their home numbers. I'm sure you have them. I can get the number of the DA's office easily enough."

"Not a problem, Fred. How exactly are you going to do it?"

"Leave that up to me. I think it best you don't know. I'll let you know when the job's done, okay? Don't worry. I'll keep you posted."

"Sounds good to me," Nevlin said and hung up.

Once Fred knew he could get the bugs, he thought about an old buddy he knew from the military. He remembered Leroy lived in New York and worked for the state telephone company. He called him.

"Hey, Leroy! It's me, Fred. And I'm here in the city."

Fred told him the circumstances without getting into too much detail over the phone as to what brought him to his friend's hometown.

"Leroy, may I take you to dinner tonight? My treat. I have a favor to ask."

"Sure," Leroy said. "Would love to. What is it, may I ask?"

"I'd prefer not to say. Let's talk about it over a nice meal at the Tavern on the Green."

"*The* Tavern on the Green?" Leroy said. "In Central Park? That highfalutin place? It's pretty darn expensive. Are you sure you can afford it?"

Fred laughed. "It's not me who's paying. I'll explain when I see you. Can you meet there around seven?"

Fred thought he heard Leroy choke.

"You're not joking me, are you? Sure. I mean, I'd do anything for a chance to eat in that place. Lived here all my life but never had the bucks to afford it."

"Well, now you'll have a chance to see the park from a different perspective," Fred said. "I'm looking forward to the experience myself."

"Okay, not a problem."

The two old friends talked about what they had been doing since the military, when they'd last seen each other. Fred learned Leroy had become a widower and had moved into senior housing. Fred shared he and Lucy had lived in the same house on the Northside of Jacksonville ever since their wedding.

"It will be good to see you again, Leroy," Fred said.

"Yes," said Leroy. "And you as well."

At the restaurant, while waiting for their food, they began talking about some of their 'Nam experiences. They shared their army stories and some of their most dangerous missions. It was time for Fred to interrupt and get to the crux of the matter.

"Leroy, I'm afraid what I am about to ask you is illegal," Fred said in a low tone.

"Really?" Leroy said. "I'm not too sure about that, but it does sound intriguing. What have you got in mind?"

"Well, to ease your mind," Fred said. "This will be nothing like 'Nam. I will be paying you well. The man who is footing my bill is generous and rich. He's paying for our meal tonight and has lots more where this came from. He'll do anything to avenge his best friend's death."

Fred went on to tell the story of his good friend Michael

Briscoe and his attorney, Wade Nevlin. Fred explained further why he was in New York and why Nevlin believed Mr. Briscoe's daughter was in danger.

"I'm supposed to be tailing them to see that no harm comes to her or her fiancé. However, I can't do that unless I know their every move. That's where you come in."

"What do you mean, that's where *I come in*?" Leroy said.

"Remember the phone lines you built in 'Nam and how we were able to bug the enemy's communications with each other? Something like that. You see, I can't follow them unless I know where they're going every day. I only know where they work and where they live."

"I see now," Leroy said. "You want me to bug their place!"

"Oh, hell, no!" Fred said "I would never put you in any kind of danger. I'm getting some bugs sent to me, and if you show me how to install them, I can do the rest myself. I just want you to *teach* me. Leave the rest to me."

"You're right," Leroy said. "That *is* illegal. I see why you need my help. Sure, I can show you how it's done. Anything else?"

"I'll let you know. I came here with some disguises. If I need something else, I figured I'd get it from a thrift shop. Maybe you could point me in the right direction to one of those."

"Sure thing, old buddy."

"Thanks, Leroy. I appreciate your willingness to help. You know I'll pay you. How much would you need to live comfortably now?"

"If the truth be known," Leroy said. "I could use a few months' rent. That would help me get back on my feet. It's been rough since Louise died."

"I think I can manage that," Fred said. He knew Leroy would be happy with the sum they agreed upon, plus some extra. He could tell by Leroy's clothes and their conversation that his old friend wasn't in the best of shape financially.

—⚏—

The bugs arrived a few days later in the mail. Fred called Leroy to set up a time for his lessons on how to make them work. In the meantime, he realized he needed to get his new disguises ready, but there were some preparations he had to do first. He took a taxi to the kids' apartment building. He went inside and checked out the locations of the custodial closets. Several were empty before he struck gold. He saw extra jumpsuits hanging in a fifth-floor closet.

He wore a business suit today and brought an empty briefcase. He took one of the extra jumpsuits, stuffed the uniform in the bag, then carefully exited the closet without being seen. Fred ran down the hallway into the lobby elevator. He walked out the front door with a big smile on his face. One disguise completed and another to go.

He called Leroy again and asked for one more favor. Fred wanted to know if he had an old telephone company uniform in his closet. Leroy didn't, but knew where Fred could get one.

"Are you sure you don't want me to do this for you?" Leroy asked.

"No, thanks. I told you. I don't want you to get into any trouble. Just let me know where, and I'll get one."

Fred got his disguises already to go with appropriate shoes, caps, mustaches, etc. The following day he'd bug the

95

kids' apartment pretending to be a maintenance worker in the morning. In the afternoon, he'd go to their place of business and pretend he was from the New York Telephone Company checking out a complaint an employee had made. Everything was in place for the following day.

He called Leroy to tell him how proud he was of himself. "Leroy! Thank you so much, pal. My plan went easier than I thought it would."

"Anything for you, ol' buddy. What's next?"

"Well, now I can follow them to work in the morning like always. Then go back to my hotel room or hang around in the city until late afternoon. I'll be listening to see if they call each other about their after-work plans. They usually pick up carryout like Chinese from Mr. Chen's or somewhere else. Neither one of seems to like cooking. I never see groceries go in their apartment."

"Okay. Got it. Let me know if you need anything else."

"Thanks. I will. Appreciate it."

—⚏—

Fred continued his daily boring routine. Even after the bugging, nothing seemed to happen. Evenings were just as Fred had explained to Leroy. The kids worked, ate takeout, and spent the weeknights at home. Now he had the advantage to follow their every move on the weekends.

On Saturday, Megan made plans to shop with her friend Veronica. The next weekend, the kids planned a Saturday and Sunday trip with some friends to the Finger Lakes. That was almost a five-hour drive from town. Fred got the okay from Nevlin to come home for the weekend.

Fred enjoyed his weekend with Lucy, and she enjoyed the extra cash he brought home with him. He didn't look forward to flying back to New York to the same boring job that was paying him a lot of money.

Chapter Eleven

INVESTIGATIONS IN GEORGIA

One of Alvarez's officers happened to drive by Christy's apartment. He saw a garage sale happening outside the building. He stopped his patrol car and approached the landlord supervising the sale.

"What's going on here?" he said.

"What does it look like?" the landlord said. "One of our tenants stopped paying her rent and isn't coming back. She told me to sell her stuff."

"That tenant didn't happen to be Christy Fields, did it?"

"Yeah, officer," she said. "How did you know?"

"Didn't the police tell you to notify them if you saw her again?"

"Well, come to think of it, they did, but that was months ago. I mean she *called* last week. I never *saw* her."

"Damn it!" the officer said. He shook his head. "Well? What did she say?"

"I told you. 'Sell all my stuff,' and that's exactly what I'm doing. She also said I could keep half of the money for my

98

efforts." The landlord smiled.

"Well, what did she say about the other half? I mean, is she coming back to pick it up? Are you to send it somewhere?"

"She gave me a strange name with a PO address."

"May I have it?"

The woman turned and went back into the house. She returned with a small slip of paper.

"Here you go," she said. She took a more serious tone as she handed it to him. "Sorry, Officer. I didn't realize how important this was."

The officer copied the Savannah address written to a Mrs. P. Oglethorpe, then called the chief.

"Alvarez, we got a lead on the Briscoe-Elmore case. Christy's having the money earned from the sale of her personal effects sent to a PO box in Savannah—it's to a Mrs. P. Oglethorpe, whoever that is."

"Thanks. Maybe it's Christy's mother. I know the chief of police in Savannah. I'll give him a call and see if he knows anything."

Alvarez picked up the phone and dialed his old friend, Ron Sandtrach. Ron had been a detective in Jacksonville but had transferred to Savannah after his wife had a baby. The couple wanted to live closer to the baby's grandparents, and both sets lived in south Georgia.

"Hey, Ron," Alvarez said. "I think we have another mutual case to work on. Do you know a lady named Mrs. P. Oglethorpe? She'll be getting a certified letter in the mail soon. We want to interview her before she gets it. Any idea who she is?"

"Everybody here knows the Oglethorpes! They're one of the wealthiest families in Savannah. Miss Penelope is the matriarch. She has an estranged daughter named Christy."

Alvarez broke him off. "Say no more. I thought it could be the case. I'm on my way. Christy's been involved in a burglary we've not been able to crack."

—⟋⟍—

On the drive north, Lead Detective David Alvarez and his partner, Brady Mason, had two hours to discuss the case.

"Anything happen with those surveillances I put you all on?" Alvarez said.

"Well, nothing important regarding Bryce," Mason said. "But a couple of strange things happened with Wade Nevlin."

"Tell me," Alvarez said. "I can't wait to hear."

"First, someone heard a portion of a phone call he made to Fred Jackson," Mason said. "You remember him, right? Ex-cop. Nevlin asked him to do something, but they couldn't hear what it was over the phone."

"Go on," the lead detective said.

"Apparently, Fred is doing some work for Nevlin in New York. Fred told him he wouldn't be calling him back until the deed was done."

"I wonder what that could be all about," Alvarez said.

"We're working on it, boss," Mason said.

It was late morning by the time they arrived on Bull Street in Savannah. The metro police headquarters sat nestled in the heart of the city near Monterey and Forsyth Squares. The city was loaded with squares. Alvarez and Mason had visited on numerous occasions when their cases crossed state lines.

No one would have guessed the small building hidden off the street was the police department except for the curbside name out front. The drab architecture of the building paled in comparison to the most picturesque and largest homes surrounding it.

"Hey! Ron!" Alvarez said. The men shook the chief's hands as they met.

"Follow me," Chief Sandtrach said. He showed them into his tiny office. "Have a seat," he said. "Welcome." He pointed to some folding chairs.

"Looking to find ol' Miss Penelope, are you?" Ron said.

"Who?" Alvarez said. "Oh yes. Mrs. Oglethorpe!" He laughed when he got the connection.

"Just kidding! I know you're really looking for her daughter, but that's what we call her mother around these parts. Ol' Miss Penelope."

"Sounds like there's a story behind that," Mason said.

"Yep, Ol' Miss Penelope, Mrs. Oglethorpe to you, moved back to Savannah after her husband died when they lived in Austin. The Oglethorpe family had roots here in Georgia for years until Miss Penelope was whisked off her feet by that Texas oil man.

"After her husband died and their only child, Christy, got her degree and moved away, there was nothing left for Miss Penelope to do. She moved back to her hometown where everyone knew her. The family had a reputation of old family money and connections. But now she lives like a hermit."

"Well, that's exactly what I am looking for—her address," Alvarez said. "All we got was a PO box, and we need to talk to her about her daughter, Christy."

"I got it for you while you were driving up. Here it is. But be careful. She may be answering the door with a shotgun. She trusts no one. I doubt she even trusts her daughter anymore. She felt Christy abandoned her. But the feeling was mutual. Story goes that Christy was forced to get married and then lost her baby. Christy never forgave her mother for it, and once she got her degree, she divorced her husband and severed all ties. Her goal was to find herself a rich husband on her own. Hope she isn't in any trouble."

"We just don't know," Alvarez said. "We want to question her." He paused. "Okay, Ron. Thanks for the tip about Ol' Miss Penelope. We'll watch our backs."

Alvarez and Mason left the station and drove to Jones Street—one of the wealthiest areas in town. If he remembered correctly, it was just a few blocks from Oglethorpe Square. Everything was in walking distance within the historic district.

The officers found the address of the multimillion-dollar townhome. It looked more like a mansion with cascading stairs on either side of the entries. Too bad they couldn't look around. The exterior looked like the cover of an *Architectural Digest* magazine.

As they walked up the steps to the entryway and rang the doorbell, they weren't greeted by a gun-toting grandma. Instead a butler answered the door wearing a white coat, tails, and gloves. Neither one of the men had ever seen someone dressed quite like that except in movies. *Ron must have been pulling our legs,* Alvarez thought.

"How may I help you, gentlemen?" the butler asked with an English accent as he bowed his head.

"Ah, ah," Alvarez stuttered. "We're from the Jacksonville Police Department. We're looking for a Mrs. Penelope Oglethorpe. We'd like to ask her a few questions."

Just as he was finishing his sentence, they heard a faint voice from another room calling out, "George, who is it?"

"Excuse me, gentlemen," he said. "I must attend to Mrs. Oglethorpe. She's not feeling well today. Please come in and take a seat in the library." The library, just to the left of the elegant entryway, had its own fireplace. The color scheme of the room matched the expensive beige and red Persian rug. The room's bookcases were filled with classic books, and the walls were paneled with light grain bird's eye wood. Alvarez was impressed. *Sandtrach wasn't kidding. This lady was loaded all right, with money, not a shotgun.*

George excused himself but returned within a few minutes. "Miss Penelope has agreed to see you. We'll be right back."

Miss Penelope came in gripping onto George's arm. She walked as slow and as dignified as a Southern Belle making her first public appearance. But she wasn't wearing an antebellum dress. She had on a red velour running outfit and white tennis shoes that looked like they'd never taken a run in their life. Miss Penelope's medium-length bleached-blond hair had been sprayed so nothing would be out of place should the wind catch it outside. Her wrists dripped in gold bangles, every finger had a diamond or gemstone on it, and her makeup had been way overdone.

Alvarez noticed Miss Penelope's nose had been bandaged and her eyes had the black-and-blue coloring of a recent surgery. *Must have had a nose job or face-lift.*

"Sorry to disturb you, ma'am," Alvarez said. The detectives flashed their badges.

George helped her sit in an overstuffed sofa across from the men in the leather chairs. The chintz print sofa with the same bird's-eye wood framed the back. Everything coordinated with the oriental rug on the floor.

"Good morning, gentlemen," she said. "How may I help you?"

"Good morning. Thank you for seeing us. We're from the Jacksonville PD. We're hoping you can help us with a case we're working on. I believe you have a daughter named Christy Fields. Correct?"

"Why, yes, it is," Miss Penelope said. "What's Christy gotten herself into now?"

"We need your daughter's help," Mason said. "The problem is, we can't seem to find her. We were hoping you could help us."

"Help *you*?" the old woman said with a laugh. "Well, I'll be! Good luck with that, gentlemen. I can't seem to find her myself. The 'elusive butterfly' is what I call her. I've given up. Seems she doesn't care about her dear old mother. Not that we've ever been close.

"Last time I heard from her was months ago. She told me she lived in Jacksonville and was having an affair with some rich gentleman. Seems to be Christy's modus operandi. Every time the two of us looked like we'd made amends, she would do something like this. Then I don't hear from her for a while."

"Did you get the name of the man?" Alvarez said.

"No, I'm afraid not," Miss Penelope said.

"And what do you mean by something like this?" Mason said.

"She gets involved with all the wrong men. You know. She wants to make it on her own and not take any of the family money. But as soon as any man finds out she'll inherit a load of it when she turns thirty-five or I die, whichever comes first, well, those varmints just start taking advantage of her."

The officers looked at each other.

"When was the last time you heard from her?" Alvarez said.

"I told you," she said, getting impatient. "Months back. That's how it goes with Christy. Hot and cold. Sometimes I hear from her frequently, then it stops. I assume it's whenever she goes off to find another lover."

"Well, be looking for a package. We heard that your daughter has moved again from Jacksonville. We just don't know where. But all her possessions have been sold, and half of the money collected will be coming to your PO box. If you get a letter showing her whereabouts, would you contact us?"

"Well, isn't that weird," Miss Penelope said in her sweetest Savannah accent. "That's so unlike Christy. Why in the world is she sending *me* money? She knows I don't need anything from her. She's never done anything like that before. Of course, gentlemen, I'll let you know. Lord Jesus, I wonder what's she done."

"We don't know for sure if she's done anything wrong," Mason said, trying to reassure her.

"Like I said," Alvarez added, "if we could ask her some questions, perhaps she could help us with our case. Thanks, ma'am, and here's my card."

Alvarez decided they could come back with a court order if something more turned up. In the meantime, the old lady sounded believable. She didn't have a reason to lie. She and her daughter had a long history of estrangement.

Alvarez called Ron back. "An old lady with a shotgun, huh? Very funny."

Ron was cracking up when they told him their experience. "I thought for sure you'd know I was kidding when you drove down Jones Street. It's just around the corner from the Mercer House. You know the one made famous in the book and movie *Midnight in the Garden of Good and Evil*. Anyway, was Ol' Miss Penelope able to help you with anything?"

"No," Alvarez said. "Afraid not. She hadn't received her money yet from Christy nor heard from her. Said her daughter's phone's been disconnected. But we already knew that."

"I'll stop and pay Miss Penelope a visit whenever you guys want. No need to drive up here anymore. I'll keep in touch with her."

"Great. We've got something to check on back in Jacksonville. I wonder if the man Miss Penelope was referring to was Bryce?"

"Anyone hungry?" Mason said, changing the subject. "Who wants to grab a bite to eat at the wharf? How about the Chart House? Seafood's not bad."

"Not bad?" said Ron. "It's great! Y'all go ahead. I'll be there in about twenty minutes."

Alvarez, Mason, and Ron met at the planned time. They sat together at a window table near the waterfront. Tourists walked by as the men chatted and talked about the cold case. They didn't notice a man with dark sunglasses in a navy-blue suit and highly polished shoes sitting across the room. He read his menu, never taking his Ray Bans off.

At first, the three men kept talking and paid no attention to any of the customers. Then Alvarez looked around and stared at the man wearing sunglasses. Even with his eyes hidden, the distinct, wavy, brown hairstyle was unforgettable. Alvarez got up from his group, walked over to the man in the business suit, and slapped him on the back.

"Hey!" Alvarez said. "What the hell are you doin' up in these parts?"

Chapter Twelve

POLICE SUSPICIONS

Damn it! Nevlin said to himself being caught off guard while sitting by the Savannah River in the Chart House. He'd been recognized by Alvarez.

"Hey, Alvarez!" Nevlin said, trying to pull off a sincere smile. "I could ask the same of you!"

When Alvarez smiled, Nevlin gave a nervous laugh. He wondered what he was going to do next. He didn't recognize the other people at Alvarez's table, and it made Nevlin uneasy. He never expected to bump into anyone he knew, nor was he anxious to admit the reason why he was in Savannah. He had to think of a good lie.

Months had gone by since the Briscoe burglary. He thought the police had shelved the case. *Why are the cops here?* He knew he couldn't ask.

"Come on over and have a seat with us, buddy," Alvarez said.

Nevlin was happy the detective hadn't repeated his initial question of why he was there, so ignored it.

Nevlin was curious why Alvarez acted so friendly, so he thought he'd play along. He needed to be cautious with his answers. "Wouldn't want to impose," he said, still sitting. "Looks like a business meeting over there."

"Nonsense," the detective said. "Come on. I'll introduce you to my friends." He tapped Nevlin's arm then pointed to the table by the window.

"Okay," Nevlin said, knowing there was no way he could get out of it. He rose from his chair, threw his white napkin on the tablecloth, and stood. "Wait a minute." He picked up his dirty martini and then followed Alvarez.

"Hey, guys, I'd like you to meet an ol' buddy of mine from Jacksonville," Alvarez said.

Nevlin said his cordial hellos and shook everyone's hands as they were introduced. In the back of his mind, he kept thinking. What did Alvarez's "ol' buddy" reference mean? What were his intentions? Nevlin never thought of the detective as his friend or as his ol' buddy. Something must have happened that he didn't know about.

"Hello, gentlemen" was all Nevlin said. Alvarez introduced his younger partner, Brady Mason, and Ron Sandtrach, the Savannah chief of police.

"Nevlin's the famous DA from Jacksonville who worked with my dad and now owns a private law office there."

"Y'all sure I won't be interrupting anything?" Nevlin said. He thought if he sat there awhile, he might figure out why Alvarez was so friendly. *He must have cleared me as a suspect and possibly done research of my cases with his dad.*

"You're not interrupting," Ron said. "Fact is, you might be able to help us."

109

Nevlin couldn't believe what he was hearing. *Wasn't that a twist of fate? I'm sure this is going to play out the other way around.*

"What are you guys talking about?" Nevlin asked.

Alvarez and his partner shared the whole story of the burglary and runaway suspect with Ron and Nevlin. Nevlin sat and listened to details he already knew. That was until Alvarez got to the part about why he and Brady were in Savannah. They had found Christy's mother and had interviewed her. Nevlin couldn't believe they were sharing their information with him.

"Yeah, ol' Ron here tried to scare us into thinking that Miss Oglethorpe looked like a toothless, crotchety granny with a shotgun," Alvarez said and laughed. "She was far from it. She may have looked like she'd had one too many face-lifts and bleach jobs in her day, but that spry, old woman…hell, I've got to tell ya. She may have been over sixty, but she didn't look a day over forty."

Nevlin played dumb. "I thought it was Christy Fields you were after."

"Why are you up here again?" Alvarez said. "You never answered my question."

"Oh, me?" Nevlin said and thought of the only excuse that occurred to him. "Just visiting an old friend. My wife's family is from here."

Brady apparently thought the answer innocent enough as he enlightened Nevlin further. "Christy sold all her belongings. She told her landlord in Jax to sell all her stuff, keep half the money, and send the rest certified to her mom's PO box here in Savannah."

"Christy can't be far behind, then," Nevlin said.

Brady continued. "Last Mrs. Oglethorpe heard, she was

still living in Florida. We told her to watch for that letter with a check from her daughter and let us know when she gets it."

Nevlin couldn't believe the police were offering all this evidence. *Maybe they hoped he would reveal something additional to them?* He didn't know as much as they did. Although it did seem out of the ordinary that they were confiding in him, but no matter what the reason, it made him happy.

"Mrs. Oglethorpe's communication with her daughter is our only lead," Alvarez said. "Or possibly the landlord. Not sure if we can trust *that* woman. She might sneak something in that registered package, like a note regarding Christy's whereabouts. If not the landlord, Christy might have written a note that could tell us something. Anything to give us a clue to find her."

"Too bad," Nevlin said. He wanted to change the subject before they got into more confidential territory. *Don't want the police to know how anxious I am for more information.* "Hey, guys! Ordered yet? I'm starving."

Nevlin downed a few more martinis as the officers drank their mineral water waiting for their food. Nevlin told them stories about old cases when he had worked with the senior Alvarez. With those drinks, Nevlin loosened up. He felt these officers could be trusted and were honest. Alvarez Senior had always been one of his staunchest allies, so why not the junior Alvarez?

After having dessert of Key lime pie and coffee, Nevlin told them the truth of why he was in town.

"Fellas, I must confess," Nevlin said. "I'm not here to visit an old friend. I'm here looking for Christy too. Not because of the burglary, although I did hear about it. It's because of a possible murder."

"What?" Alvarez said, putting down his Perrier and lime.

"Murder?" Sandtrach said. He leaned in farther and raised one eyebrow. "What are you talking about?"

"Yes, my client, Ms. Megan Briscoe, thinks Christy may have murdered her dad or she might know who did."

"You mean the Megan Briscoe whose father we found dead the week before the burglary?" Alvarez asked.

"Yep. The same Megan Briscoe."

"Why on earth does Megan think that? I thought the coroner's office ruled it a heart attack."

"Well, two reasons. First, when Megan's father died, she received a copy of two trusts with two letters. All from my office. My letter explained the two trusts and executors of each. She would inherit all things personal with the revocable trust. Michael assigned me the executor of the irrevocable trust for his half of the company. Included was also a private letter from him to Megan stating he thought someone was trying to kill him. I wasn't privy to the contents of that letter until later."

"Jesus!" Alvarez said. "Killed? Why on earth for? And why didn't you tell me this earlier?"

"We didn't think you'd believe us after the coroner's report. Besides. It could have been just a dying man's theory."

"Yes, I remember the report did say it was probable heart attack," Brady said. "What's the second thing?"

"On the night of Michael Briscoe's wake, Christy threw herself into the casket and kept yelling incoherent things like 'I'm sorry. I didn't mean it, and please forgive me, etc.' At Megan's request, I escorted her out of the funeral home."

The men at the table all looked at each other in bewilderment.

Nevlin continued. "The private letter that Michael wrote said he couldn't prove anything, but if he died under strange circumstances, she was to find out who killed him."

"Maybe we should take a closer look at that autopsy report," Alvarez said.

"A closer look wouldn't hurt," Brady said.

Nevlin agreed. "I'm sure Megan would not disapprove of that. I'm wondering if anyone else is thinking there's a connection between the alleged murder of Michael and the break-in? I sure am."

Ron nodded and looked at Nevlin. "Have you any other information that we should know about?"

Nevlin thought a team effort would be the fastest way to solve this case. "There is one more thing. About a year before his death, Bryce Elmore, Michael's partner, had a contract drawn up. It stated, in the event of Michael's death, all he needed was Megan's signature to take over her father's half of the business. He made allegations her dad put his half of the company in debt, but all would be forgiven if she signed it over."

"Maybe we have more than one suspect," Ron said. "Bryce and Christy would be putting on an act to get back together later. Or maybe they are already conniving as a team. Y'all better go back to Jax and question Mr. Elmore again. I can check on Miss Penelope here to help you find Christy."

"The quicker we find Ms. Fields, the better," Brady said.

Alvarez added, "It might not be a bad idea to put a security team on Megan, either. I hope she isn't the next one who gets hurt."

"Already on it," said Nevlin. "I got a PI friend of mine, Fred Jackson. You might know him, Alvarez, though he retired before you came on board. He's up in New York City now. I sent him to follow Megan without her knowledge for the past couple of months. I didn't want her spooked. After all, she might not be in trouble. But if I hadn't done anything and something happened, I'd have felt awful."

"Fred Jackson," Alvarez said. "I've heard of him. Excellent choice. Thanks, Nevlin."

The men paid their bills and vowed to work the case together. Finding Christy became their utmost priority. Nevlin felt confident Ron would be in touch with Mrs. Oglethorpe and that he would relay any further information about Christy to the Jacksonville PD.

As for Alvarez and his partner, Brady, he wondered why they were so eager to give him information. When or how could he get more information from them again?

He walked back to the bar. "Another dirty martini, please."

Chapter Thirteen

CHRISTY'S REAPPEARANCE

After leaving the bar, Nevlin decided to spend one more day in Savannah. Although it was walking distance, he drove his car a half block down to the River Street Inn on Bay Street. He hadn't lied to the police. He just held back the whole truth. It wasn't only his late wife's family who lived here but his own. Beverly and he were once high school sweethearts who continued to Florida State after graduation.

The inn had a special meaning for him, and he loved its history. It had been built by General Oglethorpe in the 1770s as a cotton factory and converted into a hotel in 1817. The four-story building still contained some of the original solid clay bricks, some of whose walls had been used in the guest rooms. It was a strange thought. The girl he was looking for must be related to the old general somehow.

After unpacking, he went straight to the bar and sat down. He wondered why Alvarez had divulged the information that he did.

"What'll it be?" said the bartender.

"I'll have a dirty martini," he said.

"New here?" the young man said.

"No, not really," Nevlin answered. "My wife and I grew up in Savannah. We had our wedding reception here, but that was over twenty-five years ago."

There was no one else in the bar, so Nevlin and the bartender struck up a conversation. Nevlin reminisced about his life in Savannah and his marriage over several drinks.

"So, where do you live now?"

"Jacksonville," Nevlin said as he picked up the tab. "I practice law there. If you ever move to Florida or have a friend who needs an attorney, here's my card."

He walked back to his room and decided to take a nap. He wondered if his new law office would be a success. It had been lucrative for two years, but he still dreamed about the Briscoe case. In one of his dreams, Megan was his daughter. The obsession with the case made his dreams feel as real as the people in the case, who had become like family.

—⁂—

The next morning Nevlin rose early. He ordered room service of a light breakfast and drank the energy drink he always brought with him. After donning his exercise clothes and shoes, he went out for a jog down Bay Street through the historic district. Running always cleared his mind and his hangover. For some reason, today the run didn't do it. Questions about the case kept flooding his mind. *Where was Christy? Had she murdered Michael?*

With sweat pouring down his whole body after a four-mile run, he walked into the hotel lobby. He was about to skip the stairs two steps at a time in the huge stairwell to the second floor, but an attractive woman caught his eye. He stopped before his first skip.

A gorgeous brunette stood talking to the woman behind the counter. The voluptuous lady wore black patent heels and a knit dress that left nothing to the imagination. Her long hair had been pulled back in a ponytail tied with a colorful scarf. Large dark sunglasses covered her eyes, but her ivory complexion and red lipstick made her look doll-like.

"Checking in?" the clerk said.

"Yes, ma'am," she said in a sweet Savannah drawl. She took off her sunglasses, caught Nelvin looking at her, and smiled.

"Name, please?"

"Christina Oglethorpe," she said as she turned to the clerk.

Nevlin wondered if she had recognized him. How could he have forgotten her? Her accent may have been thicker, but she used her real legal name. He ran to the top of the stairs and into his room to call Chief Santrach at the Savannah PD.

"Ron!" he said, out of breath. "You won't believe who just checked into the River Street Inn—Christy Fields! You better get over here quick."

"Damn it!" he answered. "Alvarez just missed her by a day. I'll be right over. Make sure she doesn't leave."

"I'll do my best," Nevlin said.

He hung up the phone and rushed to the hotel desk. He asked for a newspaper. He didn't see Christy at first, but after taking a paper from the lobby counter, he glanced toward the elevator. There she stood inside holding two small suitcases as the doors closed.

Nevlin sat in the lobby reading the paper until Ron arrived. He bypassed Nevlin, walked over to the desk, and flashed his badge. He asked for Miss Christina Oglethorpe's room number. He told the clerk he needed to speak to her on official business.

When Ron finished talking to the clerk, he walked over to Nevlin.

"The clerk said she went to her room ten minutes ago," Ron said. "Have you seen her since?"

"Nope," Nevlin said. "Haven't seen her. Bet she thought no one would catch or suspect her using her Oglethorpe family name. I wonder why she didn't go to her mother's house. She only lives a few blocks away."

"Good work," said Ron. "How'd you recognize her?"

"I met her once in the Briscoe-Elmore office after Michael died and I had a meeting with his daughter, Megan. I saw her again at Michael's funeral. Although her hair color has changed, I'd never forget that figure. Besides, I heard her give the clerk her legal name, which y'all gave me yesterday."

"I'm not sure how Christy's going to react to my request," Ron said. "Wait in the lobby for my team. If she comes willingly, this won't take long."

Nevlin watched as Ron went to her room using the open imperial staircase. From where Nevlin sat in his running clothes, he could see her room door. She'd been placed in a room across the hallway from his.

After several minutes, Nevlin heard a commotion. It was Christy struggling with Chief Sandtrach on the landing next to the staircase. Her hands had been cuffed behind her back. She didn't look happy about it.

"Officer, do we have to do this? I didn't do anything! Bryce is a damn liar!"

118

Then he heard the chief read her the Miranda rights.

"Please, officer, I'll tell you anything you want to know. I just don't want to be seen handcuffed in my hometown."

"All right, Christy. If you come with me and don't want to be conspicuous, I suggest you calm down and be quiet."

Christy didn't say another word. Nevlin saw her hang her head as she descended the stairs. She had tied her scarf around her head and was using her sunglasses to hide her face. No one would have recognized her. Chief Sandtrach ushered her to the lobby.

When they reached the ground floor, Ron waved one hand, signaling to two officers to stand back. Christy had calmed down and was cooperating. Ron had his one arm around her waist to accommodate her wishes hiding the handcuffs. He hurried her to the street and into the waiting squad car.

Nevlin knew he would be out of the loop soon. He'd led the police to Christy, and now it was their turn to take over. He felt sorry he hadn't found Christy sooner. Perhaps he could have helped her or gotten more information from her. But it was too late now. He had fulfilled his commitment to cooperate with the police.

He walked back to his room. He desperately needed that shower and something to eat. He looked forward to the rest of his day and the drive back to Jacksonville the following.

Ron led Christy into the police station on Bull Street. She never said another word in the patrol car. She just whimpered all the way there. Once inside, he led her into a small interrogation room. It consisted of four blank walls, no windows, and one door with a small window at the top. There was a rectangular metal table, two metal chairs, and nothing on the walls. Ron took the handcuffs off, handed her a box of tissues, and offered her a cup of water.

"Yes, please," Christy said.

For some reason, Ron believed Christy's plea of innocence. He thought she was clueless about knowing anything about the break-in, and he did not believe this petite lady could have murdered anyone.

Sandtrach had to remember this was not his case, and he had to remain neutral. The case belonged to Lieutenant Detective Alvarez. The suspicious facts that Nevlin shared at the luncheon had yet to be proven. Sandtrach could only hold the young lady because she was in his jurisdiction. Alvarez would have to advise him what to do next.

"Let's have her sit alone for a while," he told the other officers. "She needs to think about why she's here. Plus, I need to get a hold of Alvarez."

Ron got on the phone and called his old friend in Jacksonville.

"You'll never guess who we just arrested," he said.

"No," Alvarez said, "Christy?"

"Yes!" he answered.

"You've got to be kidding me. What happened?"

Ron explained to Alvarez how the whole arrest transpired. After Nevlin had given him the tip; he went to the hotel.

"I just wanted to ask her some questions at first. But as soon as I mentioned Bryce's name, the burglary, and that she was wanted for questioning back in Jacksonville, all hell broke loose. She went off on me, struck me, and made me chase her.

I arrested her for assaulting a police officer."

"Then what did she do?" Alvarez said.

"She explained she knew Bryce would do this. He had threatened her and said he'd blame her should anything go wrong. She swore she didn't know anything about any burglary. When she left his office that night with only her personal items, he was still there.

"Have you questioned her?" Alvarez asked.

"No," he said. "That's the reason why I called. We've put her in a room. I wanted to know what more you'd like me to do."

"Just keep her there. I'd appreciate it if you could fill out the extradition papers for me. As soon as I get off the phone, Brady and I will be on our way to pick her up and take her back to Jax.

"Good," Ron said. "I'll let her know she has a two-hour wait."

"Did she happen to say anything else?"

"Only that she felt she was being set up by Bryce. She claims she's innocent."

"Okay," Alvarez said. "Leave it to me. She can just sit there till we arrive. Don't talk to her any further. Thanks for taking care of her in the meantime."

"Sure thing," Ron said.

The cameras rolled in the interrogation room focusing on the suspect. The officers took turns as they watched the film of Christy and commented on her weird behavior. One minute she would be sitting at the table with her head down sobbing; another she would be up pacing the floor. As time rolled on, she took off her shoes and started to do jumping jacks as she counted. Ron told them he thought she was just bored and doing anything she could to make the time go faster.

Ron thought his officers' conduct proved just as funny as Christy's. One minute, he saw them looking busy; the next minute, they'd be walking past Christy's room just to sneak a peek at whatever she'd do next. Ron never had a suspect like Christy before. He didn't know what to make of the beautiful, buxom Ms. Fields. Could she really be a robber or a dangerous killer? She didn't look like one.

Besides Alvarez, Brady, and Nevlin, the only other person who knew about the murder theory was Ron. He didn't care to share the theory with his staff. From what he observed, he doubted the sweet thing had done any of what she'd been accused. To him, she was just an innocent girl caught up in something bigger than what she could fathom.

—ɷ—

On the drive up I-95, Alvarez and Brady had time to talk about the case.

"So, what do you think about Wade Nevlin?" Alvarez said. "I know he was a friend of my father's. But there's something about him that makes me feel uneasy. He always seems to show up in the most particular places."

"Yeah," Brady said. "First, the funeral, then the church, then Savannah. He does seem to pop up wherever a suspect happens to be."

"Church? What church?" Nevlin asked

"Didn't our surveillance guy tell you? He and Laura Elmore met at the basilica a few weeks ago. It was only for a moment. It seemed like a coincidence. Perhaps that's why our guys didn't say anything. It was right after you asked them to put surveillance on Nevlin and Bryce."

"Interesting. Guess we'll have to keep it up."

Chapter Fourteen

PIER 86, NEW YORK CITY

After spending his last night in Savannah, Nevlin decided to take another jog. The morning run was uneventful, but everything changed when he got back into his hotel room and the phone rang.

"Where have you been?" someone yelled at him.

Nevlin didn't recognize the loud voice. "Who is...?" he said.

"For cryin' out loud, Nev. It's me, Fred. You've got to come up here now. Yes, New York. Megan ran into Bryce in Soho yesterday. They'll be meeting tomorrow afternoon. I think I overheard something about signing some papers."

"Jesus, Fred. Why didn't you call me?"

"I've been trying to get hold of you since yesterday and this morning. Sally wouldn't tell me where you'd gone. But I figured it out. Savannah's River Street Inn. It's where you always go to hide."

"Sorry," Nevlin said. "I'll have to drive back to Jax and get on the next flight out from there. You can tell me the details when I get up there."

Nevlin made his reservations and called Fred back with his flight plans. Fred gave him the hotel address. Nevlin's flight would not arrive until dinnertime, and he'd take a taxi to the hotel.

With all the plane tickets, hotel rooms, and meals, this case had cost him more than anticipated. On the flight north, he thought about how much money he had been spending. He'd never had a problem with money before, but now was finding it hard to budget.

"It sure took you long enough to get here," Fred said when he opened the door to his room.

"You'd never believe what happened yesterday," Nevlin said.

They walked to a restaurant on Broadway and exchanged stories over dinner. Nevlin explained how he found Christy and the details of her arrest. Fred described Megan and Bryce's plans to meet the next afternoon. When they returned to the hotel, they walked to their separate rooms. Nevlin sat on his bed and called Megan.

"Hey, Megan," he said. "Wade Nevlin here. How's it going?"

"Now, isn't this a coincidence!" Megan said. "First, I run into Bryce day before yesterday, and now you call. What's up?"

"I have a couple of things I want to discuss with you. First, I wanted you to know that the Savannah police just found and arrested Christy."

"Wow! In Savannah? What was she doing there?"

"Her mother lives there. The police department held her until Lieutenant Alvarez arrived and took her back to Florida."

"You said you had a couple of things. What else?"

"Well, it's about Bryce. Remember what you said about a coincidence? I don't mean to scare you, but this is not a coincidence, darlin'. I came up to warn you. I think Bryce may have come here to harm you."

"What?" she said. "Really? Erick and I planned to take him sightseeing tomorrow. We have tickets to take the *Intrepid* tour at Pier 86. Then a riverboat ride on the Hudson. He seemed nice and friendly. He told me he'd love to see the city as he'd never been to New York."

"Megan, there is no way I'm going to let you and Erick meet him. I'll be taking your place. And the part about him never being in New York before. That's a lie."

"What? Where are you? Aren't you in Jacksonville? How are you going to meet him?"

"No, I'm here in New York. Please trust me. Let me meet him instead. Did he happen to say anything else?"

"Yeah," Megan said. "He wanted me to sign the papers granting him half the business."

"Even if you've been thinking of that, I wouldn't do it. I found something in the paperwork you left me."

"You did? What was that?"

"After some more digging, I found out Bryce's friendly face is nothing but a facade. He's been swindling money out of your father's half of the business and gambling it away. He made it look as if your father was doing it and not him. Your dad found out about it, and...with you out of the way too..."

"He'd get it all," Megan finished his sentence.

"Don't worry," Nevlin said as he heard Megan sniffle. "It'll be all right. What time did you say you were supposed to meet him?"

"Noon, by Pier 86. We arranged to visit the *Intrepid* first."

"None of that is going to happen on my watch," he said.

"You and Erick need to stay put. I know where the piers are."

"Wait a minute," Megan said. "Why don't we all go? I'd really like to face the bully."

"No, it's better I go alone," Nevlin said. "No need to cause a scene. If I can halt any problems, or whatever he has planned, the better. I'd like to leave you out of it and let him know he is to leave you alone. You'll have a chance to face him in court."

"Though I'd really like to go, I understand," Megan said. "Okay, we'll do as you say. Thanks, Mr. Nevlin."

"Thanks for trusting me," Nevlin said. "I'm sure this plan is better. It's for your safety."

Nevlin hung up the phone and went down to the bar. Although it was early afternoon, he thought he'd make time for a drink. Things weren't the same since his wife had died. Her death had hit him hard, and drinking was becoming his only release. If only Megan didn't remind him of a young Beverly. He'd become slowly strapped, avenging Michael's death. He couldn't stop now.

The next day, Nevlin put on his suit and tie and hailed a taxi to the pier. He wanted to look his professional best when he surprised Bryce, looking like a city businessman and not a tourist. New York had crisp air with clear skies. It would have been a great day for an outside tour. He wished he'd had the ticket for the *Intrepid*. He had always been fascinated with WWII aircraft carriers. But a tour would have to wait.

The skyline of the city loomed in the background. If you stood by the piers looking east, the skyscrapers made the city look majestic. There was no other city in the world like New York, thought Nevlin. It was such a contrast between this city and the smaller one he just came from.

He got out of the taxi and walked along the piers looking for his nemesis, Bryce Elmore. Although Nevlin had never been introduced to the man, he had seen him once in the Briscoe-Elmore office the same day he met Megan. His first impression of the man was unforgettable.

The guy wouldn't be hard to find. Bryce had an uncanny resemblance to him. They had a similar build, and wavy brown-blond hair, though Bryce was getting grayer around his temples. Bryce had to be at least six feet four, because he was taller than Nevlin. Their eye color made them stand apart because Bryce's were cerulean blue and Nevlin's green. Nevlin thought people might think they could pass for brothers.

Heading toward Pier 86, he spotted Bryce, right away, leaning against a flagpole right where Megan said he would be. He walked up to him.

"Nice day for a boat ride, huh?" Nevlin said, acting chummy.

Bryce didn't answer and gave him a funny look.

"You Bryce Elmore?" Nevlin said, trying to strike up a conversation.

"Hmm…yes…I am," Bryce snapped. "Who wants to know?" He looked at him closer with disdain. "Hey! Don't I know you?"

"I'm sorry," Nevlin said, holding out his hand, which Bryce ignored. "Let me introduce myself. Name's Wade Nevlin, and I believe you know my client, Megan Briscoe." Nevlin despised the man, thinking he could have been the one who killed Michael. He had the motive. How could someone so evil look like him?

"Client? Megan?" Bryce standing straighter and more alert.

"Yes, I am the executor of Michael Briscoe's irrevocable trust concerning his half of the business."

"Oh yeah. Now I remember you. You were in our office the day after Michael died. Meeting with Megan for something. Hey! Don't you work for the DA's office?"

"Not anymore. In business for myself." Nevlin paused. "I believe you came here with the intent of getting Megan to sign over her dad's half of the business. Correct?"

"Yes, sir," Bryce said with a smile on his face. "This should have been taken care of months ago, but we're just now getting around to it. Megan agreed—"

"Let me stop you there. I know you *were* supposed to meet her here to do that."

"Did you come in her place?"

"Smart man," Nevlin said with some sarcasm. Bryce looked smug. Did the man think she'd sent Nevlin to sign for her? He had to set him straight. "There won't be any signing of any papers today. She's absent on my advice because your deal isn't happening. In fact, we'll be taking you to court."

"Court? What?" Bryce stood looking dumbfounded.

"You heard me. I'll be filing the papers once I return to Jacksonville tomorrow. You'll be getting your subpoena soon. I've advised Megan not to talk to you. See you later."

Nevlin turned. He waved good-bye with his back facing Bryce. The satisfaction on his face felt good. Better than if he had visited the *Intrepid.*

Chapter Fifteen

THE EXTRADITION

After an hour of sitting alone in the room with only a couple metal chairs, a table, and fluorescent lighting, Christy pounded on the interrogation room door.

"Let me out!" she shouted. "How much longer do I have to be in here?"

Sandtrach opened the door. He brought in an officer named Pam to avoid any future complaints. A woman could help make the game of good cop/bad cop play easier. They sat across the table from her.

"You might as well get comfortable, missy. It's going to be a while longer," he said.

"Why? What for?"

"Because Detective Alvarez from Jacksonville PD is on his way, and it'll take him another hour," Pam said.

"You get one call," Chief Sandtrach said. "Would you like it?"

"Of course not," Christy said. "You know I don't live here, and I don't know anyone in Savannah except my mother. I won't be calling her. Leave my mother out of this. She has enough troubles of her own."

Pam added, "Would you like some water, sweetie?"

"Yes, please," Christy said. "And could you get me a cigarette too? I'm going stir-crazy in here!"

"I'll see what I can do." Pam left to get the requested items.

Sandtrach was alone with Christy for a few minutes. "You know, you could help yourself if you write a confession for us." He put a steno pad and pen on the desk. He knew Alvarez told him not to question her. He didn't intend to, but he did want to help her.

"Forget it. Confession? I have nothing to confess, and I'm not writing down anything."

"Suit yourself," Pam said as she came into the room with the cigarette and a cup of water. Christy gulped down the full cup.

"Are you sure you don't want that call? Perhaps to your mother?"

"Didn't you hear me?" Christy raised her voice. "Leave her out of this! Where's my light? And I need another cup of water."

Pam and the chief left interrogation and entered the observation room. They talked about the case while they watched Christy.

"Chief, there's something funny about that girl," she said. "From what I saw through the window when I left earlier, she couldn't sit still. The whole time you spoke to her, she either walked around the room or was up or down. When she sat, she fidgeted, twirling her hair with her fingers. Then paced the floor again. Now she wants more water. What do you think?"

"Yep, those may be signs of guilt, but about what, I'm not

sure. I know she's not telling us everything. At the hotel, she wanted to talk and explain her relationship with Bryce. When I arrested her and read the Miranda rights, she shut up like a clam. Hasn't said a word more. Not that I care, because Alvarez told me to leave it to him. He'll take care of it."

"Want to see what I can do alone with her, Chief?" Pam said.

"Be my guest. But tread lightly. Alvarez's orders." Sandtrach gave her an underhanded circular wave toward the door.

After getting the okay, Pam walked into the room bringing more water, another cigarette, and a light. "Just so you know, Christy, as the chief said, things will go a lot easier if you tell us everything. The courts may be more lenient if you show cooperation. Please think about it."

Pam left. She wanted Christy to think about what she had said to Sandtrach earlier, and maybe within the hour, she might change her mind. However, the accused just stared at the paper and continued her nervous routine. When Pam walked in minutes later with more water, she asked Christy another question.

"Anything else?" Pam said.

"Yes," Christy said. "I want a public defender."

"We can get that for you," Pam said. "I'll call the court and see who we can get."

A half hour later, a tall woman with long, dark hair, wearing black horn-rimmed glasses and a navy pinstripe suit opened the police department door.

"Hey, Chief!" she said as her stiletto heels clicked on the tile floor. The attractive woman's ponytail swayed as she walked. "I understand there's a young lady here who wants to see me."

"Hey, Madeline," Ron said. "Got a sweet young thing in room one for you. She told Pam she wanted a public defender. I'm sure glad they sent you!"

"My pleasure," she said. "Good to see you too, Chief."

Madeline Werner walked over to the room as another officer unlocked it for her.

"And who are you?" Christy said with a little sneer as the woman entered.

"Name's Madeline Werner. I'm your public defender."

"Oh yeah," Christy said, embarrassed. "Sorry. Thanks."

"How can I help you?"

Christy warmed to Ms. Werner and explained everything in detail. *Finally, I'm talking to a lawyer. It took them long enough to get me one.* Now that she'd spent a few minutes sizing her up, she hoped Madeline would work in her best interest. Christy thought she was a good judge of character. Maybe not in men but women. She wasn't going to write anything down for the police in Georgia, but she felt comfortable talking to this attorney.

She told Madeline about Bryce, their affair, the "helpful" coffee creamer, Michael Briscoe's death, her outbursts at the funeral home, and how she kept the nest-egg money plus the car Bryce had given her. She swore that was all she kept. She didn't rob the safe at Briscoe-Elmore and Associates and had not heard about it until the Savannah PD told her she was being arrested for it.

"I'm being framed for all of this by Bryce," Christy said. "Sure, I admit putting that liquid in his partner's creamer. Bryce told me it was an energy drink. Michael had agreed to it. As for the safe, sure, I knew it was there, but I didn't know any combination. Bryce lied about that, fired me, and threatened me.

"I have no reason to steal Bryce's money. Yes, I hate him, but I wouldn't steal or hurt anyone. Once my mother dies, or if I turn thirty-five prior to that, I'll inherit a lot of cash and property. Until that time, I can make it fine on my own. Always have. Always will. The only things I took were my personal belongings. I didn't even take all my things from my apartment. Bryce scared me. I wanted to get away as far as possible. I never want to see that bastard again."

"Okay, sweetie, calm down. Where and when did all this happen? Jacksonville, right?"

"Yes, it all happened in Jacksonville, months back. I came here to visit my mother. I'd been living in Baton Rouge until now with a friend. I wanted to see my mom for a couple of days. She just had surgery."

"Oh, I'm sorry," Ms. Werner said. "How is she?"

"I never found out. But don't be sorry. It was just a nose job. My mother's always having some type of plastic surgery. I guess she can't think of anything else on which to spend her wealth. Though she does give back to her community with her charities." Changing the subject, Christy added, "Will I have to spend more time in jail here?"

"Sweetheart, they could keep you up to thirty days if they wanted to, but lucky for you, they're anxious to get this case resolved in Florida. The detective is on his way right now to pick you up. I suggest you waive your right to an extradition hearing and go with him willingly. It will show your cooperation, and they'll take that into consideration in Florida. Agree?"

"Upon your advice, yes, I agree. Does that mean I'll be put

in jail in Jacksonville?"

"Unfortunately, yes. Until the judge sets bail if it is granted. Let's hope so. Right now, everything looks circumstantial."

"Thank you, Ms. Werner. I'll sign that waiver. I need to get this over with. I'm innocent."

The attorney left with the signed waiver in her hand. When the door opened, Christy overheard some men talking in the hallway. Chief Ron had been talking to Alvarez, who had arrived with his partner, Brady. Ms. Werner handed the chief the waiver.

"She's ready to go," she said. "She's going to need a public defender in Jacksonville too. The gal has no money to hire an attorney and refuses to accept a dime from her mama."

"Yep. Heard that loud and clear before you got here," Sandtrach said. "What—" He started to ask another question, but Ms. Werner interrupted him.

"Chief, you know I can't tell you anything my client said in there. I've advised her not to say anything more until she gets back to Jax and gets her next attorney. I left the steno pad in there just in case she changes her mind. But I doubt she'll use it."

Alvarez looked at Ron. "I told you she would ask for an attorney," he said. "She may look dumb, but she's one smart cookie."

"Thanks, Madeline," Alvarez said to her. Then he turned back to the chief. "If she writes anything in the way of a confession, could you have it typed up for me before we leave?"

"Sure thing," Ron said. "We can do that. Let's have a cup of coffee in my office while the paperwork is being typed and filed before y'all leave."

—⟊—

After Alvarez and Brady left for Jacksonville with Christy in the squad car, Ron gave Ol' Miss Penelope a call. He felt she needed to know, especially if she'd been expecting Christy. He didn't want her to worry.

"Miss Penelope," he said, "this is Chief Ron Sandtrach from Savannah PD."

They exchanged their Southern pleasantries over the phone before Ron got to the reason for his call.

"Sorry to be the bearer of bad news, but we just arrested your daughter at the River Street Inn this morning. She was on her way to see you but got caught."

"Caught?" Miss Penelope said. "What on earth do you mean by that?"

"Someone on the case alerted us as to her whereabouts."

"They told me all they wanted to do was ask her some questions," Miss Penelope said.

"Well, yes, they did at first," Ron said. "They didn't want to upset you, but there was more to it. I had to arrest her for resisting arrest and assaulting an officer."

"Resisting arrest? Assaulting an officer? For what? And whom?"

"Miss Penelope, *I* arrested your daughter for the burglary of her office in Jacksonville. That was me."

"Why, you obviously don't know my daughter," Miss Penelope said. "She would never steal anything from anybody. As for you, what did you do to my little girl?"

"I'm afraid she wouldn't come willingly," Ron said. "As for the Jacksonville PD, they have enough evidence to proceed with the case. I'm sorry. She asked for a public defender, and we got her one. Her attorney advised her to waive her right for extradition. She was taken to Florida several minutes ago. Christy left voluntarily and didn't want to get you involved. For what it's worth, Miss Penelope, I believe your daughter's innocent. She kept saying it was all a misunderstanding and her ex-boyfriend framed her. She left with Detective Alvarez. I believe you met him already?"

"Yes, sir. Nice young gentlemen with his buddy, right?" she said. "They were the ones who came here a few days ago looking for her."

"I'm sure they didn't tell you because they didn't want to scare her from her hometown. They didn't lie. They did have some questions for her."

"Lordy! Lordy!" Miss Penelope said. "My poor little girl. What has she gotten herself into this time? I wish she would have asked me for the money. I'd have gotten her the finest attorney."

"She's too proud," Ron said. "She didn't want to disappoint you anymore than she felt she already had. Ms. Madeline Werner was her public defender. I believe you know her."

"Good. Yes, I know Ms. Werner," Miss Penelope said. "Thanks, Ron. That's Christy for ya. Smart sometimes, naïve the next. That other cop told me I should probably take the next plane down there to help my little girl."

"You mean, Brady?"

"No, that other man who came by himself," she said.

"*Another police officer?*" Chief Ron said.

"No. Wait a minute. I sometimes get things mixed up. Let me get his card." Miss Penelope excused herself for a few minutes and came back on the line.

"Sorry, he wasn't an officer. He was a lawyer. Mr. Wade Nevlin. Heard of him?"

Christy slept the whole way in the back seat of the black-and-white, which gave Alvarez and Brady a chance to talk. They knew she was sleeping as she snored delicately and didn't fidget like the Savannah cops told them she had done in their precinct. The thought of the petite woman in the tight knit dress doing jumping jacks barefoot had been a humorous story and a vision they couldn't get out of their heads.

The Jax squad car rolled into the PD parking garage at Regency Square shopping mall. Alvarez's department was patrol zone two, where they had to check in. Christy's alleged crimes had been committed in the subdivision of Arlington. The suspect accepted her fingerprinting and DNA swab. Then she was escorted to a new cell. Next, she asked for a Florida public defender and waited.

It took the city several days for someone to show up. One afternoon a tall, good-looking man with curly, sandy hair and green eyes arrived.

Chapter Sixteen

CHRISTY'S NEW LAWYER

"Are you my public defender?" Christy said behind the bars of her cell. She sized him up and down. "You look mighty familiar."

"No, ma'am," he said. "I'm not your public defender, but I am your new attorney. Name's Wade Nevlin. Your mother hired me."

"That's where I saw you," Christy said. "In Savannah! When are you people ever going to get it? I thought I told everyone I didn't want my mother to get me out of this mess."

The guard came over and unlocked the door.

"Thanks," Christy said. "Does this mean I can leave? Am I free to go?"

"No," Nevlin said. "Afraid not. But you're free to come with me to another room. We need to talk."

Nevlin and Christy walked through the long hallway and found a private room for themselves.

"Before we begin," Christy said, folding her arms across her chest, "I don't want any of my mother's help." Nevlin saw her

139

squint her eyes at him studying his face.

"Well, this case has nothing to do with your mother. I was hired a long time ago by Megan Briscoe's father, Michael, before I even knew anything about you, Bryce, or your mother. Michael Briscoe was a dear friend of mine. As for my help, I'm afraid you've got me whether you want me or not."

"Hey! Now I remember you. You came to visit Megan after her father died. Right?"

"Right," he said.

"Wait a minute. I'm confused. Are you representing me because of my mom, Megan, or yourself?"

Nevlin explained how he got involved from the beginning. He told her of his short time in Savannah. He clarified how he accidently ran into detectives Alvarez, Brady, and Chief Sandtrach while looking for her.

"I had hoped to find you before they did as I wanted to question you myself," Nevlin said. "A day later, your mother called me and told me about the arrest and extradition. She also told me she wanted to fly here, but I told her that wouldn't be necessary. I was already on the case, and I would be glad to help. I promised her you would be well taken care of."

"Why are you doing this?"

"Christy, I believe you are innocent and there is someone else behind this."

"Well, thank God!" she said. "Somebody who believes in me."

"Megan, your mother, and I do not think you robbed your company or had anything do with Michael's death. You had no motive. You had a good relationship with Michael, didn't you?"

"I loved him like a father. I put that energy drink in his

coffee creamer to make him feel better. That's all. Bryce told me to. I also gave those copied papers to Michael when I thought something didn't look right."

"I'm hoping," Nevlin said, "with your help, we can put Bryce behind bars. We need the paper trail to prove it, and we'll also need you to testify against him. Will you?"

"Hallelujah! I will. That will make my day. It's what I've been hoping for. Put that son of a bitch behind bars. But how can I help when I'm in here?"

"Just follow my instructions," Nevlin said.

"I really don't know what got into Bryce," Christy said. "He was so sweet to me in the beginning. I didn't date him for the money. I honestly thought he loved me. I never thought he'd turn mean, until I saw he had a temper whenever he was cross."

"Don't worry about that right now. Let me take care of getting you out of here first. I need to have the judge post bail, and we'll go from there. In the meantime, I need all the information you can give me about the business and how much you knew. Tell me what you did daily from the beginning. I know about your affair with Bryce, but I want to know more details." Nevlin loosened his tie. Not all the conference rooms in the county jail had air-conditioning and if they did run, they were noisy and inefficient. He got out his pen and steno pad from his briefcase.

He laid the two items on the table plus a small tape-recording machine. "Mind if I record our conversation?" Nevlin said. "Remember. This will only be between you and me."

"Okay," Christy said, sounding unsure.

"I swear. This is between you and me. It's called attorney-client privilege. We can start whenever you're ready." He turned on the recorder, and after the tape started to roll, he stated the date, the time, and names of the two people present. "Ms. Fields, when did you start working for Briscoe-Elmore and Associates?"

"Ten years ago," Christy said.

"When did the affair with your boss, Mr. Bryce Elmore, start, and when did it stop?"

Christy answered Nevlin's questions with short answers. She threw in a few cuss words every now and then to describe her boss. She talked nonstop for over twenty minutes. When she was finished, she looked exhausted. Nevlin stopped the tape.

"Let's take a break," Nevlin said.

Christy started to cry. "I thought I knew the guy better that that. How could I have fallen for such a jerk with all his lies and gifts?"

"Because you wanted to believe in him. *In love*," Nevlin said. "Understandable. You fell for the fairy tale he used to lure you."

"I guess," Christy said. "But it doesn't make me feel any better. I feel used and abused." Christy stood from the table and walked over to the high, small window in the middle of the room. Nevlin observed her trying to get a peek between the bars that crossed the bulletproof windows. After her unsuccessful jumps to see what was outside, she turned around, frustrated, and sat back in her chair.

"Let's get on with this," she told Nevlin.

Nevlin pressed the recorder button and started to ask more.

"So, how was your relationship with Bryce when you first worked for the company?" Christy admitted she liked both her bosses, Mr. Elmore and Mr. Briscoe, but as father figures. Her father had died when she was ten.

"I barely knew my dad," Christy said. "I do recall he was kind and generous. He always gave me nice presents for my birthday and at Christmas. He showered me with love until the day he died. I was his only child."

Christy went on to explain that after eight years, her bosses called her into an office and gave her a promotion with a big raise. They told her she had been an outstanding employee, honest, faithful, and deserved to have an administrative assistant title with a salary to match.

"Soon after that promotion, my best friend died in California," Christy said. "I felt like I would have a nervous breakdown. I had no close friends in Jacksonville with whom I could confide. It started to affect my work. Knowing I couldn't afford the flight to California for the funeral, Bryce offered to take me, and I accepted his offer."

"Is that when the affair started? During that trip?" Nevlin said.

Christy broke down crying again.

"Can we stop for a while, Mr. Nevlin?" she asked.

Nevlin turned off the tape. "Would you like to finish tomorrow?"

"No," Christy said, sniffling. "Do you happened to have some tissue in that briefcase?"

"No," Nevlin said. "But you can have this." He pulled out a monogrammed handkerchief from his inside pocket.

After Christy wiped away a few sniffles, she told Nevlin

she was ready to begin again. He turned on the recorder again, and she started where she had left off, filling in the rest of the details.

"Did your job description change after that?" Nevlin asked.

"No, everything stayed the same," Christy said. "I had already acquired the promotion, so another would look suspicious. Bryce told me to keep our affair confidential as fraternization was not allowed in the company. Last Christmas, however, things got out of control. He bought me a new car and got me a better apartment. Our relationship started to move faster than I could comprehend. Something had to have happened for him to have that windfall. But I was so overjoyed, I couldn't help but show my affection in the office."

"How so?" Nevlin asked.

"Well, I couldn't help but hug and kiss him when he bought me an expensive necklace for my birthday. He gave it to me in the office. It was after-hours because he was afraid someone would see us. What was I supposed to do? Shake his hand? He didn't like my public display of affection and got mad."

"What did he do?"

"We had our first big fight. Imagine that. Right on my birthday! I told him it was his fault, and he shouldn't have given it to me there. But I went too far when I remarked, 'Where did you get that?' and 'How could you afford this expensive gift?' Then he really blew up. He told me never to question how he could afford anything again or where his money came from, *ever*, so I never did."

"Let me get this straight. The relationship between the two of you was a secret in the office until *after* Christmas, right?"

"Right. It was a secret until after my birthday on February

5. We had that rough patch during the winter, but we made up in the spring, and all was forgiven. Even though we had cooled it, people started to get suspicious."

Christy explained their relationship had been going fine, or so she thought, until Bryce asked her to put the energy drink in Michael's coffee creamer. Then in the summer, their relationship ran cold.

"It seemed it was always me instigating our meeting places. When I asked, sometimes he would come meet me, and sometimes he gave excuses. If you ask me, I think he was going to the greyhound track. He told me once how much he loved to see those dogs run. I know he couldn't have afforded it any other way without his wife knowing.

"I thought we had a special thing going. I didn't understand why things started to unravel. Besides the expensive gifts, he gave me thousands of dollars to put under my mattress to keep for our wedding day. He said things like 'There's plenty more where that came from,' and, 'We're goin' be rich one day, babe.' I didn't want to argue, so I never said anything about his comments.

"Then Michael died. That forced me to ask questions again. Bryce became more pissed. He got all weird on me, and then our relationship spiraled out of control."

"How so?"

"For one thing, he stopped talking to me at work. He kept his office door shut. He'd send work for me to do via an email or walk past my desk, throwing the assignment down with a note. After hours, he avoided my phone calls. I didn't know why. But to me, he was acting suspicious.

"One day, unexpectedly, he told me he changed his mind

about leaving his wife. I didn't believe him. Laura seemed to be the most unloving person. He never showed her any affection when she came around. Nor the other way around. She never called him at the office. In the past, I tried to convince myself what Bryce told me was true. He was in a loveless marriage, and he was going to leave her for me. I couldn't believe he changed his mind. It didn't make sense."

"Is that when you suspected Bryce had been stringing you along?"

"Not really. The only time I saw Laura at the office was when Michael's wife got sick. Then more so after she died. It looked to me like Laura came to the office to support Michael rather than to be with Bryce. Guess I was wrong. She must have been a sincere, nice person."

"Did you notice anything else?"

"Yeah. Come to think of it. Laura did stop by after work on occasion to see Bryce. But he often seemed too busy for her. I had suspected she really came to see Michael. Maybe I'm too suspicious, and it was what I wanted to believe. I did see Laura and Michael chatting through the window in his office a few times. They would be laughing and sometimes having a glass of wine after hours."

"I didn't know about that," Nevlin said. Christy choked up again. He saw what a difficult time she was having confessing her story. "There, there," he added. "You sure you don't want to stop for the day?"

"Oh no. It's just that I feel so ashamed," Christy said. "Laura's actions could all have been purely innocent."

"What about the business?" Nevlin said. "Anything suspicious going on there?

"Bryce had been making some bank transfers, about the same time we were on the outs. They were done once a month over the past six months. That's when I noticed things out of the ordinary."

"Bank transfers?" Nevlin's eyes became large. "What kind of transfers?"

"The kind I don't normally make…the kind from his side of the company to Michael's side and vice versa."

"And you didn't ask him about it?"

"I did. But caught hell for it. He told me to keep my mouth closed if I knew what was good for me. Bryce isn't the type who likes to answer questions. He's the boss, and his actions cannot be questioned. I didn't want to push it since I still wanted a life with him. I loved him, and his money didn't matter to me.

"I did think Bryce's, Laura's, and Michael's relationships were strange. Bryce always assured me that everything would be all right in the end and not to worry. He reminded me I was their confidential secretary and needed to keep it that way. We all worked for the same company, and everything would balance out in the end."

"Did you ask him what he meant by that?"

"No," Christy said. "Remember? I had to stop asking questions."

"Prior to that, did you have any suspicions your relationship would end?"

"Not in the slightest. Bryce kept telling me he'd get his divorce. Then we'd get married, and I'd have his babies. I could be a stay-at-home mom. I'd never have to worry about anything ever again."

"Those transfers you were speaking about earlier. Did you

happen to make any copies?"

"Why, yes, I did. When he began giving me the cold shoulder, I knew there had to be something in those papers. It didn't seem right. I went to the Xerox room and made my own copies when he wasn't paying attention. Michael just happened to drop by, so I made a set for him too. But I told him not to tell Bryce I gave them to him."

"So." Nevlin stopped midstream. The puzzle pieces started coming together in his mind, but he wasn't going to share his thoughts. "Thanks, Christy. You've been a big help. I'll be back in a day or two. I hope to get you out of here soon."

Nevlin came back the next day to prepare Christy for court. It had been three days since she had been captured in Georgia. She'd been extradited to Jacksonville on charges of suspicion of burglary and resisting arrest. Nevlin knew she had to make her first appearance in court within seventy-two hours. He explained to her how the court would go. She'd stand before the judge and enter her plea of not guilty. He told her to let him do the talking. There was one caveat that had to be explained.

"Christy, I must forewarn you," he said. "The judge isn't going to take kindly to you trying to flee the state twice already. Once to Baton Rouge and the other to Savannah. He might think you'll flee again. A high bail could be set. Unless you want to sit in here until your trial date is set, you might want to change your mind about asking your mother for money. Since I work for myself, I might not be able to afford an extravagant bail."

Christy started to balk. Nevlin held up his hand, signaling to stop.

"You have the night to think it over," he said. "Maybe you'll want to wait and see what the judge has to say. He may be lenient, after I explain what an exceptional employee and person you have been until now and that you have never been in trouble with the law."

"Okay," she said. "I promise to think it over."

Chapter Seventeen

NEVLIN GETS ASSISTANCE

*I*t had been cloudy and overcast all day. The chance of rain in the weather forecast matched Nevlin's mood. He didn't know how he was going to tell her the bad news. The only way he could get her out of jail was with more evidence against Bryce. He hoped she could get it for him.

When he got to the jail, Christy's mood made it worse. She appeared happy and more jovial than he'd ever seen her.

"What are you so happy about?" Nevlin said.

"I've made up my mind," Christy said. "I'm not going to ask Mother for help. I'd rather let the judge determine my fate."

"But, Christy," Nevlin interrupted, "I came here to tell you that our only hope is to get a copy of those photocopied papers. We need them as soon as possible. It's your ticket out of here, and your case depends on it. Does your roommate know where you've hidden them?"

"No, but if you call Denise, I can tell her where she can find them."

"Does she know anything about this?" Nevlin said.

"No, but she will after I explain everything," she said.

"Will she have a problem sending them to my office FedEx?"

"I don't think so. She'd do anything to help me."

He pulled out a brick-size object from his briefcase. It looked like a walkie-talkie.

"What in the world is that?" Christy said.

"It's the newest technology called a cell phone. Pretty handy for me. Not many people can afford them. They're quite expensive." He handed Christy the phone.

"What do you want me to do with this?"

"Please ring up Denise," Nevlin said. "Just press the buttons like a regular phone and talk normal into it. Explain where you've hidden those papers and what she's to do with them. Then hand the phone back to me. I'll give her my address. Got it?"

Her friend was at home. "Denise," Christy said, "listen carefully. I'm in jail in Jacksonville, and my life depends on those papers you're going to get me. You know the old fireplace in my bedroom? When you told me it didn't work, I put my important stuff up the chimney on a ledge. Pull out the manila envelope. Go get it and come right back."

Denise came back to find Nevlin on the phone. He gave her his office address so she could overnight them. They hung up.

"Christy," Nevlin said. "I don't know how much longer you'll have to stay in here. As soon as I get those papers tomorrow, I'll study them. When I come back, we'll make our next plan. Okay?"

Christy nodded, disheartened yet hopeful. She left the

private conference room with the guard to walk her back to her cell. Nevlin left the prison hopeful.

When Nevlin received the papers as expected, he studied them. The more he read, however, the more he thought it wasn't going to be as easy a case as he thought. It wouldn't be a misdemeanor of stealing. The papers showed more than that. The crime was too big for him to try.

Bryce had embezzled over $100,000 from his partner and tried to cover it up. The extent of the embezzlement would be labeled grand theft felony in the first degree in the state of Florida. The most Nelvin could wish for would be second chair if the state prosecutor would allow him. The good news was that Christy's story proved it happened just as she had explained it. She hadn't fully understood what it meant.

Nevlin called up an old friend, Mike, from the district attorney's office. The papers provided proof of malice and showed how Bryce took money from his partner's half of the business, little by little, which he gambled. It also showed how Bryce made it look like Michael was indebted to him, not vice versa. In the paper trail, there was also the plan on how Bryce intended to pay it back in increments.

"Hey, Mike," Nevlin said. "I have a favor to ask. Could we possibly meet for lunch or dinner today?"

"What's the urgency?" he asked.

"I have some documents I'd like you to take a look at," Nevlin said. "They're papers one of my clients gave me. They belonged to her former boss. It looks to me like they show proof of embezzlement. Are you free?"

"Sounds pretty serious. I'm busy today, but could you bring them over to my office? Say, around 4:30. Will that work?"

"Great!" Nevlin said. "I'll do that. See you then."

Nevlin was anxious to tell Mike the whole story. As he parked behind the courthouse and walked to Mike's office, it brought back old memoires. Mike and he had tried cases together for several years before Nevlin ventured out on his own. He didn't know how much time Mike had but hoped it was enough to tell him the Briscoe-Elmore story.

When Nevlin arrived, they shook hands, and Nevlin sat opposite Mike's desk. He talked nonstop, summarizing the case as succinctly as possible.

"Hey, Nev," Mike said. "Slow down. Take it easy. What's your hurry?"

"Sorry, Mike," Nevlin said. "It's just that this case has taken hold of me…"

"I understand," Mike said. "I have time. You were always interested in getting those wrongly accused out of jail. But, hey, we haven't seen each other in a long time. Tell me about yourself. What've you been doing since you left our office?"

"After Beverly died, I tried to be more of a presence in our sons' lives. They do grow up before you know it. It's been almost two years since I ventured out on my own."

"Yes, I'd heard you went solo," Mike said.

"Yep," Nevlin said then paused. He was at a loss for words, not wanting to bring up the past.

"And what happened?"

"Well," Nevlin said. "It happened to be my very first case, which started with two simple trusts for a friend. Those turned out to be not so simple. Quite complicated, in fact. My friend died rather young under some strange circumstances, and it's taken some time and money. It may wind up a murder case if I can pin it on his partner.

"I'm trying to exonerate my client Christy, whom I think is innocent of any crime, and I'd like to give closure to Megan, the daughter of my departed friend. Although the coroner's office said it was a probable heart attack, I think otherwise. I believe the partner who did the embezzling had something to do with it."

Nevlin had worked with Mike long enough to trust him. He knew Mike would give him sound advice. He tried steering Mike away from talking about old times, as he was anxious for him to listen to this new case. But it looked like Nevlin would have to be patient.

"Remember that case we had in the early '80s?" Mike said. "The one they called Operation Hardcash. This new case of yours can't be as complicated as that one. There were so many offshore companies involved, with money transfers in the Caribbean. All that money laundered and then the arrest of the former assistant US attorney. Remember that? Are you sure your case is as complicated as that?"

"When you look at it that way, no, you're right. However, there are some added complex problems. Megan wanted to remain friends with Brittney, so in good faith and giving Bryce the benefit of the doubt, before she left Jacksonville, she gave Bryce two verbal agreements. First, she told him he could take her father's name off the company logo and legally change the name to Elmore and Associates. Second, she gave him the authority to manage the company until they'd be able to settle her dad's half of the business."

"Go on," Mike said. "I have a feeling there's more."

"Yes. Months later, Bryce became anxious and couldn't

wait any longer for a settlement. He flew to New York to rush Megan into signing the business over to him."

"What did she do?"

"Luckily, I'd hired a private investigator to follow her in New York. I didn't trust the guy as much as Megan did. Fred, the PI I had hired, forewarned me, and I was able to intervene. I felt her life was in danger. After the verbal agreements, I deduced if he was as evil as I thought he was, he might bring harm to her to inherit the business. I flew to New York, confronted Bryce with a lawsuit, and sent him back to Jacksonville."

"Okay," Mike said. "I agree from briefly looking these documents over that this would be a grand theft felony case. Let me read them closer and get back to you. If they do, I'll see if a friend of mine at the state office can take it and get the judge to issue a subpoena."

"Thanks, Mike. I'd appreciate it."

Chapter Eighteen
BRYCE'S SURPRISE

*M*egan called Bryce. The conversation was brief.

"Sorry, Bryce," Megan had said. "Just wanted to let you know I'll settle the company business when I can come back to Jacksonville again. Currently, I don't know when that will be, but until that time, I'm putting you in charge, temporarily, until we get everything straightened out. Nevlin will keep you informed."

"Okay, Megan," Bryce said. "Just let me know what you want me to do."

Megan proceeded to give him a list of things, which Bryce was more than happy to do. First, he was to change all the stationery to read Elmore and Associates, and then he was to change the marque in front of the building to the same.

Bryce took pride in himself now that he ran the company, if only temporarily. His skills had nothing to do with it. Megan would never have let this happen if she knew the company was close to bankruptcy. No one else knew except Christy and him, but she was gone.

Bryce had a new plan for his cover-up and takeover. If he had enough time in his momentary position and could turn the finances around, he could possibly get Elmore and Associates in the black.

The first of his plan was to burn the old books and keep only the cooked ones he had saved. He had to make sure he could fool Megan and her attorney into believing that the company had been running smoothly all along.

Bryce tore up the old contract he wanted Megan to sign in New York. He didn't want proof of that. Upon returning from the Big Apple, he wondered why Nevlin never approached him like he'd threatened. Megan had made that initial call and sent him some contradictory emails making him believe that she now trusted him. Why else would she let him take the company over temporarily? What were she and Nevlin up to? Run the company until they settled later in court? Could it be as simple as not wanting the company to have a reminder of her father?

Bryce started to feel lucky. He brushed off Megan's convivial behavior as innocent. She acted like the old Megan he once knew. Perhaps she didn't take Nevlin's advice. Unofficially, the company became one entity in Elmore's eyes. There seemed to be only one problem, and it had a name—Wade Nevlin. He was the man who had tried to persuade Megan to sue.

Now that he was in charge, he thought of himself as the new CEO of the company. He needed to make some changes, and the first was to replace Christy. He'd grown tired of the incompetent gals the temp service had been sending over. He needed a woman more refined and skilled for the secretary/bookkeeper position. He wanted to save money by hiring someone who required less of a title with less responsibility. Someone he could control while he revamped the office configuration.

He put an ad in the newspaper and after a few interviews thought he'd found the right person. Her name was Molly, and she looked older than his mother. She wore her black hair short and had a frail appearance. Bryce figured she couldn't weigh more than one hundred pounds. She came in wearing a plaid pantsuit, and her eyeglasses sat perched on the tip of her nose. There was a strictly business, no-nonsense demeanor about her. Bryce took an instant liking.

At the end of Molly's interview, Bryce said, "I think you're the right person for the job." After looking at her resume one last time, he tossed it on his desk. "I don't need to look any further."

"Does that mean I'm hired?" Molly said.

"Yep," he said. "Can you start the first week of January?"

"Why, yes, I can," Molly said. "Thank you. See you then." They stood and shook hands. Molly started walking out his office door.

"Merry Christmas!" Bryce yelled to her as she reached the threshold. She turned around and waved back. He thought he'd done the right thing by hiring someone totally different than Christy. Molly wouldn't pose a threat. She accepted the salary he offered, which was half of Christy's, and of course, her age wouldn't be a risk to his virility.

December in Jacksonville brought more cold weather and rain than usual. Although the weather was dreary, the décor of the city shone brightly. Colorful Christmas wreaths with festive lights of green and red hung on streetlamps across town. Some windows displayed blue and silver candles for the coming of Hanukkah. Residences displayed their own holiday decorations with Christmas trees or candles in their windows or on their lawns.

Seeing the city all decked out put Bryce in a playful mood. He thought things were finally starting to look up. He'd planned a huge soiree at the office the second week of the month. He had plenty to celebrate. He'd hired Molly to replace Christy, he had created a plan to get the company out of debt, and he would soon be on his way to claiming Elmore and Associates as his own.

The Christmas party would be his last financial splurge of the year. After that, he'd tighten the company finance's belt. He told all the employees they could leave early that Friday afternoon, if they promised to come back at eight in the evening for the annual staff party. Although he could only afford meager bonuses, he assured them they'd have the next two weeks off. That was the least he could do.

The employees started to trickle into the Victorian house, which had become known as the Elmore and Associates office. Bryce had enlisted Laura to help with the decorations, and to his surprise, she was happy to do it. Laura put in the right amount of time and effort to make the place look spectacular. Bryce was glad decorating had always been her forte. It came in handy at times such as these. He hired the gourmet caterer to serve the food and bring in a magnificent ice sculpture. He thought, by going all out, it might take away some of the gossip regarding the loss of Michael and the disappearance of Christy.

Bryce's strategy worked. He only heard remarks like:

"I miss Michael and his famous eggnog." And "I wish

Christy were here. Her vivaciousness was always infectious!" And "I loved their Christmas carol sing-alongs!" If Bryce heard words or phrases like these, he ordered Laura to float around with a drink tray and offer some bubbly along with a change of subject. Bryce did the same, and the plan worked. He'd been pleased Laura agreed to help with the preparty arrangements and her willingness to participate in the revelry. He thought she looked ravishing while having a good time.

When the clock struck twelve, it seemed like everyone had turned into Cinderella. They acted like they had to get somewhere fast. Perhaps they didn't want to stay and help clean up like always? Maybe they didn't like their paltry bonus or couldn't wait to get their time off started.

"Bryce, I'm too pooped to clean up tonight," Laura said. "I want to go home, relax, and go to bed. If you want me to come back in the morning to help you clean, I'd be more than happy to."

"Thanks, hon," Bryce said. "I have a few things I need to do here before I leave. I'll catch you later."

"Okay," Laura said. "Thanks. See you later." The two hugged before she left. *Why did she hug me like that? She gave the biggest hug—willingly.* That gesture had been the most intimate they'd experienced in a long time. The feelings he had for his wife, which had long passed when Christy was in his life, were now adding up into months of growth of fondness.

Laura had looked stunning for the party. She had styled her hair in a new french twist, had on more makeup than usual, and had worn a Christmas green dress made of velvet. Bryce could hardly take his eyes off her. Could his Christmas wish come true? Could this be the start of getting back to a more intimate relationship when he got home?

With those thoughts in mind, Bryce thought about rushing home and putting off the cleaning like Laura had said. Maybe he'd get lucky. But there was time for that another night. He had work to do, and he had to do it fast to get rid of the evidence.

The fireplace had been roaring all evening during the party. It had been the perfect ambience, thriving next to the decorated Christmas tree. Now it would serve a greater purpose for Bryce. He stoked the fire, adding some papers between the logs.

The tinder he used was the paper from Christy's old accounting books. He had rolled them into starter wads and threw them in the fireplace. The more he threw in, the more the fire roared, and the more he smiled.

"They'll never catch me now," he said to himself as he continued shredding the rest of Christy's stuff and laughing as he threw it in the fireplace.

The house's living room held a few secretaries' desks. They had been pushed against the walls to make space for the employees to stand and mingle. When he was done shredding and burning, he pushed all the desks back to their original places.

He became tired and decided to have one last nightcap before heading home. He locked up all the rooms and made sure Christy's desk was barren. He wanted it ready and empty for Molly. He poured himself a glass of Scotch on the rocks and sat at his desk with his feet up.

"Ahh," he said to himself. "The perfect evening to end the perfect year. No more two sets of books, no more energy drinks, no more secrets, and I definitely won't be having an affair with Miss Molly, Grandmama!" He grinned and took a slow spin in his leather chair. It stopped in front of the oil painting of the inn at Atlantic Beach.

"And to you, my friend." He talked to the painting as if it could answer him. "A toast! You've been a blessing in disguise. I don't know who stole that money, but I know you do. I salute you!" Bryce raised his glass, drank the rest of it, then poured himself another Cutty.

"You saved my life," he said, still talking to the oil painting. "I pinned the heist on Christy knowing full well she didn't do it. Christy got arrested for it, and I'll be getting the insurance money soon. *That* will sure help me get back on track."

He opened the safe behind the Sea Turtle Inn picture frame. There it was, still hidden behind a secret panel the burglar or burglars had not seen. It was the long velvet box with the yellow diamond bracelet he'd failed to give Christy the night of the quarrel and firing. He hoped Laura could be happy with him again and forgive him once she saw this exquisite gift. He wanted to show how much he loved her and apologize for being a jerk. He'd never admit it was once meant for Christy. And he'd never explain he won it betting at the BestBet Orange Park dog track.

It was time to go home. He put the jewelry box in his inside suit pocket. He made one last spin around the office. He gloated, saying the company would be his soon. His happiness caused him to be giddy with a slight skip in his step while securing the rooms.

He walked out the front door. Just as he turned around to put his key in the lock, he was tapped from behind on the shoulder. Startled, he jumped and turned around.

"Bryce Elmore?" said a man in dark clothes.

"Who wants to know?" Bryce said, not recognizing either of them. "May I help you?"

The two plainclothes men, one tall, the other short, identified themselves as they flashed their badges.

"You're under arrest for grand theft," the tall man said.

"Florida Statute Number 812," the shorter one said.

"What?" Bryce answered in a daze. It was now after 1:00 a.m. He'd partied all night. "There's been some misunderstanding. Please, officer, you're making a big mistake."

"Sorry, bud," said the taller cop as he handcuffed Bryce. "Turn around and put your hands behind your back."

"You'll have plenty of time to tell your story," said the short cop. "But we're the wrong guys to tell it to." The officers laughed.

The three of them walked to the car as the tall one read Bryce his Miranda rights.

Chapter Nineteen
Bryce Meets His Attorney

*O*n the short drive across the Matthews Bridge to the police station, Bryce never said a word. He rode in the back seat of the officers' car looking at the St. John's River, thinking. He needed a criminal attorney, but he wasn't sure how he'd get one. He didn't know any. He wondered if he should phone Alan, the company's attorney, or perhaps Father Pat? No, he'd telephone his wife, Laura. She'd be worried about him and wonder why he hadn't come home now that it was two in the morning.

Once photographed and fingerprinted, he was allowed his first call.

"Honey?" Bryce said.

"Where are you?" she said, sounding half-asleep.

"I'm in jail."

Bryce got straight to the point without divulging any details. He explained how the officers surprised him at work. He didn't realize how serious it was until he heard them quote a Florida state statute of embezzlement and mirandized him.

"Call Father Pat," he said. "I'm sure he'll know what to do."

Before he said anything else, the police hung up his call and escorted him to the cell where he'd spend the rest of the night.

—⁓—

The next morning Laura made the call to the rectory at Assumption Catholic Church and asked for their parish priest.

"May I please speak to Father Pat?" she said to the woman who picked up. "Tell him this is Laura Elmore, and it's an emergency."

"Yes, just a minute, I'll see if he's available," the woman on the other end replied.

A few minutes later, Father Pat picked up. "Hello, Laura," he said. "What's wrong? I heard this was urgent. You okay?"

"Oh, Father," she said, sobbing as she plopped into her easy chair with relief. "Thank heavens you're in. It's not me; it's Bryce. He's in jail for a crime he didn't commit. Can you help us?"

"What?" the priest asked. "What in God's name did he do?" Without giving her a chance to answer, he continued. "Why, yes, of course, I'll help you. What would you like me to do?"

"Bryce needs an attorney, and we don't have one. A good criminal one, that is. Is there anyone in the parish you can recommend?"

"Anything for Jesus's flock," said Father Pat.

"He's being accused of embezzlement. I can't imagine Bryce ever doing anything like that. He and his late partner Michael ran the company fifty-fifty. Bryce swears he didn't do it."

"I'll see what I can do," Father Pat said. "After I make some calls and find the right person, I'll call you back."

"Thank you so much," Laura said. She then poured herself

a drink even though it was only ten in the morning. Her nerves had been shot since she heard the news the night before. "I'll let Bryce know."

"And tell Bryce," the priest said, "I'll be over soon."

When Laura called Bryce later that day, he wasn't thrilled about Father Pat visiting. He knew he'd have to tell lies to hide the truth. It'd be much easier lying to a lawyer than a priest. Although he went to church every Sunday with Laura and they tithed, he wasn't in the mood for any kind of confession. Why should he be? He was innocent. That's what he'd swear to anyway. He didn't want Father Pat to know he wasn't the godly man he appeared to be.

The next day he got a call from his priest. "I've got you the help you requested," Father Pat said.

"Hallelujah. Thanks be to God," Bryce tried to say in a convincing manner. He was happy to get an attorney, but he knew it wasn't any of God's doing.

"His name is Ray Solomon, and a pretty good criminal attorney," the priest said. "The problem is he can't get over there for another week or so."

"Oh my God!" Bryce said and then caught himself. He needed to be more appreciative and not use the Lord's name in vain to a priest. "Sorry, Father. I meant to say, thank you very much. I really appreciate it."

Ten days went by slowly. Bryce didn't like the idea that he'd have to spend his first Christmas Eve and the holidays in the county jail with all the Jacksonville drunks, lowlifes, and misfits instead of his family. His anger mounted with every day that passed. He felt the walls closing in on him as he watched the cheap paint peeling or listened to the conversations of the other men. With each passing day, he found it harder to keep his sanity together to protect himself from the others.

When Roy Solomon came for his first visit, Bryce took an instant liking to the guy. He had a friendly way about him that was reassuring. He looked like any other attorney, with one exception. The man wore black framed glasses with thick lenses. Bryce doubted the man could see in front of him without them, and they made him look comical even though he talked all business. After their introductions, Bryce asked his new attorney what was most disconcerting.

"Solomon, how soon do you think you can get me out of this place?" he said. "I can't take it anymore. I've never been in jail before in my life. It's been rather unsettling."

His new attorney assured him it shouldn't take too long, but with the holidays, Bryce had to remember that things moved slower than usual.

He had a long talk with Solomon, telling him what had happened with the money. He explained how Michael and he had two separate accounts and how he had "robbed Peter to pay Paul." But it'd been a gentleman's agreement with a handshake. Michael knew about it. Bryce had intentions of paying back the money he borrowed, but it became harder to accomplish as he got deeper in debt. He told Solomon the truth about his gambling problem, but he had paperwork to show he had a plan to pay it back.

"Where can I find this paperwork?" Solomon said.

"I kept those papers in a folder in my office safe," Bryce said. "My wife has the combination. She can take you over there to pick them up."

"Okay," Solomon said.

"Could you do me another favor?" Bryce said. He thought about his family celebrating Christmas without him. "When you talk to my wife, would you ask her to tell my family I miss them, love them, and that I'm terribly sorry? But please spare them any details."

"You can do that," his attorney said. "I'll let them celebrate Christmas and will call her in the next few days."

Bryce felt guilty attempting to take the coward's way out. He had told Laura the bare minimum. But that's the way he wanted it. She and the family would learn soon enough once the trial started.

"Solomon," Bryce pleaded again. "Isn't there any way you can get me out of here?"

"I know a judge who owes me a favor," Solomon said. "The problem is, it's the Christmas recess. I'm not sure if he'll see me. But I'll try."

Solomon left the jail. Bryce stewed for hours in the jail cell, pacing, with his mind racing. What was he to do if his attorney couldn't post bail for him?

Just then the guard came over and said, "Your attorney's back to see you." Bryce got excited. He thought seeing Solomon twice in one day and coming back so soon was a good sign.

"So," he said, "what's the good news?"

"Sorry," Solomon said. "I talked to the judge, but I couldn't get you bail. I got the next best thing. I'm here to make sure you're moved to another facility."

His attorney explained the judge would not permit bail, as he considered Bryce a flight risk.

"What the hell?" Bryce said. "Why would he think that?"

"Because it's a high-profile state's case," Solomon said. "You have the means, money, and a passport to flee. You should be happy I'm getting you out of here."

"Oh yes," Bryce said. "I am. But can't say I'm not disappointed."

"As soon as you get moved and settled, you can call your family. Tell them I'll be over there first thing in the morning," Solomon said. As he left, he added, "Talk to you later."

"Thanks, Solomon," he said. "Will do."

Within a few hours, Bryce was moved to a state facility and called home.

Brittney answered. "Dad?" she said, choking with emotion. "Is that really you? How ya holding up?" She put the phone on speaker.

"Better now, hon. I just got moved to Montgomery Correctional Facility. Don't worry. Solomon is taking good care of me. Can I speak to your mother?"

"Tell him I'm in the middle of cooking," Bryce heard Laura yell from the kitchen. "We'll stop over to see him later."

"Did you hear her, Dad? We'll come over after dinner, okay? Love you."

"Love you, too, Brittie," he said as he heard the phone hang up.

Bryce couldn't believe it. His own wife was too busy cooking to talk to him. *I guess I deserve it,* he thought. If only she knew about the diamond bracelet that had been in his pocket when he was arrested. *I was only an hour away from giving it to her. Damn it! Wonder if I'll ever get it back. She's never going to forgive me.*

He sat in his cell thinking about the last twenty-four hours and how it would effect his holidays. He'd missed the family's midnight Mass the night before, the traditional opening of presents on Christmas Eve, and dressing up like Santa for his grandkids. *How could I have gotten caught? I was so close to getting away with it all.*

The next day Solomon went to visit his client. He wanted more information from Bryce before his arraignment.

"I swear I never did any embezzling," Bryce told Solomon. "I believe it's Christy who's behind this. She managed the books and had everything to gain. She made it look like I skimmed the books, so she'd have a secure future with me. She didn't plan on my breaking up with her. I'm sure that's why she stole the money from the safe. Sure, I lied to her, and you could say I was a jerk, but I didn't love her anymore. Shit happens. Last I heard, lying is not a crime, and neither is having an affair."

"We'll get down to the bottom of this, Bryce," Solomon said. "If all your paperwork proves otherwise, everything should be fine. I must tell you, however, I've heard some rumblings from the prosecution. They're looking into the death of Michael. They have a feeling it wasn't natural causes. You weren't involved in that were you? No worries. It's an allegation I won't let them bring up in court. They can't unless they have solid proof."

"What the hell are you talking about? I'd never hurt Michael. He was my best friend. Someone must be lying."

"Okay," Solomon said. "I'll check out your papers once Laura gives them to me. Let's hope you're correct and the proof is there. That's all of it, right?"

"Damn straight. I don't know what they're talking about. The papers will prove my innocence. I'm pleading not guilty."

"Good. One more question. Where did you get that

four-carat diamond bracelet the police found in your suit pocket when you were arrested?"

"Oh, that. It was a Christmas present for my wife," Bryce said. "I'd been a shmuck for several years and wanted to make it up to her. I bought it at Underwood's and still have the receipt to prove it. Want it?"

"Well, no. I wasn't talking about *where* you bought it. I was referring to how you were able to purchase it."

"I can't lie. I like the greyhounds. A bookie over at the BestBet in Orange Park lets me know when there are some good 'run-ins.' The kind of dogs that run the *inside* of the track. I seem to be lucky when I bet on them. Gambling doesn't make me a killer, does it?"

Chapter Twenty

THE VISIT

*I*t wasn't until later that evening, Laura and Brittney arrived for their first visit together at the state prison.

"How's it going, Dad?" Brittney couldn't believe her eyes. It'd been almost two weeks since she'd seen her father. His unshaven face and gaunt look made him look older than his years. His appearance scared her. If she didn't know him and met him on a dark street, she'd be afraid of him.

Brittney didn't know what was going on in her mother's mind. Her mom showed no expression, acted sullen, and reserved. Was she in shock? This wasn't like her. Perhaps her silence was a way to show him her disappointment? The last couple of years of their marriage had been rocky to say the least, Brittney thought.

The two women sat down behind the plexiglass bulletproof window. They shared a phone to listen. Brittney spoke first. "Dad, how did you get here?"

"Like Mom probably already told you. The police arrested me after everyone had gone home from the Christmas party and I was locking up the place. I'm charged with embezzling the company. I don't have a damn idea how they could think that. I swear to y'all I didn't do it. But my lawyer, Solomon, is on top of it."

Bryce looked at Laura. "He told me to tell you something. He'll be calling you soon. He wants you to get him something out of my office safe. He'll call you with the date and time. You'll need to open the safe and give him the only folder that's in there. It's proof I didn't do this."

"Did he tell you anything else?" Laura said.

"Yes," Bryce said. "It's a bit of bad news, I'm afraid. He told me the judge won't be granting bail."

"What?" Brittney said. "No bail? How can he do that?"

"It's a state case, sweetie. Because of the amount of money stolen and the amount of money we're worth, the judge considers me a flight risk."

"What does it mean if you're found guilty?" Laura said, skipping straight to a negative scenario.

"It means, honey, if I'm convicted for grand theft felony in the first degree, I could get up to thirty years in prison and possibly a $10,000 fine."

"Oh my God!" Laura said. "That's ridiculous! What's Solomon's plan?"

"He told me it's going to take some time for the trial. During which he'll see what the prosecution has and compare it with my records. My records should prove my innocence. Solomon hopes to bring this to trial by March. "

"This has to be a huge mistake," Brittney said. "Right, Dad?" She couldn't hide the tears rolling down her face as she brushed them away with her hands.

"Darlin'," Bryce said. "Don't cry; that's exactly what I hope Solomon can clear up and prove it's all been a misunderstanding."

"Dad," she asked, this time looking him directly in the face. "Are you positive?" Brittney wasn't sure she could believe him. He had kept many lies from his wife over the past few years, so why wouldn't he lie to her?

"That's all I know," Bryce said. "I swear. Until we find out what the prosecution has, there's nothing more to say."

"Girls," Bryce continued, "I think I have a good idea who's trying to pin this on me. But I'm not saying. Let Solomon build his case, and we'll go from there."

"Let's go, Mom," Brittney said with an angry look on her face. "I can't take this visit anymore. Sorry, Dad. I need time to digest all this."

The two women stood, mouthed their good-byes, and waved. They walked to the parking lot and got into Laura's Mercedes.

"What's going to happen to Dad?" Brittney asked her mother as Laura got behind the wheel and Brittney slid into the passenger seat. Laura grabbed some tissues from her purse and handed them to her daughter.

"I don't know, sweetheart," Laura said. "I really don't." She patted her daughter's leg to comfort her. They drove the rest of the way home in silence. It was a longer drive than the city jail. But they were happy that Bryce had been moved to a white-collar crime facility.

When they arrived home late, they expected Steve would have put the children to bed. Instead, when they walked in the front door, the women found everyone all cuddled on the

sofa. They'd been watching the family's favorite Christmas
movie, *Heidi*. But their special movie couldn't keep them
away from Grandma Laura. Whenever she came in the front
door and yelled out "Hugs!" they all raced to her.

The kids' stampede almost knocked the young grandmother
down. But after everyone got their "lovin' sugar," as they called
it in the South, they ran back to the living room to finish the
movie.

"How'd the visit go?" Steve asked, standing in the foyer
as the women took off their coats and put them in the closet.
"How he's holding up?"

"I don't think so great," Brittney said. "It looked like he was
keeping it together just for us."

"I agree," said Laura, turning to her son-in-law, Steve. "Let's
talk about this tomorrow. I'm beat. The kids need their sleep.
I'll come back tomorrow. We can talk it over at lunch when the
kids are outside. I don't want them to hear our conversation
anyway. Brittney can fill you in."

The next day Laura brought over some Christmas leftovers,
and they all ate a smorgasbord of turkey sandwiches with some
side dishes. The weather was perfect for the children to play
outside. After lunch, they raced outdoors to see who could get
on their new bicycles first.

"Brittney explained what happened last night," Steve said.
"That poor guy. Isn't there anything we can do to help?"

"Apparently not," Laura said. "Nothing but pray. It's all in
the hands of his attorney, Ray Solomon, and his team to get
him acquitted."

"Dear God, I hope Mr. Solomon is the top attorney
everyone says he is," Brittney said.

"Father Pat says so," Laura said, "and I trust him. I also believe if we pray hard enough, justice will prevail, and Dad will be out of jail before you know it."

Chapter Twenty-One

THE TRIAL BEGINS

A settlement could not be agreed upon at the pretrial hearing. As for bail, despite Solomon's best efforts to plead his case, the judge would not budge and wouldn't allow it. The arraignment would be in ninety days.

The only new face to the scene was the addition of the state's prosecutor, Jonathan Martin. Martin had agreed to accept Nevlin as his second chair, since Nevlin knew so much about the case and the witnesses. They had developed an amiable working relationship, thanks to Nevlin's friend, Mike, who had introduced them and encouraged the arrangement.

The afternoon following the pretrial was when it all began. After the bailiff had escorted Bryce back to the jail, Nevlin invited Mr. Martin to lunch at Harry's. They were to meet Mike, but he had to cancel at the last minute.

"Great!" the tall, handsome African American attorney had said. "I know right where that is. Meet you there in twenty minutes."

They met at the restaurant and sat down at a table by the waterfront.

"Thanks, Martin," Nevlin said. "I appreciate you giving me the opportunity to be second chair with you."

"Not a problem," Martin said. "I'm happy you will be working with me."

"Have you had a chance to go over the paperwork I've forwarded to your office?"

"Yes," Martin said. "I have. The discovered hidden papers Megan had given you were the exact match to those Christy had in her possession."

"Fantastic!" Nelvin said. "Do you think we'll have any problems proving our case?"

"No," Martin said. "Without any unforeseen discoveries, it looks solid. At least that's how I see it."

At the pretrial, the Martin and Nevlin team succeeded in adding the crime of murder. Solomon objected, stating this crime needed to be separated. However, Martin argued, stating prior case numbers that connected embezzlement to murder, proving it was all a part of Bryce's greedy plan.

The judge allowed it with fair warning to the prosecution.

"I don't need to tell you both: this needs to be proven beyond a reasonable doubt."

"No, Your Honor," the men said at the same time. Martin and Nevlin had been forewarned. They knew they had their work cut out for them. Proving the murder case would be trickier than the embezzlement. They hoped they could somehow get more time to prove their theory.

"The trial will begin on June 1," the judge said as he hit his gavel. This meant that the attorneys on both sides were granted two extra months to put the double crime cases together. The prosecution team decided Martin would do the questioning with the police or any special technical questioning required of any witnesses, and Nevlin would question the witnesses with whom he'd already worked.

After several months of prep work on both sides, it was time for the trial to begin. Jury selection proved difficult, and Nevlin saw the frustration on Solomon's face. He was running out of jurors. It seemed there hadn't been anyone in the city of Jacksonville who hadn't heard of Mr. Briscoe or known of his philanthropic activities. Solomon requested a change of venue.

"If you want a speedy trial, Mr. Solomon, and I'm sure your client does, then you'll have to find an agreeable jury with the prosecution," the judge said. "Change of venue denied."

After several more rigorous weeks, a jury was finalized. But other things kept getting in the way. It got on everyone's nerves. One postponement after the other occurred for different reasons with even a continuance applied by the judge *sua sponte*, without prior motion or a request from either party. The judge had become ill. It couldn't be helped. It was to Nevlin's advantage the case dragged on. He had more time to find evidence to prove the murder charge.

The day of the trial, Attorney Jonathan Martin made his opening statement for the prosecution. After common introductions, he presented his case to the judge and jurors.

"We have evidence shown in Exhibit A, the original contract written and signed by the defendant and the deceased. That contract, and nothing legal was found to have been made thereafter, showed no mention of any verbal agreement referring to borrowing against each other's portion of the company.

"In Exhibits B and C, we have different sets of documentations provided by two witnesses that corroborate the authenticity of them. Those papers prove Mr. Elmore had been embezzling from his own company for years.

"Ms. Megan Briscoe, daughter of the deceased, will testify under oath that the papers she discovered after her father's death belonged to him. They were found in a locked compartment under his desk.

"In Exhibits D, E, and F, Ms. Christy Fields, Mr. Elmore's previous secretary and mistress, will not only testify the other copy was in her possession but also show photographs of her and the defendant with a new car and expensive jewelry, paid for by the defendant. She will also testify and admit to their adulterous relationship.

"Our theory is that Mr. Elmore wanted the company to himself, no matter what it took. When his embezzling got out of control, he ordered Ms. Fields to help in the process. Unbeknownst to her, the substance she put in Mr. Briscoe's coffee creamer wasn't the energy drink she thought it was. Then he had her copy documents he'd altered making it look like Mr. Briscoe took the money. He destroyed the originals and put fake ones in their place. Luckily, Ms. Fields made copies of those originals.

"The crimes committed by Mr. Elmore were committed out of greed. We'll prove beyond a reasonable doubt he embezzled the money to such an extent he had no choice but to kill his partner. He'd made a subsequent plan to inherit it all and rob Mr. Briscoe's daughter of her rightful inheritance."

Now it was Solomon's turn to dispute what Mr. Martin had said. Solomon had a smooth opening delivery. The short attorney with his thick glasses had not a single hair on top of his head but a gray ponytail down his back. He was a striking contrast to the debonair Mr. Martin. Nevlin thought Solomon's cavalier attitude was a bit off-putting, but the jury looked like they hung on the flamboyant attorney's every word.

"Ladies and gentlemen," Solomon said, "there's a simple explanation for my client. He didn't embezzle any money, nor did he murder anyone. The money was half his. It was a simple misunderstanding. Bryce owned half of the company. The two partners had been the closest of friends and always worked well together.

"A verbal agreement had been made years ago, explaining that each had the right to borrow money from the other's account. If borrowing ever happened, they'd pay it back whenever they could. Bryce's paperwork will show examples of this during the trial.

"No matter what the prosecution may say, and about some of which we agree, Mr. Elmore was not a greedy man but a fair man. Yes, he became an adulterer, and yes, he did gamble. Who doesn't have a fidelity slip or go to the dog track occasionally? My client may be these things, but he is not an embezzler, and he's not a murderer. Our case will prove it.

"My client has no dispute over the documents that were first drawn in 1970," Solomon said. "Mr. Elmore agrees that the stipulations and laws within these documents in Exhibit A were legally signed and notarized by the deceased and himself."

At the end of Solomon's opening statement, the judge told the prosecution to call their first witness.

"I call Megan Briscoe to the stand, Your Honor," Nevlin said.

Megan, looking nervous, walked toward the witness box, put her hand on the Bible, and was sworn in. After letting her get settled, Nevlin asked her to introduce herself.

"Please state your name and your connection to this case."

"My name is Megan Briscoe, and my father owned half of the original Briscoe-Elmore and Associates company."

"Will you please tell the court why you have brought this case to trial?"

Megan explained how she had known Bryce Elmore her entire life and how he and her father had become partners. She added that the wives and daughters had become close growing up, and the families often vacationed together.

"Would you say that you have remained friends with the defendant?"

"No."

"What happened?"

"After my father died, my relationship with Mr. Elmore cooled, though I've remained friends with his daughter and wife."

Solomon jumped up. "Objection. Relevance."

"Sustained," the judge said. "The relationship between Ms. Brisoce and the defendant has nothing to do with the crime. Ask another question, Mr. Nevlin."

"Ms. Briscoe, how is it that you came to know me?"

Megan explained when her father died, and without her knowledge, her dad had set up two trusts.

"One was a revocable trust with me as executor and the other an irrevocable trust for Dad's half of the company with you, Mr. Nevlin, as executor." She paused. "But I didn't know any of this existed until my father died mysteriously."

"Objection!" Solomon said and stood again. "Ms. Briscoe's father died of a heart attack. I move to strike that last sentence."

"Overruled," the judge said. "Mr. Solomon, this is within the legal limits of questioning in this case."

"I'll rephrase, Your Honor," Nevlin said. "Exhibit G is the coroner's report that says that your father died of a heart attack. Correct?"

"Yes, that is correct."

"What else was in that package that I sent you with the trusts, Ms. Briscoe?"

"You mean besides your business introductory letter?"

"Yes," Nevlin said. "Besides that."

"There was a letter from my father addressed to me with the words, 'For Your Eyes Only' on it.'"

"And what did that letter say?"

"It said if I was reading it, it meant someone had succeeded in killing him."

The jury gasped.

Solomon popped up another time. "Move to strike, Your Honor. What someone thinks is not any proof in a trial."

"Overruled," the judge said. "The jury will disregard that answer. Ask another question, Mr. Nevlin."

"Yes, Your Honor," Nevlin said. "Megan, how did you come across your father's papers shown in Evidence B?"

"I found the papers in my father's desk after he died, when I was cleaning out his office. The papers were hidden in a locked compartment under the top drawer. I found the key and opened the drawer to obtain those papers."

"No more questions," Mr. Nevlin said and turned to sit at the plaintiff's table.

Solomon approached the stand for direct examination.

"Megan, before your father died, would you say that he was of sound mind?"

Now it was Nevlin's turn to stand.

"Objection, Your Honor," he protested. "Calls for speculation. Michael's state of mind has nothing to do with this."

"Overruled," the judge said. "You may answer the question."

"Yes, I do," Megan said. "I spoke to him frequently on the phone and had talked to him two nights before he died. He sounded fine to me. I also submitted his medical records, which prove he was in good health."

"Do you think your father would be able to change the company's documents to make it look like Bryce was stealing from him?"

"Objection," Nevlin protested. "Calls for speculation, again."

"I'll withdraw the question." Solomon said. "No more questions."

Nevlin couldn't believe it. Solomon looked like he was winning by putting doubt in the jury's mind about Michael's health, his mental capabilities, and the possibility *he* had changed the financial records. Although it was overruled by the judge, the jury would still have some doubt in their minds. Megan was excused from the stand, and Nevlin thought she look dejected. He looked at the jurors, but he couldn't read their faces as to what they were thinking.

The judge pounded his gavel, "Mr. Nevlin, please call your next witness."

Nevlin stood. "I call Christy Fields to the stand."

Chapter Twenty-Two

THE TRIAL CONTINUES

Christy hadn't been in the audience per Nevlin's request. She stood out in the hall waiting to be summoned. One of the bailiffs opened the back doors, and the petite blond struck a short pose before sauntering in, swaying her hips like Marilyn Monroe in her movies. Her hair was coiffed to perfection, her makeup glowed, and her chiffon dress showed off her bronze tan. Her long tresses were dyed the golden color they once were. As her curls swung around her face under the breeze of the ceiling fans, everyone heard the clicking of her patent leather stilettos on the courtroom floor.

Christy took the stand with more confidence than she had ever shown before. Her self-assuredness made everyone sit up straight and pay attention—especially the men.

"State your legal name, please," Nevlin said.

"Christina Lauren Oglethrope Fields," she said. "People call me Christy in these parts. It's Tina in Louisiana." She glanced at Bryce, giving him a dirty look. She spent the rest of her time looking straight at Nevlin as he had directed her to.

"How long did you know Mr. Elmore?" Nevlin said.

"For the same amount of time as Mr. Briscoe—ten years."

"Did you ever work directly with Mr. Briscoe?"

"Of course, but not as much."

"How do you mean?"

"Mr. Briscoe liked to do his own secretarial work, but I always did the books for both of them."

"Anything else?"

"Well, if something urgent happened or needed to be done that Mr. Briscoe didn't have time for, then I'd help him out."

"Did you ever socialize with Michael?"

"Only at parties in the office," Christy said. She twirled her curls with her red-painted fingernails and looked down to admire them when asked a question. "But I wouldn't call that socializing."

Her statement brought laughter in the court room and the judge had to pound the gavel on the podium several times. "Get on with it, Mr. Nevlin."

"Sorry, Your Honor. I'll rephrase the question."

"Ms. Fields, were you and Mr. Briscoe friends?"

"Yes, of course, we were friends, but like I said, we didn't socialize outside of the office. He was more like a father to me."

"And how would you describe your relationship with the defendant?" Nevlin said.

"We had a very good relationship until the last few years I worked there," she said.

"Then what happened?"

"Do I have to spell it out for you?" Christy said. "Okay. First, I was his employee, then I became his lover, and the next year I wasn't. His lover, that is, nor his employee. When the affair ended, so did my job. He fired me, but that was last year."

"And now?"

"I haven't seen him since the day we broke up. I moved to Louisiana the same day he fired me."

"Prior to the breakup, how would you describe your professional relationship?"

"I suppose you would say it was good. I had worked for the two men over ten years and always received excellent evaluations."

"Do you remember doing any personal business for Mr. Elmore? Outside of the realm of the company?"

"I'm not sure. 'Outside the realm?' I did copy some out-of-the-ordinary papers for him on several occasions. Is that what you mean?"

"Yes. Could you describe these papers for us?"

"Well, they looked like nothing I'd ever seen before. Bank statements and spreadsheets. When I asked Mr. Elmore about it, he told me it was none of my business and to keep my mouth shut."

"What did you think those papers meant?" Nevlin said.

"Objection," Solomon said while scribbling in his notebook. "Cause for speculation."

"Sustained," the judge said. "The jury will disregard the question. Mr. Nevlin, you need to go elsewhere with your questioning."

"Sorry, Your Honor. Let me rephrase. Did Bryce ever ask you to do anything other than your job description?"

"Yes, I did transfer monies several times from Mr. Briscoe's account into Mr. Elmore's account. I thought that was odd too. I'd never done that before. When I asked him about it, he gave me the same response. Keep it between the both of us."

"Wasn't it your responsibility to make sure the books stayed balanced, Ms. Fields?"

"Yes, sir, and I did."

"No more questions for now, Your Honor," Nevlin said as he smiled at Christy and turned to walk back to his seat.

"But...but..." Christy wanted to interject more information, but the judge wouldn't let her.

"You may step down, Ms. Fields," the judge said in a harsh tone and banged the gavel. "I'm calling for a two-hour recess for lunch. Mr. Solomon will have his chance for cross-examination in the afternoon."

—⚏—

Nevlin and Christy went for lunch at a less popular place than Harry's. He knew of a little out-of-the-way place on the Northside that had good barbeque.

"Christy," Nevlin said, after they sat down to order their lunch, "you cannot interrupt me, the judge, or anyone else while you are on the stand. This afternoon, Solomon is going to try his best to discredit you, so remember what I said. Tell the truth but only in short answers. And whatever you do, for God's sake, don't tell a whole story to go along with it."

"Okay, Mr. Nelvin," Christy said as they finished eating their barbeque chicken sandwiches, peanut slaw, and hush puppies.

Nevlin had a few beers while they sat outside on the wooden benches and tables. The shade of the Southern Live Oaks and the breeze from the river were comforting. Nevlin made an effort to keep Christy calm, so he changed the subject to lighter conversation. He wanted her comfortable and ready to face the afternoon of tough questioning by the defense. They talked about Louisiana, her mother, her friend Denise, and her plans for after the trial.

As they drove back to the courthouse, they marveled on what a beautiful day it was.

"I think it's an omen," Christy said.

"I certainly hope so," Nevlin said. "Just remember what I told you, and we'll be good."

They entered the courthouse to a room full of people, many of whom had not been in attendance in the morning. Nevlin noticed Laura and Brittney sitting behind Bryce. There was nothing strange about a wife and daughter supporting each other as well as giving support to their husband and father. But one thing did look strange. Brittney was dressed as if going to church, and Laura was dressed like she'd just strolled off the tennis court. Nevlin wondered what that was all about.

The judge came into the room, and everyone stood when the bailiff called, "All rise."

"Court is now in session," the judge announced as he sat. "You may call your witness, Mr. Solomon."

"I call Ms. Christy Fields," he said.

Christy was sworn in again and walked up to the witness box. Solomon recapped the morning's testimony.

"Now, Ms. Fields, before lunch, you were telling us about your relationship with your two bosses. Correct?"

"Yes," she said, following Nevlin's prior directions.

"You stated earlier you didn't work for Mr. Briscoe as often and only on a few occasions. Did you ever have many conversations with him?"

"Yes, we had many."

"Do you ever recall having a conversation with him about Mr. Elmore's bookkeeping?"

"Yes, there was a conversation."

"Ms. Fields, you have admitted you balanced the books for the firm of Briscoe-Elmore and Associates, haven't you?"

"Yes."

"If you were responsible for that, then why were you talking to Mr. Briscoe about it? Hadn't you been doing that job for years?"

"Yes."

"Did you ever do anything illegal with those bookkeeping records?" Solomon said.

"Objection!" Nevlin said. "He's badgering the witness!"

"Sustained," the judge said. "You don't have to answer that, Ms. Fields."

"I'll rephrase," Solomon said. "Ms. Fields, did you ever do anything with the books that you didn't understand?"

"If I were told to do something I didn't understand, I would ask Mr. Elmore. Yes, there were a few times."

"What were those?"

"Those were the times I saw transferals of funds. I asked Bryce about it, but he refused to tell me. He said Michael knew about it, and they were with his approval."

"Did you believe Mr. Elmore?"

"I wasn't sure. But something told me the math wasn't right. I went to the copy room later and made my own copy. I also made one for Mr. Briscoe when he came into the room."

"What did Mr. Briscoe say?"

"Nothing really. He looked at the papers and thanked me.

He asked me if Mr. Elmore knew I was copying them. I told him no."

"What did he say to that?"

"He was very calm. He told me to keep it between us. 'No need to worry Mr. Elmore,' he said. Mr. Briscoe assured me he would look at them and take care of it. That everything was probably fine. I believed him, and we never talked about it again. He died a week later."

"No more questioning, Your Honor," Solomon said.

"You may step down, Ms. Fields," the judge said. "Court will adjourn for the weekend. We will resume first thing Monday morning. Court dismissed."

Chapter Twenty-Three

THE TRIAL ENDS

On Monday morning, the trial continued. Nevin's clever questioning showed Christy had been more than willing to rat out her ex-boss. But Solomon's questioning put doubt in the jurors' minds. She had admitted she copied all the original documents. Nelvin couldn't wait until it was his turn to prove they matched the documents Megan had in her possession. The combined documents verified Bryce had embezzled the money and tried to make it look like Michael had done it. But Solomon had not finished grilling Christy.

The defense attorney stood and walked over to the box to continue his cross-examination.

"Isn't it true, Ms. Fields, that you had something to gain by doing everything your boss told you to do at the company?"

"What do you mean?" Christy said, shrugging her shoulders and lifting her palms up as she flashed her eyes toward the jurors.

"I mean, wasn't it to your benefit that Bryce stole the money to splurge on the expensive gifts he gave you?"

"I never asked him to buy me those presents. In fact, I asked him to *stop* doing it. I didn't think he had that kind of money. When I accused him of doing something illegal, he became angry and offended. He told me to never question him like that again. So, I didn't."

"Did you ever have any conversation about an energy drink?"

"Yes, I did."

"Did Bryce tell you to put it Mr. Briscoe's coffee creamer?"

"Objection!" Nevlin stood up. "He's leading the witness." *That line of questioning should be mine, not his. What is he doing?* Nevlin was not pleased with where this was going. He could foresee Solomon's future questions or comments and where they would go next.

"Overruled," the judge said. "Mr. Solomon. You may continue."

"Thank you, Your Honor," Solomon said. He paced back and forth in front of the witness.

The intense look on Solomon's sunburned face and the way he furrowed his eyebrows frightened Christy. He took his glasses off and threw them on his table.

"So, you admit to changing the books and copying them, and now you are saying you admit putting arsenic in Michael's coffee creamer?" Solomon said.

"Objection," Nevlin said as he rose. "Move to strike, Your Honor. He's not only leading the witness but badgering again."

"Sustained," the judge said. "I'm instructing the jury to disregard Mr. Solomon's question. Mr. Solomon," the judge continued, "I'm warning you. If you go any further with this, I may hold you in contempt of court."

"Sorry, Your Honor," Solomon said. "I'll rephrase. Did Bryce ever instruct you to put something in Mr. Briscoe's coffee creamer?"

"Yes, he did. It was an energy drink."

"How did you know it was an energy drink?"

"Because that's what it said on the little pink tube," Christy sighed in frustration.

The people in the jury box laughed, and the audience chimed in. The judge used the gavel a second time to call order.

"Let me get this straight. What you're saying is you believe everything that's written on a bottle and you believe everything people tell you as the truth?"

Nevlin jumped out of his seat, but before he could say anything, Solomon interrupted him.

"Never mind, Your Honor," Solomon said. "I'll withdraw. No more questions." Solomon walked back and sat next to the defendant.

At first, Nevlin didn't like the gratified looks he saw at the defense's table but was glad he had a chance to redirect. He had prepared himself for this line of questioning.

"Christy, do you remember how much liquid you put in the coffee creamer daily?"

"Hmm… The little pink tube said it measured one tablespoon. I would put the whole tube in every time Michael brought a new pint of creamer to work. I stopped doing it in June."

"You stopped in June? Why?"

"After a few months, it looked to me as if Michael appeared sickly. I didn't know what was making him sick, so I told Bryce I quit. Bryce assured me the energy drink was helping him, not hurting him. Bryce didn't force the issue and told me he'd continue doing it."

"And did he?"

"I assume so, but I really didn't pay much attention and never saw him do it."

"Okay, let's go on to another question, Ms. Fields," Nevlin said as he held a photograph in the air. I have here Exhibit F, a picture of you at the Briscoe funeral. You did attend, right?"

"Yes, I attended."

"And didn't you make an odd gesture there?"

"Yes," Christy said, "I suppose I did."

"Can you explain what you did and why you did it to the jurors?"

"I put my arms in the casket around Mr. Briscoe's corpse. I apologized because of that energy drink and told him I didn't mean to hurt him."

"What did you mean by that?"

"I loved Mr. Briscoe," Christy said. "Like I said earlier, like a father figure. I'd heard he had a heart attack. I was afraid I might have done something to trigger it."

"No more questions, Your Honor," Nevlin said.

Solomon stood up to cross.

"Did you ever discuss with Michael what it was you were putting in his coffee creamer?"

"No. We never talked about it," she said.

"Why not?"

"Bryce had made me promise to never mention it. Especially not in front of anyone else. He said he didn't want everyone in the office 'getting in on his special drink.' I only saw Bryce put it in that one time. The same day he asked if I would continue doing it for him, which I did."

Christy started crying harder and dabbing her eyes with her embroidered, white handkerchief. Her cries became uncontrollable, so the judge excused her and ordered her to step down.

When Christy left the witness box, the judge spoke again. "The defendant's attorney will have time to finish the cross-examination later. We'll have a brief recess, including a break for lunch. Court is dismissed until two o'clock. All attorneys will meet me in chambers directly after dismissal."

Solomon, Martin, and Nevlin walked into the judge's chambers.

"This questioning is getting us nowhere," he said. "Where do you intend to go from here, Mr. Solomon? Do you or your client have any more evidence to reveal?"

Solomon didn't say a word, so Martin interrupted. "Excuse me, Your Honor. The prosecution would like to ask for a continuance."

"What for?" Solomon objected. "Everything has already been submitted into evidence."

"You brought it up, Counselor," Mr. Martin said. "Although the autopsy report had been suppressed, you mentioned the word *arsenic*. We want to have the body exhumed and tested with more bloodwork."

"I've already gotten signed permission from the family in New York, but since Mr. Briscoe was buried in a Catholic cemetery here in Jacksonville, we'll need the church's permission," Nevlin said. "That could take months."

"Anything else?" the judge said.

"After the exhumation, we'll want to have a new toxicology

report and a different ME as a witness to explain it."

"Any objections, Mr. Solomon?" the judge said.

"Objections!" Solomon said. "This is ridiculous!" He turned and pointed his finger at the prosecution. "This is outrageous. What are you two trying to prove?"

"You did open the door, Counselor," the judge said. "I'm going to allow it. Your objection is noted. Let's see what else we can find out. Although we may get proof Mr. Briscoe was poisoned, we still need solid evidence who did it. No more pointing at each other's clients without evidence. Don't waste anymore of the court's time. How long do you think you'll need, Counselors?"

"Six months should be sufficient," Martin said.

"Six more months my client has to rot in jail?" Solomon interrupted. "Absurd!"

"Request granted," the judge answered. "Any more outbursts from you, Mr. Solomon, and I'll hold you in contempt!"

"Thank you, Your Honor," the prosecutors said in unison.

Solomon swung around and left the building grumbling.

Martin and Nevlin departed the building discussing the case.

"Call Alvarez," Martin told his partner, "and get him up to speed. I'm going back to my office."

Nevlin called Alvarez from the courthouse. He was under the impression the two of them had become buddies since Bryce had gone to jail.

"Can you meet me at Harry's for lunch?" Nevlin said.

"Sure," Alvarez said. "What time?"

"As soon as you can get there. I want to share some big news with you."

Nevlin was suspicious of Alvarez's welcoming attitude. He hoped he'd find out soon. The two met at Harry's Bar and Grill. When Alvarez came in, Nevlin was already sitting at the bar drinking. They moved to their usual place by the river and ordered food. Nevlin filled him in on what had transpired in the morning. Nevlin was happy Solomon put doubt in the jurors' minds as to what was in the creamer. That was the prosecution's plan. Nevlin had the exhumation in the works. If the answers were there, it could mean he was poisoned. But who had the better motive to kill Michael—Bryce or Christy? The defendant's attorney was trying to pin the robbery and the possible murder on his client's mistress.

"I can't believe you are having the body exhumed," Alvarez commented. "You've gone through a lot of trouble just to prove your innocence."

"My innocence?" Nevlin said. "What in the world are you talking about? I'm trying to prove Christy's innocence."

"For a long time, I've had the suspicion that you and Christy had a thing going," Alvarez said. "You always seemed to pop up whenever that damsel was in distress. At the funeral, you came to her rescue. The night she was fired, you were parked outside of the Briscoe-Elmore company. Then you find her in Savannah! I could never put my finger on it, but now I understand why. To prove Bryce's guilt, you had to prove her innocence first."

"What?" Nevlin said and started laughing. "Me and Christy? No way. I'm just trying to find out who murdered my friend. He *was* murdered you know. Good thing I entered Megan's personal letter into evidence. It all fits. Bryce's plan to overtake the company by getting his partner out of the way and embezzling the money."

"Exhuming the body was the last piece I needed to prove your innocence," Alvarez said. "Very good plan. No one would do that if they were guilty."

"Thank goodness you believe me. Your testimony will weigh heavily on this case. I appreciate the proof you'll bring forth about Bryce being the only person who had reason to steal from his own safe. Martin will also bring that up Christy had no motive to steal or kill Michael. He'll question you about your trip to Savannah and what you found out from her mother."

"Right," Alvarez said "We already went over this. But what else was so urgent?"

Nevlin informed Alvarez about the continuance. "We've requested a second set of blood work from the exhumation. Normally those reports take a month. Is there any possibility you could speed up that toxicology report?"

"I'll see what I can do," Alvarez said. "Anything else?"

"We'll also need the best medical examiner to concur with the report. Had there been enough arsenic to kill him or was it a heart attack?"

"Let me make some calls," Alvarez said. "I know some people who owe me some favors."

"Thanks so much," Nevlin said. "Let's celebrate!"

Alvarez, being on duty, continued to drink his mineral water, and Nevlin downed a few more of his favorite dirty martinis. His drinks were becoming a dirty habit.

Chapter Twenty-Four

THE VERDICT

What should have been a six-month hiatus turned into more than a year. During that time, Nevlin and Martin found out that they would be getting a new judge, the Honorable J. Jones. The new judge approved the exhumation of the body, including the request for new evidence with the laboratory reports with a new ME. The information was shared with the defense. Martin and Nevlin felt lucky to catch this break.

It was now the summer of 1990 and almost three years since the crimes had been committed. The Jacksonville federal courthouse had a foreboding entrance. The six-story gray structure that once had been white looked more like a prison than a courthouse. Nevlin noticed the building's construction date cemented into the wall. *Wasn't it a coincidence that 1933 was also the year of Bryce's birth?*

The courthouse began to fill with people, most likely to support Megan Briscoe and her father's legacy. The bailiff ushered in Bryce last. Nevlin thought he looked worse than the outside of building. He shuffled in wearing handcuffs, chains around his feet, and a wrinkled jumpsuit. His hair had turned solid gray, which matched his long beard. He was not the dashing, middle-aged gentleman he once was. Nevlin was curious why Bryce looked ill. He hadn't heard anything about his health.

Nevlin's years in the DA's office made him feel comfortable. It may not have been the same courtroom, but similar marble floors and wood-paneled walls gave him the confidence he needed. He had no fear of standing before a new judge. They waited for everyone to take their places.

Martin and Nevlin thought they were ready for any argument Solomon would throw their way. They were clothed in their fine suits and ties, expensive shoes, and briefcases. They dressed completely opposite of Solomon, who looked outlandish. Their opponent's short stature had become thick like his glasses and his gray ponytail behind his bald head longer since they'd last seen him. Today Solomon wore a beret instead of a cowboy hat he usually wore with his cowboy boots and suede jacket.

Next, the bailiff walked to the front side of the judge's bench to make his announcement.

"All rise for the Honorable Judge Judith Jones." When everyone stood, Nevlin had to force stop his jaw from dropping. He knew they were getting a different judge but hadn't expected a woman. He wasn't sure she'd be in their favor. In all the years he'd practiced law, he had never stood before a woman.

The judge announced at the very beginning about a new discovery.

"My apologies for the trial being postponed. The exhumation and the reports from it were conclusive. There wasn't enough arsenic in Mr. Briscoe's body to kill him. Nothing abnormal was seen regarding the energy drink. The probable cause remains a heart attack."

There was a sigh of relief from some members in the audience and a low groan from the prosecution. The trial went on for several more days. Solomon dragged out more about the dirty details of Christy's affair and tried to make her look like a gold digger. She was the one who could have fixed the books. At the least, whomever did them, she looked the other way.

Next Solomon took the testimonies of the family to build his case that Bryce couldn't have done this. He called Bryce's wife, Laura, to the stand. This time her appearance had more of an older, more distinguished woman's look. Her answers were short and concise.

"Yes, I'd known of the affair," she said, sitting in a crisp blouse and pin-striped suit. "Longer than Bryce knew I did. I'd forgiven him that Christmas after I found out he'd broken up with Christy. I thought maybe we might have had a chance being a couple again, but then he was arrested. The distance made it too difficult to start over again. I moved on." Tears rolled to Laura's chin, but she never made a sound. Occasionally, she dabbed her eyes with a tissue while Bryce never looked up from his hung head.

Nevlin had a chance to cross-examine her. "Isn't it true, Ms. Elmore, that after your husband went to jail, you took over the company until it was time to settle with Ms. Briscoe?"

"Yes, sir," she said.

"And isn't it true some papers were found to show there had been some money transfers regarding a 'takeover'?"

"Yes, I did find some deposits that were made into Mr.

Briscoe's account after his death which I did find odd."

"One more question. Is it true you remarried while your husband was in jail?"

"No," she said. "Not yet. We are engaged, however." She looked at the huge rock and spun it on her left finger.

"Never mind," Nevlin said as he walked to his chair. "I'll withdraw. No more questions, Your Honor."

"I call Brittney Elmore-Warren to the stand," Solomon said. This time Brittney's appearance was like her mother's the first time. She was dressed as if she had walked off the Jacksonville Beach with her skimpy sundress and sandals.

Brittney stood up for her father with her statements. "Dad may have had an affair, but he definitely would never hurt Michael physically or financially. This embezzlement theory is a joke. It's been false from the start. My father would never embezzle or hurt anyone. The Briscoes and Elmores had been family friends for years, until this trial started. It was Dad's and Michael's practice to borrow from one another since they started the business."

When Solomon had no more questions for her, Nevlin rose and had his chance to cross-examine.

"Ms. Elmore," Nevlin said, "I have here in Exhibit A the evidence of the contract your father and Mr. Briscoe signed in 1970. Nothing in this contract mentions anything about a verbal agreement nor are there any addendums that were attached. How can you be so sure?"

"I swear I saw Daddy writing a new contract up." Brittney looked at Megan with tears in her eyes.

"You may have seen him write a contract," Nevlin said, "but nothing's legal, unless both parties have signed. That never happened. No more questions, Your Honor."

It was Solomon's turn again. Brittney continued to support her dad and believed the "embezzlement fiasco," as she referred to it, had all been a mistake. The Briscoes and Elmores had been friends forever, and her father would never do anything to harm his best friend.

In closing arguments, Solomon tried to convince the jury Bryce had done nothing wrong. This client admitted he transferred money from one side of the company to the other, but Michael knew about it.

"As for Bryce accusing Christy of killing Michael? It was all a ruse to get his mistress out of town so he could mend his marriage. This wasn't embezzlement, like his family said. It was only borrowed, so Bryce could pay off his gambling debts. The photocopied documents prove nothing. Anybody could have changed them. Christy or Michael could have doctored those books."

Solomon ended closing with "You heard it yourselves. There was no murder. There was no embezzlement. You need to acquit my client."

Martin had his chance for closing arguments. He produced the evidence of the by-laws, which had been signed and notarized by the partners in the 1970s. Nothing legally had been changed since then. There was no verbiage there about any borrowing.

He also brought up Bryce's surprise New York visit to get Megan to sign a contract turning the company over to him. It was another contract, which Bryce tried to cover his tracks, which Nevlin squelched. When he fired Christy, he accused her of killing Michael to make sure she'd leave town.

The only thing Michael was aware of was Bryce's gambling and cheating on his wife. But he had no clue of his partner's nefarious bookkeeping until Christy gave him the papers to prove it. Stealing from his company made it a crime.

The jurors had copies of the paperwork provided by both sides. It was time for them to decide which side had the more credible witnesses. They went back to their chambers and deliberated. It took just two days for them to come to an agreement.

In the end, Nevlin and Martin were able to prove without a reasonable doubt Megan's and Christy's testimonies were more believable. They also found discrepancies in the bookkeeping that Bryce Elmore had kept. Solomon couldn't prove his Mistake of Fact case—that is, that the property he took had been legally his own.

When the jury came back with the guilty verdict, the shock of hearing the decision devastated the whole Elmore family. Brittney looked at Megan, squinted her eyes, and mouthed, "How could you?" Then she fainted. Laura gave Megan a dagger-eye look before she and her son-in-law, Steve Warren, helped Brittney walk out. Laura cried her silent tears again as the Elmore family left the courtroom. They never once looked back at Bryce to say good-bye as he was escorted out. *How weird,* Nevlin thought.

Months later, the sentencing happened with no surprise. Bryce was penalized with the maximum. Nevlin felt no total satisfaction, however, knowing Bryce would be behind bars for the rest of life. Even the substantial settlement for Megan did not make him happy. The disappointment in the dropped murder case made him drink to excess.

The finances of the pro bono case had consumed him. His checking account had dwindled, and his savings were gone. He'd dug himself into a hole while failing to try and prove his suspicions. He couldn't afford his office suite in the Independent Life Building and was forced to look for space elsewhere. He found himself a two-room office in San Marco. He set up his business in a storefront on River Road. No matter what he did, he couldn't find happiness. He'd never been able to shake his belief that Bryce not only embezzled the company money but murdered his friend too.

Chapter Twenty-Five

ROCK BOTTOM

Months turned into years. Nevlin continued to spend endless nights working on a case the police considered cold. He accepted fewer and fewer clients and started ignoring the ones he did have. If he felt like a break on the weekends, he spent his nights alone at the Chart House bar. He'd sit waiting until someone sat next to him. On occasion he would engage in a conversation.

"Know anyone interested in a five-bedroom home in Deerwood?" he asked whenever a stranger sat beside him.

The weekends were like a Groundhog's Day movie. They kept repeating themselves. Nevlin would ask whomever he met if they wanted to buy his house or his boat. He needed the cash to make up for his heavy spending on booze and at the track.

When he finally sold his house, he found an apartment in San Marco close to his new office. The U-shaped building had a center walkway filled with Palmetto trees. His second-floor location had a view of those trees on the north and the St. John's River to the west. The apartment was just the right size for a single person with small necessary rooms plus a single bedroom. He loved the fact he could walk or jog to work.

Nevlin felt alone and sorry for himself. He struggled with his drinking, and his business started to falter. He didn't care about anything but the case he couldn't prove. One day he got a letter from Christy.

"I'd like to invite you my wedding," she said. "What I'd really like is for you to give me away. Please tell me you will. You are the closest person I feel who could fill this spot. I hope you'll think about it and come to Savannah. The wedding is six months away." The letter went on, telling him how she met her fiancé and the plans for the wedding, which she assumed, according to her mother, would be one of the biggest in Savannah's history.

Nevlin threw the letter down on the small desk in his bedroom. He didn't know how or if he would respond. He was in no condition to make a decision. This would be the second wedding he'd have to miss. He had been on a bender the weekend of Megan and Erick's. In his present condition, the answer would be no, but he didn't know how to tell Christy, so he avoided a response, just like he did to Megan's invitation.

A year later, he received a letter from Megan. She wanted him to come to New York.

"Erick and I will be having a baby this year. I hope you will consider being the godfather of our son, Michael. Please come to the christening. Hope to hear from you soon." The card stated the date and time. Nevlin threw down this letter, too, and ignored it like the others.

He rarely heard from them except at the holidays, and now he was surprised their letters had such personal requests. How could they expect him to be a big part of their lives now? He didn't understand, nor did he want to. He'd been thinking he had no purpose in life and nothing to live for. What was he doing with his life? Was there any way he could salvage it? Surely not before these big events.

Nevlin felt ashamed of himself. He'd tried to rekindle his relationships with his sons but never regained the closeness they once had. He always had reasons why his life had turned out the way it had. Everything went downhill after his wife died and then Michael shortly thereafter. He blamed his drinking problem on losses and hated not being able to convict Bryce of killing his friend.

His sons had moved out of state after law school. They had tried to keep in touch, but Nevlin let their calls go unanswered too. When the two boys tried to get their father to visit them, he always had an excuse not to. He regretted he hadn't taken the time when he had the money. But he couldn't visit them now even if he wanted to. He was broke.

At least Sally, his secretary, had stuck around. She had been the one true friend he could count on. She was the one bright light in his life.

"Honey, you need to get yourself together," Sally said one day. "You're not fooling me. Listen to what I'm about to tell you." She paused. "Sit down," she added louder, pointing to a chair.

"Whoa!" Nevlin said. "You sound serious." Nevlin sat where she'd pointed.

"Damn straight I am," she said. "You know Joe and I've had our problems over the years, right? And you knew he was an alcoholic too, didn't you?" Sally didn't wait for any answers and kept right on talking. "Now, after thirty plus years of marriage, he's decided to quit and go to AA meetings. Lordy, I've been praying for this day forever."

"I'm so sorry, Sally," Nevlin said. "No, I didn't know." He hung his head in shame. He had been oblivious to other people's troubles instead of drowning in his own.

"Well, tell you what. Just think about this. My church holds AA meetings on Tuesday nights. Why don't you go with Joe? I'm sure he'd be glad to have the company."

"No, thank you," Nevlin said. "I don't need time to think about it. I'm not going."

"Well, just so you know," Sally said, "that door will always be open to you. A good friend of Joe's invited him. He was stubborn at first too. Then one day he thought he'd try it, and he's been going ever since."

They dropped the subject, and each went back to work. A week later, Sally approached Nevlin again and had another heart-to-heart.

"Nev', darlin'," she said. "Can't you see? You're digging yourself into a bigger hole every day. I'd say you're about to lose your business. You haven't paid me for a few weeks now. Honey, I love ya, but I think it's about time we parted ways."

Nevlin tried to interrupt her, but she held up her hand with one finger over her pursed lips to shush him.

"Now, I won't hear any more," Sally said. "This Friday will be my last day. It's time for me to retire anyway. I'll have everything organized for you by matter of urgency. You'll know how to take care of everything. There's not much here."

They gave each other a hug. Nevlin swore he saw her eyes well up, as his did.

"I'm sorry, Sally," he said. "I didn't realize how much I'd screwed up."

Nevlin knew Sally was right. There was not much to organize. A few old cases, which had been pushed aside, and some recent things he had been working on. He thought about what she had said. It wouldn't take much time before his little company would be closed for good or replaced by a larger one.

What in the world had he been doing? Why had he deserted his family? His friends had abandoned him. There was hardly anyone left in Jacksonville with whom to socialize. He thought about Fred Jackson. He'd never forgotten him, but like his kids, he failed to keep in touch.

He thought about the assignment he had given Fred years ago in New York. But he hadn't spoken to him since the trial. Nevlin decided to call and see how his old pal was doing.

"How's it going, Fred?" he said.

"Hey! Nev, ol' buddy! Where've ya been? How's it going?"

"As a matter of fact," Nevlin said, "not so hot. That's why I'm calling. Would you like to go to dinner and catch up? For old times' sake?"

"Sure. Does that mean we'll meet at the Chart House again?'

"Heck, no," Nevlin said. "I can't afford that place anymore. Can we meet at Luigi's? Pizza's more my style now."

"Sure thing. Shall we say five thirty? That will give me enough time to get to my AA meeting across the street afterward," Fred said.

"Great. See you then."

The men agreed to meet for dinner in the old-town section of Nevlin's new neighborhood. He was happy he could walk there. On the way over, he hoped Fred would suggest they split the bill.

"Hey, Nev!" Fred yelled as he left the San Marco Fountain parking lot and crossed the street. Nevlin had seen him park his car and walked in his direction.

The men shook hands and exchanged hugs with several pats on the back.

It was the first time Nevlin felt embarrassed by the way he looked. The extreme casual clothes of a Hawaiian shirt and pair of shorts were much different than the expensive three-piece suits he usually wore when he used to meet Fred. He also hoped Fred hadn't noticed what he wore on his left wrist. His shiny diamond Rolex he'd inherited from his father had been replaced by an inexpensive, digital Casio.

The men grabbed a booth in the back of Luigi's for privacy.

"So, what's up, buddy?" Fred said. "I haven't heard from you in years. Since the Briscoe-Elmore case, right?"

"Right," Nev said. "Sorry I've been out of touch. I haven't been myself of late." He fidgeted with the short beard he had grown and hesitated. There was an awkward silence. At first, Nevlin couldn't find the right words to say to his friend.

"Fred, I've been thinking of something you told me years ago," Nevlin said. "I believe you used the phrase 'hitting rock bottom'? Well, I'm there, Fred, and I need your help."

Fred patted his friend's shoulder. "You've come to the right guy, Nev."

"Thanks, Fred," he said. But he couldn't look Fred in the eyes as he stared at his own shoes. The pricey sandals from Rosenblum's Nevlin prided himself in wearing had been replaced by fake replicas.

"I can't seem to find work," Nevlin continued. "I've been drowning my sorrows with those damn dirty martinis. I'm having melancholy dreams about still being married to Beverly when we had the boys. I've been going to the track and betting on the dogs with money I don't have. I've lost most of that, my self-control, and my self-respect. Sally warned me I was headed in this direction. Now she's left me too."

Fred put his arm around Nevlin's shoulder. "It's okay, Buddy. Remember? I was once there myself. Tried to drown myself in booze after my dad died. We all do it for different reasons. But in the end, we're all addicts. Why don't you come with me to my AA meeting tonight?"

"That's what I was thinking," Nevlin said. "Let's enjoy some pizza then go together."

"I'm glad you called me. Can you believe it? I'll be getting my ten-year chip this evening. It'd make me happy if you were there to share my joy."

"That's great!" Nevlin said as he congratulated his friend and ordered Cokes with their food. During the meal, Nevlin felt comfortable confessing the details of his downfall. He didn't remember it happening suddenly. His kids told him it evolved over the years. First, he couldn't pay his bills. Then, he had to sell his boat, his watch, and his house. When he couldn't acquire more clients, his debt became bigger, and the vicious cycle began.

"Word also got around the courthouse about my drinking and excessive spending," Nevlin said. "I thought I was a functional alcoholic, as they call it. I thought I was in control when I saw other attorneys having celebratory drinks after big wins or drowning themselves after huge losses. I should have known when I totaled my Mercedes last year. When I awoke in the hospital, I didn't remember a thing. When I got out, I went home and drank to forget it."

"I'm so sorry, Nev," Fred said. "Now I understand why you didn't come to me sooner. But I think what you're saying is you're ready for a change, right?"

Nevlin nodded, and the men finished their dinner. To Nevlin's relief, Fred picked up the whole tab. Nevlin thanked his friend.

"Why don't you ride with me?" Fred said. "The church is right down the street. I'll drive you home afterward."

"Sounds good," Nevlin said. "I guess you noticed I was on foot?" Nevlin saw Fred nod with a wink. "Thank you so much," he added.

The two men arrived at All Saints Episcopal Church. The meeting was held in a large back room. About twenty men set up the chairs in a semicircle. The facilitator, named Doug, stood behind his chair and talked to one of the men. The others pinned on their name tags, using first names only, and greeted each other. People knew Fred had been coming for years, and tonight he'd receive a major chip. They congratulated him with enthusiasm.

In a few minutes, it was time for everyone to get their drinks and close in the circle. The church didn't allow smoking inside, so the men on the lawn finished up their smokes outside before coming in. They grabbed their coffee or colas and joined the others.

After everyone got seated, Doug welcomed the group and addressed the man at the opposite end of the circle. "I see you have brought a friend with you tonight, Fred," Doug said.

"Why, yes, I have," Fred said, as he stood and pointed to Nevlin.

Nevlin stood too. He knew they used first names only, so he said with a smile. "My name is Wade, and I'm an alcoholic."

Chapter Twenty-Six

NEVLIN'S NEW GOAL

*N*evlin was grateful Fred had brought him to the AA group. The two of them rekindled their relationship and became like brothers. From then on, they attended all their AA meetings together. It had been a struggle for Nevlin the first couple of years. But after getting his second-year chip, Nevlin felt like a new man. He didn't have any urges for his daily dirty martinis anymore. Rarely did he have bouts of melancholy or have to fight his old demons with the impulse to drink.

He stopped going to the track, and his business picked up. He had a positive outlook on life and started a savings. He had a goal in mind, which motivated him. He didn't work on the Briscoe case nightly but only on occasion. He didn't let it consume him and stayed focused on his job and on the course toward his new goal.

One weekend, after years of attending AA, Fred and he fished off the north shore's beaches and discussed his plan with his friend.

"Fred, I'm thinking about moving to the Keys," Nelvin

said. "Ever been to the Key West?"

"Can't say I have," Fred said. "Always wanted to go. But Lucy and I never had the money to travel that far away."

"It was the dream I once had with my old pal, Michael. We were planning on setting up a charter business together down there. I thought I'd follow the dream I discarded years ago after he died. This time I thought I'd do it solo."

"Sounds like a great idea to me," Fred said. "I always loved being on the water. Could only afford my little fishing boat over there, though." Fred pointed to the small outboard Nevlin and Fred had used to motor over to their favorite fishing spot. He smiled. "Lucky for me, this old Tracker outboard was enough to make my wife happy."

With years of sobriety, Nevlin became more self-confident. After saving, working, and staying sober, he received his five-year chip. Fred and his AA friends were there to cheer him on. The men in his group had heard of his new plan and encouraged him to purchase a charter fishing boat and move south.

One evening, he called up his son in Chicago. Todd wasn't into fishing, but he loved the water and outdoors as much as his dad.

"Hey, Todd, how ya doing?" Nevlin said.

"Great, Dad," he said. "How've you been?"

"Fantastic! In fact, I just wanted to call and tell you about the boat I just bought. It's for the new goal I've been saving for."

"Oh yeah?" Todd said. "What kind did you get, and what goal are you talking about?"

"I purchased a thirty-six-foot Bayliner cabin cruiser, like the one I used to have. Only this one was used, and I could purchase it on credit."

"I'm so proud of you, Dad," Todd said. "Sounds like you are finally getting your life in order."

"Thanks, Todd. I appreciate that."

"Was purchasing that boat the new plan, or was there something else? That's a pretty big one."

"As a matter of fact, you're right. Remember when I had planned to move to the Keys with my friend Michael?"

"Yes. How could I forget that?" Todd said with a little sarcasm.

"Well, since it never came to fruition, I've decided to move there alone and start up the charter boat business myself. I think I can do it."

"Good for you, Dad," Todd said. "I think that's a great idea. On another note, have you talked to Dan lately? I think you should talk to him about this. That would be nice."

"You're right, Todd," Nevlin said. "I'll call him. It's been quite a while since we've talked." He tried to forget the memories of when he drank too much and became too critical of his son Dan. He hated the fact it seemed their personalities had always clashed when Nevlin had too much to drink. He'd said words to this son that he deeply regretted.

"Dan and I have talked," Todd said. "He's proud of you too, getting sober, but he's too proud to be the first one to pick up the phone. I'm sure he'd be happy to hear from you."

"You're right," Nevlin said. "I'm glad Fred helped me take that first step joining AA. He saved my life. I'm still working on all those recovery steps, especially with Dan. I know I'm the only one who can turn my life around, and I'm glad I am.

"The Briscoe case did a number on me. Losing your mom and then Michael so soon afterward was hard on me. I wanted justice for him, and for his daughter, Megan, in the worst way. Money didn't matter. I loved that girl like a daughter. I was sorry I couldn't get closure for her. I couldn't handle the fact the murder case was never solved. It hurts me to this day."

"Don't let it eat at you, Dad," he said. "Just remember how well you're doing. I'd hate for you to lose your sobriety again. Maybe more counseling?"

"Don't worry, son," Nevlin said. "Perhaps you're right. In the back of my mind, I'm still not satisfied. Bryce Elmore reminds me of several other cold cases. He went to prison for embezzlement but not for the murder of his partner."

"Come on, Dad," Todd said. "Take care of yourself. Forget about this for the time being. Sorry, I must get back to work. I can't wait to hear more details of your great idea later. And don't forget to call Dan."

"Okay, son," Nevlin said. "I'll get back to you once my plans are finalized."

Nevlin got off the phone and walked from his small office on the St. John's River to his apartment on San Marco Boulevard. For the first time since sobriety, he had both checking and savings accounts with substantial monies and no credit card debt. He was happy knowing he didn't owe anything to anybody. Fred and his new AA friends had saved him from destruction.

When he arrived home, he decided it would be a good time to call his other son, Dan, in California.

"Hi, Dan," he said. "Before you say anything, I want to

apologize for being the rotten father that I've been."

"You haven't been a rotten father," Dan said.

"Please, hear me out," Nevlin said. "I know you and Todd have been talking. I'm sorry I haven't picked up the phone to talk to you. I want to make amends for all the times I called you names and embarrassed you when I was drunk."

"It's so good to hear you say that Dad," Dan said. "I know things have been hard on you, losing Mom and then Michael."

"I know, but that was no excuse for my behavior. I want to make it up to you. I've been thinking about this for a long time. First, I wanted to tell you I bought a boat. A Bayliner like the one I used to have, only bigger. Second, I've decided to move to the Keys, like Michael and I once planned."

"The Keys?" he said. "Really? I thought that idea fizzled out years ago."

"Yes, Dan, it had," Nevlin said. "But it's come back now that I have my life together again. Did Todd tell you I received my five-year chip?"

"Well, yes, he did. That's swell. But he didn't tell me any plan."

"I told him not to," Nevlin said. "I wanted to tell you myself."

"This doesn't really surprise me. I've known since I was a kid how much you loved the water. I'm happy for you, Pop, and I hope your plan succeeds."

Nevlin was overjoyed to hear his son call him by the nickname he used as a child. "Yes, I've missed my boat ever since the day I had to sell it when I lost everything."

"I know, Dad," Dan said. "But let's not talk about the past. Only the future."

"Okay, good. I've been putting away most of my money a little at a time for this move to Key West. I want to own a charter boat business. I'd have the best of both worlds. Take folks out snorkeling, fishing, or diving while I'm behind my boat having fun in the sun. I'd make some money while I'm at it too. Call it my semiretirement."

"I think that's a great idea, Dad," his son said.

"Good," said Nevlin. "Does that mean I have your approval?"

"Dad, you don't need my approval," Dan said. "I just hope you've thought this through. You have, haven't you?"

Chapter Twenty-Seven

THE SURPRISE VISIT

*B*efore Nevlin moved to the Keys, he wanted to make one last trip to Savannah. He'd never made it to Christy's wedding. At the time, he was too drunk to even attend it, let alone give the bride away. The new father-in-law had filled in for him. Nevlin felt he needed a visit to make amends.

He called Christy first. "I'm so sorry, dear, for what I did those years ago," he said." Not giving you away was one of the biggest regrets of my life."

"That's okay Mr. Nevlin," Christy said. "I thought something was wrong, by what you wrote me."

"You're right. There was something wrong. I'd become an alcoholic. But now I'm sober and would like to visit you and your husband, Matthew. If that's all right?"

"We'd be glad to have you! When do you plan on coming?"

"Is this weekend too soon? This Saturday? Just for a few hours."

"Sure. That'd be great. Would love to see you again. I'll tell Matthew you're coming."

There was another reason for his visit, but he didn't want to say over the phone. Other than asking for her forgiveness, he wanted to say good-bye too.

He booked a room at the River Street Inn like usual. Maybe he'd stop and say hello to Ron while in Georgia. He wondered if Ron still worked there. Nevlin hadn't heard from him in over five years.

Late Friday afternoon, Nevlin drove for two hours north on I-95 to Savannah. He reminisced, thinking about the good and bad times he'd spent there. Memories floated through his brain until he reached the hotel.

He had to keep his mind straight. Being clean and sober, he had to refer to AA solutions on how to handle these recollections. He would have to fight the urge to drink every time nostalgia overcame him. He needed to use the mind games he learned to turn the thought around. As soon as he got to his room, he opened some Perrier from the pay fridge. He drank it and decided to take a run. That always cleared his mind.

When he returned, he made a reservation at the Chart House for a late dinner. Then he showered and took a nap. When he woke, he shaved, put on his casual dinner clothes, and decided to take a walk in the city before going to the restaurant on the river.

Nevlin felt refreshed as he strolled to Lafayette Square where Christy had her wedding. The basilica was the largest Catholic church in town and the same one where he and Beverly married. The warm breezy evening made for a perfect stroll in the evening. The smells of blooming honeysuckle and lilacs filled the air. He swore the aroma was what put smiles on everyone's faces as he passed them, looping back to the Chart House.

When he arrived at the Chart House, he asked to be seated by the window and ordered a drink.

"I'll have a Perrier and lime, please," Nevlin asked the waiter. "Any specials this evening?"

"We have a lobster that's delicious and a veal cordon bleu, sir."

"I'll take the veal," he said.

The waiter left. Nevlin always enjoyed looking out the window as the boats went by. He thought again about his memories of Savannah, and the fact he knew he'd never return. Caught up in that reverie, he hadn't noticed the family who had walked into the restaurant. There were an older couple and a younger one with two small children. As he finally caught the older gentleman's eyes as they sat a few tables over, the man stood and walked over to Nevlin.

"Well, isn't this déjà vu?" he said.

"My good Lord!" Nevlin said, not recognizing him at first. But then he stood and shook the man's hands. "Why, if it isn't my old friend, Alvarez. Good to see ya, buddy! Have a seat."

"Nice seeing you again too," Alvarez said and laughed as he sat across from him. "What on earth brings you up to these parts?"

Nevlin explained how he had hit rock bottom after the Briscoe murder case ran cold. That he had to sell everything he owned and downsize. And with the help of his friend, Fred, and AA, he became sober and rebuilt his business.

"Sobriety did the rest," Nevlin said.

"I did notice you were drinking Perrier."

"Yep, mineral water is my drink now. No more 'dirties,' as I called them. Used to love 'em, but I'm far better without 'em.

What about you? I'd heard you'd retired and moved to Georgia, but I didn't know it was Savannah."

"Initially it wasn't. We moved to Atlanta to be by our kids and lived there for several years. That's my daughter and husband with their kids. My son-in-law got a new job down here last year. We missed the grandkids so much, we decided to move closer to them. We needed to downsize anyway."

"Glad I ran into you," Nevlin said. "I was going to stop by the old police station to see if Chief Sandtrach still worked there. Does he?"

"Sorry, pal," Alvarez said, "but he died a few years back. Heart attack. Stress of the job. You know. What did you say you were doing here?"

"I didn't," Nevlin said. "But I came up to see Christy."

"Christy?" Alvarez said, shocked. "What on earth for? I heard she got married several years ago. Had one of the biggest weddings Savannah has ever seen. Married some wealthy dude."

"That's right, and I missed it. Came to make amends, as they say," Nevlin said. "Also heard Miss Penelope died. I wanted to give Christy my condolences and meet that new fellow of hers. Will stop in for a visit tomorrow. She told me they're living in Miss Penelope's condo until their house is built."

"Yes, I heard that house is going to be big too." Alvarez said. "And what do you know about Bryce? Still in jail?"

"Far as I know," Nevlin said. "Haven't heard otherwise. I've kept in touch with Megan and Erick in New York. Was godfather to their second baby last year."

"Nice. What are your plans next?"

"I'm changing careers to start a semiretirement business in Key West. I already purchased a boat there and will start a charter business. You know I've always had sea legs that beckoned me to the ocean."

"Sounds perfect for you," Alvarez said. "Good luck. Nice seeing you again. Enjoy your dinner."

"You, too. Get back to your family. They must be wondering what's taking you so long."

"That's okay," Alvarez said and smiled. "They know me. When they see me talking to old friends, they know it always takes a while."

"Before you leave," Nevlin said, "please give me your new address and email, so we can keep in touch. Once I get my new business started, I'll invite you down on my charter boat."

"Will do, and that boat ride sounds fantastic!" Alvarez said as he walked back to his family's table.

Nevlin's dinner came. He ate it slowly, trying to make it last long for the memories. After paying his bill, he stopped by the Alvarezes' table. The retired detective introduced his friend to everyone then handed him a card with his personal information.

"Here's where you can get in touch with me," he said. "Now, don't forget. I'll be looking forward to that deep-sea fishing excursion you promised."

"Thanks," Nevlin said and looked at the card. "I won't forget."

The next morning, Nevlin took his morning jog, almost passing the police station. He stopped for a moment. He gave a nod and salute to the man who helped him prove Christy's innocence.

The visit with Matthew and Christy was intimate. "I have a surprise of my own to tell you," Christy said as she opened the door and rubbed her belly. "I wanted you to see for yourself and not tell you over the phone."

Nevlin gave her a hug and kissed her on both sides of her cheeks. "If I had known, I would have brought a gift for the baby! Congratulations!" He gave his condolences for the loss of her mother and congratulated her again on her marriage and unborn child.

After a few hours visit with conversation over sweet tea and freshly baked cake, it was time to leave. As Nevlin approached the door, Christy said, "Oh, by the way, we're going to call her Penny Marie, after our mothers. They were the ones who introduced us."

Nevlin smiled and gave her another hug before he left. It was time to drive back to Jacksonville.

The late Saturday afternoon drive back to Jacksonville along Interstate 95 calmed him. There was little traffic on the freeway. He had driven that route many times before for business and pleasure. He had an idea on the way home to make a detour down memory lane. He drove past his old office location in the Independent Life Building. He shuddered as the memory was too painful to think about.

He drove across the Matthews Bridge and turned down a side road called Seabrook Cove Parkway. He needed to shake the bad thoughts and recall happier times when Beverly and he lived in the apartments on a canal off the St. John's. It was there he had moored his first small motorboat. They were young and in love with no kids and had a little rescue dog named Snoopy. He laughed as he remembered the acronym that people used in the 1980s. They were called DINKS, which stood for Dual Income No Kids. The friends they made there were the same.

The apartment buildings looked different because management had painted them a different color. He felt it was the sign he needed to forget the past. He drove out of the Seabrook Cove apartments and onto Atlantic Boulevard toward his own apartment.

As he pulled into his parking space at the San Marco building and stepped out of his car, he felt a weird sensation blow through him.

He couldn't explain the feeling, but he sensed something ominous. For some reason, after spending two splendid days in Savannah, he felt his emotional high freefalling. He perceived danger lurked inside.

What could be wrong? When he unlocked the door, order was not what he saw. Someone had been inside and trashed the place. Although it appeared nothing of value had been stolen, it looked like whomever was in there had been looking for something. Every drawer was pulled and turned over. The closet was also a mess. But what were they looking for? And why?

Nevlin called the police to report the strange break-in. The officers arrived at the scene within minutes. They looked around, dusted for fingerprints, and took some photographs.

"Unfortunately, sir," the officer said, "there's been a string of robberies in the area. Have you noticed anything stolen?"

"Not to my knowledge. I can't for the life of me understand why anyone would break in, make a such mess, and not take anything."

"Think. What do you suppose they could have been looking for?"

"Nothing," Nevlin said. "All my legal documents and valuables I keep at my office in a safe."

Nevlin thought a moment. "Oh, Christ!" he said. "My office! Please, officer, may I leave? I need to get over there right away. My landlord can lock up for you. She's on the first floor right below me in room one. My office is on River Road, two blocks over. I need to get there now."

With the police's permission, Nevlin ran to his office and braced himself before opening the door. Just what he suspected. It looked like his apartment but much worse. Someone *had been* looking for something. But what? He called the police again, gave them the address, and told them to come right over. Every file had been ripped out of the cabinets and thrown helter-skelter around the office. It would take him several hours to try and figure out what was missing.

The police came and followed the same protocol with pictures and print dusting. After the police left, it was late, so Nevlin decided to lock up and close his business for a few days. He took his Rolodex of addresses and phone numbers home. He'd call his clients on Monday to reschedule their appointments. He'd concentrate on his house first. Maybe there *was* something missing he'd overlooked.

Nevlin didn't want to worry his kids, so he didn't tell them what had happened. He wasn't too worried himself. Hopefully, it was what the police said. Perhaps kids just looking for money for drugs. Maybe it was a past criminal he'd put away a long time ago and who wanted to make things more difficult for him. No messages of any kind had been sent like letters, emails, or phone messages. This looked more like an annoyance tactic than a threat of any kind.

It didn't take long to clean the apartment. Being in a small place did have its advantages. He was lucky the perpetrator had left his television, his pricey Bang and Olufsen stereo components, his record collection, and his few pieces of jewelry. *Strange they didn't take anything of any value.*

What could this person have been looking for? Maybe the person didn't know Nevlin had already sold most of his expensive stuff. But who would know that? Was it something in his office?

The next morning, Nevlin decided to take his daily jog and get some fresh air. The fall breeze was crisp, and the leaves had turned their vibrant colors. In the South, he loved that fall came in December a few months later than in the North. He took his four-mile run down past Luigi's and into the subdivision behind it. He circled around toward River Road before stopping at the office.

He sat on a bench and rested before walking inside. When he finally went in and started to clean up, it didn't take long to notice what was amiss. After putting all the *A*s back that in their place, he started on the *B*s. He found the Babcock, Bailey, and Barnsdall files, and… Oh, shit! Every case paper as well as any evidence in the Briscoe file case were gone. That had to be it. It was the only cold case still open. All his private notes, including the court rulings about the embezzlement and what information he had on the alleged murder of Michael Briscoe, had disappeared.

Before he put anything back, he sat down at his computer and typed up everything that he remembered. His photographic memory came in handy when it came to things like this. He remembered every bit of paper, where it had come from, plus its size and color. He became angry when he realized it would be harder now to prove anything without those hard copies.

Then he had a glimmer of hope and remembered what he had done before he closed his penthouse office. Prior to his move, he had Sally take photos of everything in the Briscoe files before he put them in his safe deposit box.

Chapter Twenty-Eight
THE SAFE DEPOSIT BOX

*T*he night after the robbery, Nevlin dreamed he and Michael had gone to the Keys as they had once planned. Michael and Nevlin were having a lazy afternoon with just the two of them fishing on his boat. He couldn't remember what they had been talking about in his dream but most likely about fishing, running or FSU, like the conversations they always had. He awoke with a smile on his face, thinking about what a nice guy Michael had been. But soon his smile turned to anger when he remembered somehow Bryce turned up in the dream too. He didn't understand why. Suddenly he had a gut feeling of urgency to work on the cold case again and avenge his friend's death.

Why do the good die young? He remembered a song by Billy Joel with a similar title. He thought about how he once compared himself to Bryce when they were younger. It was the day they met on the pier in New York. However, the last time Nevlin had seen him at the courthouse, they were far from looking the same. And they may have been similar in stature and hair coloring at one time, but their personalities were completely different. Bryce was a criminal.

Being clean and sober for several years, Nevlin realized he wasn't anything at all like the person he considered his nemesis in looks or in morals. The dream made him wonder if Michael's instant friendship with him anything had to do with the falling out with his long-time friend, Bryce. *That guy can rot in jail for all I care.*

Nevlin had to stop thinking these absurd thoughts and go for a jog. He needed some fresh air to think about the facts of the break-ins at his office and home. It reminded him of the weird break-in at Bryce's office many years ago. He felt the cool breezes against his face as he ran along San Marco Boulevard then made his turn down River Road. Living by the river with all the palm and fir trees was somewhat bucolic.

Fall was Nevlin's favorite time of year when the leaves had turned their vibrant colors of orange, red, and gold. He had a strong feeling the Briscoe break-in, his own burglary, and Michael's murder were connected. He wanted to find the underlying cause of whoever did this. Bryce couldn't have. He was still in jail. Did he have someone else on the outside to orchestrate this?

He looked again for the Briscoe file. Maybe he had missed it. It wasn't in the usual spot, but perhaps it just got misplaced. After checking all over the room to make sure that hadn't happened, he confirmed it was gone. All his notes, including the closed court rulings about the murder and what he had done to solve Michael's murder, had been taken.

He called the police and was connected to the officer in charge of the San Marco break-ins. "Any hits on those prints you found in my office or home?" Nevlin said.

"Well, as a matter of fact, there were," the officer said. "And you wouldn't believe it."

"Hey, don't I know you?" Nevlin said. "Your voice sounds awfully familiar. What's your name?"

"Mason is the name," he said. "Brady Mason. "Yes, we've met before when I was Alvarez's partner. In Savannah."

"I thought I recognized your voice," Nevlin said. "Now, what's this about fingerprints and something I wasn't going to believe?"

"First, I took over as lead detective after Alvarez retried," Steve said. "And second, as for those prints. We found only partial ones—inconclusive at best, but they belonged to Bryce Elmore."

"Bryce? What the hell? I thought he was still in jail."

"Nope," Brady said. "We thought so too, until we called the pen in Blountstown. Come to find out he'd been released two weeks ago. They'd taken years off his initial sentence due to good behavior."

"I knew it! I had feeling it wasn't the San Marco burglar or a copycat. We've got to get this guy. I know he killed my friend, Michael. I just need someone to help me prove it. This could be the break we need. We now have proof he ransacked my home and office and stole my Briscoe file. He can be arrested, right?"

"No," Brady said. "Wait a minute. You know we can't hold someone on a partial print. We can only bring him in for questioning. They could have been old prints from before, right?"

"No," Nevlin said, "there wouldn't be any reason Bryce's

partial prints would be on those papers found in my house or office. He didn't have access to them." Nevlin paused. "How do we catch this guy, and what did he want with my Briscoe file?"

"Sorry," Brady said. "I'm not sure how we can catch him. I'll have to get back to you on that."

Nevlin, though disappointed, thought of all the proof he once collected. He called the bank to see when he could get into his safe deposit box.

"Anytime the bank is open, sir," the teller said. "Just make sure you have your key and a photo ID with you."

"Okay," Nevlin said. "I'll be right over."

Nevlin was happy he was born with a photographic memory. When he took out the box, he saw that every item he had identified on his computer he had remembered from that file. What stumped him was what was in those papers Bryce needed and why?

The only way to find the underlying cause would be to entrap Bryce somehow and ask him directly. Now that he knew Bryce was out of jail, he needed to think of a way to do that.

Nevlin got up the next morning and sat at his computer mulling over the papers in the box concerning the Briscoe case. Most of it made his mind turn to Michael. His friend had been innocent of nothing more than trusting his old friend, Bryce. Nevlin had lost everything because of that case. Would he be willing to do it all over again? He had to protect himself. He couldn't afford to spend a lot of money again. He only had what he'd saved for his boat and the move south. He had to be smarter to catch Bryce and possibly an accomplice.

He promised himself he would never risk it all again. Besides, in a few months, he would be living the semiretired life in Key West with his charter boat company. He wanted more than anything to forget everything he once lost in Jacksonville and live a simpler life in the Keys.

He decided to call Fred. Maybe his friend would have some ideas.

"Hey, Fred," Nevlin said. "Can you meet me at the Chart House tonight for dinner? I have something I need to discuss with you."

"Sure. Is everything all right?" Fred said. "You sound a little nervous."

"No worries. I certainly don't need a drink. I hope that's not what you're insinuating. Everything is fine. I wanted to talk to you about the Briscoe case. But it's too long to discuss over the phone."

Many years had gone by, and Fred and Nevlin's bond had become closer than ever. Fred had become Nevlin's AA sponsor, and seeing each other on a regular basis had sealed their friendship.

"Why would anyone want to trash your apartment and office?" Fred said after he sat down to dinner. "Why would Bryce want to steal that file?"

"Since the Briscoe case had been singled out from all the rest of the *B*s, it has to be Bryce," Nevlin said. "He's guilty and wants to get rid of the evidence, I suppose."

"Geez, Nev. But with what evidence? None of that was enough to convict him of murder in court, remember? Do you suppose he thinks you have something else on him?"

"That's exactly what I think. Remember, I always thought Bryce was guilty of his own break-in and he also killed Michael. It may not have been arsenic, but it could have been something else. We need to find out it was. A clue has to be in that box."

They finished their dinner and decided that they would meet the next afternoon at Nevlin's office.

Fred came over after lunch, and Nevlin had the photos from his safe deposit box and the sheets of paper he had typed up with additional information.

They went over everything together and looked at all the copies of the records. They couldn't seem to find anything in the Briscoe file that Nevlin hadn't already memorized and typed on his computer the day before.

"Fred, I'd like you to help me. Let's look over these photos and papers again. Something has to be here."

As the two of them shuffled the papers and looked through the copies Sally had made, they talked about everyone involved in the case.

Most had gone on with their lives and were living them happily. In New York, Megan and Erick had gotten married and started a family. Christy had married the wealthy young man from Savannah. Brittney and Steve had a rock-solid relationship with their boys, and Laura hadn't wasted any time getting engaged and living with her new fella after Bryce went to prison.

"We only have the Elmores to look at," Fred said. "The rest of these people live too far away. No one else could have done this."

"I know. I know," Nevlin said. "That's why I'm sure it was Bryce. No one else had a reason. But it has got me thinking."

"About what?" Fred said.

"The *cause* of Michael's death. Could it have been something else? Maybe I've been looking in the wrong place. Maybe Bryce wasn't the murderer. Could it have been someone else?"

"What do you mean?"

"I remember another old case from Georgia. A lab tested for the wrong chemical on a person's body, only to find out later the person in the lab had missed something. I mean, what if there had been another drug that killed Michael? Perhaps we should have the lab test for something other than arsenic."

"Oh, geez, Nevlin. What if this, and what if that. Do you think they still have samples?"

"I'm sure they do. They'd have to because it's still evidence in a cold case, Fred. Someone *did* mess up my apartment, right? And they *stole* the Briscoe file, right? A thief doesn't search for something, find it, and keep it for no reason. They steal it because they found what they were looking for."

"Yeah," Fred said. "You're right. Now, what do you plan to do about it?"

"We need to look through everything again and not stop until we find something," Nevlin said.

The two went over everything again and kept brainstorming.

"How are we going to prove Bryce did this?" Fred said.

"I'm not sure, but there's got to be a way. We've got to be missing something."

"Have you talked to the police about the break-in? Any leads?"

"Yeah, they still haven't found anyone. Of course, they questioned Bryce, and he denied any involvement. They had to let him go even though he couldn't explain why his partial print was on one of the papers."

"Sounds exactly like the Briscoe burglary," Fred said. "Did you ever think of that?"

"Yes," Nevlin said. "That thought did cross my mind. Only a partial print. Hmm. That does seem odd."

They looked at the contents of the box once again. One piece of paper stood out. It was one of the papers left on a piled stack on Michael's desk. Fred set it aside.

"This is like trying to find a needle in a haystack," he said. "What do you make of this paper?" Fred pointed to the paper he had pulled out and laid aside. "If it wasn't Bryce, then could it have been Laura or Brittney?"

"Hey, Fred," Nevlin said. "I think you are on to something. Laura was a registered nurse who worked in a hospital lab when Michael died. She would have had access to any poison."

"Nev, look at this paper. I know you said that Megan thought it was spilled wine. But what if Michael was trying to spell Laura's name?"

"Fred!" Nevlin shouted. "That's it! Laura! You're right. To the naked eye it looks like a check mark of spilled wine, but perhaps Michael *was* trying to tell us something. I bet anything she's the one behind all this."

"She had a motive alright," Fred said. "Gain control of the company by killing her husband's partner and frame Bryce for the murder. She must have found out he was already embezzling from the company."

"Now this is making sense," Nevlin said. "Bryce was so desperate to pin the murder on Christy he didn't even see what Laura had been doing. She had access to different drugs at the hospital, and she also had access to the office safe. She could easily have poisoned Michael by putting something in his wine.

"Witnesses said Michael had been staying late in the office the week he died. He must have let her in. He would have known and trusted her. They must have talked and had a drink like usual. When he wasn't looking, she must have slipped it in his drink. She was the only other person who could have reset the alarm and make it look like a heart attack. Therefore, no foul play had ever been suspected."

"Brilliant!" Fred said. "Now how do we catch her?"

"I'm not sure, but it might take some time. I'm not going to tell the police my theory yet. If correct, we might have to force her into a confession."

"How the hell are we going to do that?" Fred said.

"Well, I'm not sure. But I'll think of something. In the meantime, I'm going to let the police do their own detective work as to who did the robberies. Besides, I have some work of my own to do. I need to close my office and buy a new business in the Keys."

—✺—

Within a few months, Nevlin had closed out all his cases in his small one-man law office. He met Fred at an AA meeting a few days later and explained his progress.

"Fred," Nevlin said. "I want to share with you how I'm going to entrap Laura. I decided to send out invitations for her and her family for a free trip to Key West. They will spend the weekend in the Keys and the Fourth of July on my fishing boat. The only thing is she and her family will be the *only* people winning the trip besides the police.

"Once we get offshore, you'll be my copilot and I'll get her to talk. The police will be wired. Once she confesses, they can take her in."

"Sounds like a great plan," Fred said. "If she falls for it."

"Oh, she will. She goes anywhere her daughter goes. If Brittney and Steve go, then it's a sure bet Laura will go too. Plus, she gets to bring her soon-to-be husband. I think she'll feel safe with no one else aboard except two old fishermen. I'm positive she'll confess."

"What a great way to start your new business!" Fred said. "Finding the real killer of Michael."

"Now that *would* be exciting, wouldn't it?"

Chapter Twenty-Nine

THE INVITATION

rittney, Steve, and the kids had their usual Friday night pizzas at Luigi's. Most of the time Laura and her fiancé, Gregg, would join them. The couple had been together for several years. Laura filed for divorce shortly after Bryce went to prison. The year it became final, Gregg moved in with Laura, and they got engaged.

Brittney liked Gregg enough, but he'd never be a replacement for her dad. She was always cautious around her mother's boyfriends, as they seemed to come and go like the wind. However, Gregg's commitment was lasting, but she wondered if her mother's plans would ever become permanent.

Brittney knew Gregg had asked her mother several times to marry him, but Laura always declined. First, she said it was too early in the relationship, then it was too soon after the divorce, and later there was always some other excuse. Brittney asked her mom about her relationship in front of the group.

"Honey, we're engaged, and we live together," Laura said. "What more do you want? A piece of paper? Why would I want to mess up a good thing?" Laura smiled and made light of the serious question and conversation. She looked straight at Gregg and said, "I like things just the way they are." Then she blew him an air kiss. He caught the imaginary object and put it on his lips.

"Hey!" Gregg said. "I've got an idea! Maybe we could all go to Vegas and get married there."

To which Laura, answered, "We'll see."

Everyone laughed, and Laura changed the subject.

"Hey, Brittney," she said. "I got a strange invitation in the mail last week about a fishing charter boat in the Keys. Guess who it was from? That lawyer, Nevlin, who put your father in prison. I thought that was kind of odd."

"Oh my God," Brittney said. "I got one too, but I threw it away. I don't want anything to do with that man or Megan ever again. You know she and I have never spoken since the trial.

"As for Mr. Nevlin, Mom," Brittney continued, "I know there's been no love lost between you and Dad. Maybe Nevlin knew it, but he has a lot of nerve. After all, he knew how loyal I'd been to Dad throughout the whole case. Maybe he doesn't know I still believe in his innocence."

"Nevlin?" Gregg said. "I've heard of that guy. Isn't he the attorney who lost everything in that case? The man who went into debt trying to pin Michael's murder on Bryce?"

"Yep," Steve said. "He's the one."

"Well, maybe since he couldn't prove anything," Laura said, "he's given up on that idea. I sure hope so. Perhaps he's trying to make amends. I heard he turned his life around and joined AA."

"I bet you are right," Gregg said. "He's sending these invitations to make amends for the wrong he did."

"I think we should all go," Steve said. "Sounds like a fun trip. I've never been to the Keys, but I've always wanted to go."

"Okay," Laura said. "Let's take a vote. Are we all in agreement?" Everyone's hands went up. "Brittney, do you remember the date on the invitation?"

"All I remember is that it's for the Fourth of July weekend," she said.

"Perfect," Steve said. "I'm sure the kids can spend the weekend at my mother's or one of their friend's houses. They'll be plenty of things for them to do around town with parades, barbeques, and the fireworks."

"Great!" Gregg said. "So, the four of us will do it?"

"Yes, agreed," Laura said. "I'll make the flight arrangements."

"Thanks, Mom," Brittney said. "Send me that card, and I'll let Mr. Nevlin know all of us have accepted his invitation."

"Okay, sweetheart," Laura said. "You take care of the hotel reservations. Try to get us adjoining rooms if you can."

The rest of their evening was spent chatting about the future trip for the following month. They discussed the possibilities of where they might stay and other places they might want to visit. Everyone had some idea of a tourist attraction they wanted to see. Brittney wrote their ideas down. On the list were the Hemingway House, Sloppy Joe's Bar and Grill, Jimmy Buffet's Margaritaville Restaurant, and the Tortugas Islands, just south of the Keys. All of them had heard of these places through their friends. They were all excited to go.

The next day Nevlin got the call he had hoped to get.

"Mr. Nevlin, this is Brittney Elmore Warren. My mother asked me to call you."

"Yes" was all he said.

"We wanted you to know that the four of us, my mother, her fiancé, Gregg, Steve, and I, have accepted your invitation. We'll be happy to meet you in the Keys and go on your charter boat for a fishing trip."

"That's wonderful!" Nevlin said.

"It sounded great to us too," Brittney said, "considering none of us have ever been there before. Mr. Nevlin. I just wanted to ask you one question."

"Yes? What is it?"

"May I ask why you are doing this for us?"

"Well, several years ago I joined AA," Nevlin said. "Perhaps you read about it in the newspapers? No matter. Are you knowledgeable on the Twelve-Step Program associated with it?" Nevlin never gave her a chance to answer any of his questions and just kept talking. "In Step Nine, you must make amends to any people you have harmed. I've always wanted to make this up to you and your family. I couldn't until now."

"Well, thank you very much. My family is very appreciative of that. We're looking forward to it."

When Nevlin got off the phone, he had to chuckle. He'd been lying. Of course, Step Nine was as he described it. It was the correct step, but he had completed that years ago. He never had any intentions to make amends to Bryce or his family. The only thing he ever wanted to do was put the real killer of Michael Briscoe behind bars.

Chapter Thirty

THE MOVE

*N*evlin called his best friend. "Hey, Fred! They took the bait!"

"Well, what'd ya know? Now what are you going to do?"

"Besides call the police and let them in on it?" Nevlin said. "After I've explained my plan, I'll let them figure out the rest of the details. Now I need to hurry and get ready for my move. I only have a little over a month to rent a trailer, pack all my stuff, and drive it down to the Keys. I'll call you when I get there. Hope you'll come down for that Fourth of July visit."

"You better count on it," Fred said. "Perhaps for the first time, I'll leave the wife home alone."

"I think that would be best," Nevlin said. "It might be a dangerous mission."

The weather had been warming up in early June. Nevlin noticed how the alligators had been sunbathing on the backroads leading to his favorite Arnold Palmer golf course in Palm Coast. He'd often seen those critters come out from the water holes on several different occasions.

Nevlin looked forward to his new gig, as he called it. He would miss some of his golfing buddies but would make new friends farther south. He took most of his business suits and ties over to the Goodwill. Someone could still get use out of them. He promised himself that he would never wear a suit and tie again. From now on, the only thing in his closet would be his casual wear: cargo shorts or Docker khakis, T-shirts or polos, flip-flops or dress sandals with an extra pair of each on his boat. As for the few high-end clothes, he donated them to the Cancer Society thrift shop in honor of Beverly.

Next, he bought himself a used medium-size truck. He only needed one big enough to haul a small trailer behind it. It only took him a day to organize everything in piles for the donations and those he needed to pack from his apartment. Once the truck and the trailer were filled, he felt the happiest he'd been in years. He was only a day away from living his dream.

The landlady, Mrs. Hansen, who knew of his move, told him he could drop off his keys anytime. She only requested that if he left late to drop them in her mailbox. But he didn't feel right about it and felt it too impersonal.

He walked downstairs and rang her bell.

"Mrs. Hansen?" he said.

"Yes, son," she said. "What is it?"

"I know you told me I could drop the keys off in your mailbox, but I wanted to say good-bye to you in person."

"Well, of course," Mrs. Hansen said. "I wish you the best of luck, Wade. Thank you for telling me when you were leaving. I already have a tenant lined up. I'm not sure they'll be as great as you."

"Oh, I'm sure he or she will be just fine."

When he had told Mrs. Hansen of his move, she quickly called her sister in Key West. Her elder sister, Mrs. Nielsen, and her had been neighbors in Jacksonville and raised their families together. After Mrs. Nielsen became a widow, she moved to the Keys to be closer to her grandchildren. She owned a house on Front Street, and it so happened she needed a tenant as well as a handyman. If Nevlin could do the odd jobs around her house and repair her broken dock, he could live in the back house for free.

"Thanks for your keys," Mrs. Hansen said.

"Well, thank you for this great opportunity," Nevlin said.

"Whatcha goin' do next?" Mrs. Hansen said.

"I have one special stop on my way," Nevlin said. "I hope to pick up a dog at the humane society to keep me company on my drive south. I promise I'll keep in touch when I get settled in my new home."

"Please do that. I'd love to hear from you. Best of luck!"

"Thanks, Mrs. Hansen," he said and gave her a big hug. "I'll miss you too."

Nevlin went to his office, locked up, and gave his keys to the building manager. After he left River Street, he went on his way to the pound. He thought about how lucky it was that he wouldn't have to live in an apartment in the Keys.

When he arrived at the humane society, he thought about the kind of dog he wanted. He didn't care which breed. He would just go by his gut feeling and the personality of the dog. He loved dogs but had never had one since the boys were young. After that dog got hit by a car, no one ever wanted a dog again.

He walked inside the pound and looked around. He spied a shy golden retriever who was hunched in a corner in the last kennel.

"Hi, girl," he said to her. She wagged her tail a bit but refused to move.

He asked the attendant, "What's wrong with this beauty?"

"Oh, you mean Sandy?" she said. "Sad story. She lived with this man for years, and when he died alone in his house, she lay with him for days until someone found them. The man had no relatives to take the dog, so we got her. Sweet dog, though, just shy."

"And I suppose a little traumatized too. I'll take her."

Nevlin had always been a sucker for sad stories, especially any pertaining to animals. He wanted to be Sandy's next companion.

"I suppose we both could use a little cheering up and a change of scenery, huh, girl?" he said to the dog as the attendant let her out of the cage. "We're going on a long ride in the car!" The dog wagged her tail again and rubbed up against him. She looked happy to be out of the cage. She sat next to him. His heart melted when the dog looked at him with her deep-set eyes. She acted like she knew what he was telling her.

Nevlin paid for the dog, got whatever shots she needed, then paid for the license and other official papers. They went outside, and the lab went straight to the passenger side as if she knew what was about to happen. Nevlin opened the door, and she jumped into the truck. He rolled down the window so Sandy could put her head out. It stayed glued there until Nevlin stopped every couple of hours to let her out for a walk.

He had purchased a few bowls, some dog food, and a leash

before he'd stopped to get her. Nevlin laughed watching Sandy stick her head and tongue out the window. She appeared to be enjoying the ocean breezes as if lapping up salt water. They traveled down the A1A for miles past Ponte Vedra and St. Augustine before hopping on the interstate.

Seven hours later, after driving through Miami, Nevlin knew it wouldn't be long before they arrived at their destination. He had only been to the Keys once before but had never forgotten them. It was a paradise of its own—little towns on little islands called Keys with names connected only by bridges. They were so close to the water you could almost hop in the ocean from your car. Of course, there was no stopping on the bridges.

Nevlin's devoted love for the water only made it more perfect to live here. He hoped Sandy would love it just as much. He had a good feeling about his new companion. Every time they'd stop and get out of the car, Sandy would run toward the water. It seemed the lab was born to love the beach. What a great name the man had given her, Nevlin thought.

He stopped at a CVS store and purchased a frisbee. Sandy loved it. She must have played with one before, he thought. He wanted to see if she knew how to play catch. They had to wait until they drove over the seven-mile bridge just after Marathon Key, the longest bridge before Key West. He remembered the large public beach after Marathon and decided to stop.

Nevlin was right. Sandy knew what to do with the Frisbee, and they had a ball playing catch. After several minutes of romping with her, Nevlin said, "Okay, girl, only a few more miles to go! We've got to scoot!"

They arrived at Mrs. Nielsen's house shortly before dark. Nevlin had made contact with her prior to leaving. He had called her again from a pay phone in Marathon right before stopping at a burger joint to eat. He wanted to let her know they had already eaten and would be arriving soon.

Once in Key West, he knocked on her door. "Hey, y'all," Mrs. Nielsen said. "I've been expecting the two of you." She looked down. "And who's this pretty thing?"

"That's Sandy," Nevlin said.

The dog nuzzled right up to her. Mrs. Nelsen petted her head and back. Sandy jumped and kissed her, approving of the affection and attention.

"She's a great dog," Nevlin said, "and friendly too, as you can see. We've been making friends on the way down. Though it wasn't hard, I might add."

"It sure will be nice to have a dog around here," she said. "Always liked 'em, but now I'm too old to take care of one myself." Mrs. Nielsen petted the dog again, who responded with more licks of love and lots of happy wags.

"Here're your keys, Mr. Nevlin," she said. "Have a good night."

"Yes, ma'am," Nevlin said. "I'm sure we will. But please call me Wade. It'll be nice to have people call me by my first name from now on. Less formal."

"Okay, Wade," Mrs. Nelson said. "I'm sure it was a long drive and you're mighty tired."

"Yes, ma'am," Nevlin said. "Thank you!"

He turned around, walked back to his parking space, and got his suitcases out of his truck. He remembered to get his valuables from the trailer and then locked everything. Sandy followed him inside the one-bedroom bungalow, small but adequate for his needs. He had only seen pictures that Mrs.

Hansen had shown him. He and Sandy couldn't have found a better place for the two of them. He threw down his keys on the nightstand and stripped to his boxers. It didn't take long before the two of them had crashed on the queen-size bed.

They awoke the next day about six in the morning when the sun came up. Nevlin was thankful he didn't have to go out and purchase furniture. The place came fully furnished. In the short distance, he could hear people's laughter on the street and boats' horns and the revving of their engines out on the ocean. He hadn't realized how early he would be hearing those sounds at his new place.

"Time for our morning walk, girl," Nevlin said. "We need to do some grocery shopping too. Our cupboards are bare!"

The two of them walked over to Eaton Street and found a mini-mart close by. Nevlin, who had never really been interested in women since Beverly, found himself attracted to women for the first time. Everywhere he and Sandy went, women stopped and commented,

"May I pet your dog?"

"Of course," Nevlin would answer. He was happy to be living in a place where people were dog friendly. If the conversation went further, and it usually did, the women would ask if he were new in town. He always answered in the politest way how he moved to the Keys to start a new charter boat company. He met more people walking down the streets of Key West than he had anywhere else. The more he walked, the more he thought about how he was going to love his new town. Purchasing Sandy had been a bonus.

After getting the grocery items he needed, he and Sandy headed back to the bungalow. He unpacked the food and talked to his new companion.

"After I cook breakfast, it'll be time to tackle the truck and trailer," he said. Sandy lay down and put her paws over her ears as if she had understood. "It's okay, girl," Nevlin said with a laugh. "You don't have to help."

The lab gave out a sigh as if saying, "Thank goodness I don't have to help. I'm exhausted."

After bringing all his boxes inside near the front door, Nevlin decided he'd scrub the bungalow down before putting anything in it. He was sure Mrs. Nielsen had cleaned it to the best of her ability, but he'd feel better giving it another once-over.

Nevlin had been a clean freak no matter where he lived. Mrs. Nielsen told him there hadn't been any tenants in there for months. She had only done some surface cleaning for him. There wasn't much to the place. Just about a thousand square feet, like his last place in Jacksonville. The biggest difference were the abundance of the tropical fruit trees, native palms, fragrant orchids, and other sweet-smelling flowers surrounding the property. Another reason to love it.

"Time to unpack, Sandy," he said. "You stay here." The dog's behavior showed she had been well taken care of. Nevlin was happy she knew all his commands. He was thankful the previous owner had loved the dog and provided for her. Next, he prayed Sandy would love being on the ocean as well as she loved being on the beach. *Tomorrow we'll find out*, he thought.

The next day, Nevlin went by himself over to the charter boat company. He let his dog sleep on his bed while he was gone. He walked to the man's house who had sold him the charter company. He had been working for Nevlin the past few months until he got down to the Keys to take over. Nevlin was now the new owner, and the man could take his official retirement.

Everything went as planned, and all the transfer papers were signed. Nevlin had owned a Bayliner cabin cruiser before, so he knew his way around boats. The larger charter boat would be big enough to fit six or eight people for fishing. They could comfortably fit their gear either in the front or in the back, and there was plenty of room inside for those who did not want to fish. People could hook their rods, fix the bait, or ice their catch without tripping over one another.

The man gave Nevlin the keys. "Wanna take her out for a run?" he asked.

"Sure," Nevlin said. "Don't mind if I do. Care to go with me for one last ride?"

"Would love it," the old man said.

The two of them left the marina, and the man showed Nevlin the best places to take people fishing.

"How's the business been doing?" Nevlin asked.

"Just like I said on the phone," he said. "Pretty stable. Tourists love to come down here and see if they can catch a big one, but unfortunately this boat can't hold that kind of fish. Everyone seems happy, though, with whatever they catch, especially the kids. I get a kick out the little ones. Seeing the smiles on their faces whenever they land a fish of any size is amazing!"

"Sounds like I'm going to love my new job," Nevlin said.

"Oh, you'll love it," he said. "I promise!"

Chapter Thirty-One

THE NEW JOB AND A PLAN

Sandy jumped up on Nevlin, licking his face as the sun came in the window. "I love you too, gal," he said. "Today we're going to find out what kind of sea legs you have."

After his ride with the previous owner the day before, he'd been anxious to go it alone with Sandy. He'd copy the same path where Ned, the previous owner, had said the good fishing could be found. He had a map, a navigator, and depth finder on the boat, plus all the other required licenses and equipment, such as life preservers.

"Sandy, you're in for a treat today!" Nevlin said. "We're going fishing!"

They walked down to the docks and hopped on board. Nevlin couldn't wait to put the key in the ignition and start the boat. He couldn't remember the last time he felt so good. Sandy seemed to feel right at home on board the boat as well.

"Hey, Sandy!" he said. "What shall we call our boat?" The dog turned her head from side to side as Nevlin mentioned a few names. Her ears flopped as if listening and voting. The previous owner had already removed the old name, so Nevlin had a chance to call it whatever he wanted.

"Beverly," he said, and the dog barked with agreement. "Yes, that's right, girl. We're going name her after the love of my life. Glad you agree!" He talked to the dog like a person would talk to a friend. Of course, Sandy had no idea who Beverly was or the fact Sandra had been her middle name. Nevlin thought it had been another omen, however.

"Let's go, partner," he said, as he revved up the engines. "It's a fantastic day for a ride along the coast." He'd been so excited about the first ride with the dog that he hadn't picked up any fishing gear or bait. It turned out to be just a fun ride.

It was amazing. They rode out to sea far enough to see a bale of turtles in the distance. Nevlin drove around the Keys for a while longer before they headed back. Soon there was a pod of dolphins in their wake which surrounded the boat on both sides.

The lab barked at the dolphins when they got too close. Some swam away when they heard her bark and the boat sped up. Four others swam on both sides for a couple more miles. They jumped and played in the water, while Sandy barked whenever the dolphins splashed him.

"Good girl," he said. "You tell them…not too close."

It took Nevlin another half hour to get to the marina. "Wow!" he said. "That was an exciting tour!" He heard his stomach growl and remembered they'd forgotten to stop for food or eat breakfast. "Let's go get something to eat. Isn't sea life wonderful?"

He piloted the boat into the marina. "Bet you're hungry, huh, girl?" he asked the dog. "Me too! We'll eat at the first diner we see. Promise."

After docking the boat, the two of them walked into the central part of the city. Nevlin looked for a place that welcomed dogs. The more he walked, the more he enjoyed Key West and the people he met. He couldn't imagine a friendlier place.

He stopped in at the Key West Bait and Tackle Shop, which had a little café on the outside. After ordering food and drink of a soda, fries, and two burgers, he handed Sandy the plain patty from one of them.

"We'll eat our food here, girl," he said. "I can pick up the gear and bait later."

After eating, Nevlin got advice on what kind of fishing tackle he needed for his charter business and the best kind of bait. He bought what he'd been advised and strolled back to the boat. They got on board and went out again on the ocean. He wanted to try out his equipment and see if the man had told him the truth. If they were lucky, he'd catch a yellowtail or black fin tuna, but he'd settle for a grouper or red snapper. Fresh fish sounded good for dinner.

His first day out proved not to be so lucky. But it was a good day anyway. This was only the beginning, and he figured he'd have plenty more days like this to find out. He'd seen a few sharks and thought maybe they'd scared the other fish away. When Sandy and he came back to shore and docked, the two of them shopped for more groceries to grill on the barbeque at his new back house.

Later, Nevlin spoke to Mrs. Nielsen when she came out of her house. He invited her to have dinner with them, but she declined.

"Oh no, thank you," Mrs. Nielsen said. "I've already eaten. But mind if I sit and watch you grill? I could watch Sandy for you while you're cooking."

"That's mighty nice of you," Nevlin said.

While the landlady kept an eye on Sandy and watched him cook his steaks, Nevlin asked her how long she thought it would take to get a phone line hooked up.

"Oh, shouldn't take longer than a few days," she said. "Want me to call them and set it up for you?"

"Thank you. That would be nice."

While Nevlin went inside and popped a few potatoes in the microwave, Mrs. Nelsen played fetch with Sandy until they both got tired. Sandy lay at her feet while the landlord kicked off her shoes and massaged them in the grass.

Nevlin came out and said it was time for him and the dog to eat.

"Oh, don't mind me," Mrs. Nielsen said. "I have dessert for you in the kitchen. I'll be right back."

"Thank you," Nevlin said. "You shouldn't have."

Mrs. Nielsen scurried into her house and came out carrying a round dish with her hot pads. "I know you won't refuse an old lady's welcome gift of a homemade apple pie, would you?"

"Definitely not," he said as she passed him the pie. "Thank you so much."

"Care for some coffee to go with it? I just made a pot in the house."

"No, thanks," Nevlin said. "I think I'm going to have to save this for tomorrow." He turned and walked into his house. He thought it a sweet gesture of Mrs. Neilson to bake him a pie. *Just hope she doesn't become too much of a busybody,* he thought.

"We can't be eating too many pieces of these," he said to the dog once inside. "We'll get fat. Let's freeze them for special occasions." The aroma from the pie almost drove Nevlin crazy. He could smell it had just the right amount of candy apple cinnamon like the ones Beverly used to bake. But he resisted the temptation. After cleaning up the dinner dishes, he cut individual slices and put them in his freezer.

Nevlin and Sandy nestled together on the small sofa to watch TV. He looked forward to another day in Key West, but with all the bars he saw around town, he needed to look for an AA meeting more than anything. It might be more difficult than he thought. He had failed to check out that information before he had left Jacksonville. While walking around town earlier in the day, he noticed a bar located on almost every street corner. There were more bars located between every other store. *That's what I get moving to a tourist town,* he thought.

The next day he made arrangements to paint his new name on his fishing boat. He needed to keep busy before the grand opening of his new business. He didn't have a timeline as to when that would happen, but he wanted it as soon as possible.

He had found the initial stencils to paint on the boat and the brushes he needed before heading toward the docks. Sandy came bounding down to the marina after him. Nevlin thought it best to tie Sandy up while he painted. He didn't want her to spill any paint where it didn't belong. It was going to be a messy job without her helping.

He raised the boat up out of the water with his hoist and turned it around so that he could sit on the dock to do the painting. B-E-V-E-R-L-Y. The job didn't take long, but it needed several hours to dry. He put the paint and stencils back in the tackle box, and he and Sandy walked home.

"Come on, girl. Let's go for a walk." They walked around the town looking for the information center. He knew he could find a place without asking anyone. He had been correct. Instead of the tourist center, he found something better. It was a place called the Anchors Away Club on Virginia Street for recovering alcoholics. Anchors Aweigh had once been a bar, but it had been converted to a snack shop and a place for people like Nevlin to socialize.

He looked on the bulletin posted next to the door. A list of all the meeting times had been posted. There was one every day of the week. *How fantastic,* he thought. *This might not be a bad place after all.*

A few days later, his phone line had been installed in his bungalow. He called both his sons and gave them his new address and phone number.

"How's it going, Dad?" Todd asked.

"Better than expected," he answered. "I love it here. Got myself a dog too!"

"Wow! A new boat *and* a new dog! What kind of dog, and what did you name her?"

"She's a golden Labrador Retriever, and her name is Sandy. Speaking of names…can you guess what I named the boat?"

"No. What?"

"The Beverly."

"Oh, Dad," Todd said. "Mom would have loved that. How sweet."

"Thanks, Todd. Okay. Gotta go. I need to call your brother on the West Coast while the time is still early."

"Good to hear from you, Dad," Todd said. "Call me again once you're more settled and ready for the Nevlin family from Chicago to invade your privacy."

"Okay," his father said. "Love you too, son." He hung up

and called Dan.

His second conversation didn't go over as well as the first. He didn't understand why. First, he couldn't comprehend why Dan got so mad that his father had named his boat the Beverly. Then Dan questioned him as to why he would want a dog.

"Why would you want to take care of a dog, Dad?" Dan said. "I thought you were through with dogs a long time ago. You must feed them, wash them, take them on walks, and take them to the vet when they are sick. I thought this was a sort of retirement. Doesn't sound like much of a retirement to me. Won't an animal tie you down?"

"It's too late, son," Nevlin said. "I love dogs. Always have and always will. I just wasn't in the right frame of mind to have one before, and now it makes me happy. Aren't you happy for me?"

"You know I am," Dan said. "I just want what's best for you. I thought it might be too much with a new company and all."

Nevlin didn't need to argue with his son. They had had enough of that in the past, and he wanted to keep it there. They never really agreed completely. Maybe when his son came out for a visit, he would see for himself how happy he was with his business and how much he loved Sandy.

"Thanks, son, but I couldn't be happier," he said. "And Sandy makes for a great companion. We've bonded like she's been mine for years."

"Okay, Dad," Dan said. "I believe you."

His next phone call went to Fred. He knew Fred could cheer him up.

"Hey, Fred!" Nevlin said. "How ya doin'?"

"Great! How 'bout yourself?"

"Couldn't be better!" Nevlin said. "I love it down here. And

Sandy does too."

"Sandy? You got yourself a girlfriend already? You haven't even been there a week!"

"No," Nevlin said with a laugh. "Told you I was getting a dog, and she's a beauty. A golden Labrador Retriever. Wait till you come down and see her."

"That sounds great. Hey…been to any meetings yet?"

"No, but I now know where and when they are. Thought I'd go to one tomorrow night. Promise."

"And what about your plan? Have you got that figured out yet?"

"Well, not in its entirety, but I'm working on it."

"You better hurry up. The Fourth is coming up soon."

"Fred," Nevlin said, "I have a favor to ask. Go to the Jacksonville PD and ask for Detective Brady Mason. I talked to him last week about this. He let me know my theory was correct. Another toxicology report showed ethylene glycol in Michael's system. It had to be Laura. She came to his office the night after I left. They had wine, and she poisoned him with what she had stolen from her lab."

"She was right in front of our faces the whole time," Fred said. "I wouldn't have believed it, but now it makes sense."

"Yep. Bryce stole that file from my office not to hide his guilt but to prove his innocence. His wife had framed him."

"I'll talk to Lt. Mason in the morning," Fred said. "I'll make sure they're sending down a couple of officers to extradite her."

"And I'll make sure my plan is ready down on this end," Nevlin said. "Thanks, Fred."

Chapter Thirty-Two

THE CAPTURE

*N*evlin was hard at work getting his business ready to open. He made signs on his computer and walked around town posting the ads everywhere he could. Sandy enjoyed walking with him. He even mentioned it at Anchors Aweigh, where he had developed some new friendships, and at St. Paul's Episcopal Church, where he'd started attending his AA meetings. His ads explained to any who were interested to give him a call and a date would be set for a day of fishing or snorkeling.

It didn't take longer than one day to get his first scheduled appointment. Soon the calendar on his fridge with a photo of the Beverly and Sandy on top was filled for the rest of June. July had started to get filled too. He had to tell many people that the weekend of the Fourth of July was already taken.

This was his semiretirement, and he didn't want to fill up all his days. He chose to work on Mondays, Wednesdays, and Fridays, with an occasional day on the weekend. He never wanted to work full-time again, although being out on the ocean was nothing like working. He couldn't believe he finally was living the life for which he had saved.

The weekend of the Fourth was when the Elmore family would come down. He knew there would be plenty of excitement then. He called Fred.

"You will be coming down on the Fourth to help me, right?" Nevlin said.

"Of course," Fred said. "We just talked about this. You nervous?"

"A little," he said.

"Well, don't be," his friend said. "I wouldn't miss this for the world. Haven't made my flight arrangements yet, but I'll call you back when I do. You'll be picking me up, yes?"

"Correct," Nevlin said. "I'll bet I'm looking forward to this more than you are."

The days quickly passed with all his charter assignments going well. The people had been satisfied with the accommodations on board, the rental equipment he provided, plus the snacks and drinks he brought for his guests. Everything was included in the fee. His advertisement postings did mention they would be alcohol-free excursions, so his charter boat outings attracted primarily families with kids. The kids were surprised a dog was on board, and they all loved Sandy. Some of the kids got bored with fishing, so it gave them an added distraction while their parents continued angling.

The Fourth of July arrived. Nevlin had contacted the local police again and explained the story of the cold case from Jacksonville. The Keys PD told him that they had already been contacted by the police up north. They planned to send two plainclothes officers to act as other tourists on the boat.

"Great!" Nevlin said. "This puts my mind at ease. My

friend, Fred, will also be with me. He's a retired detective from Jacksonville. Glad the 'field' will be even." It was the first time Nevlin could chuckle a little about it and hide his fear of what could go wrong.

The memory of the day Bryce went to prison was as if it happened yesterday. He knew he had gone to prison only for the embezzlement. He was guilty of that. But he had been sure for years that he had also killed Michael. Now he realized he had focused his hatred on the wrong person. He wanted more than anything to get this over with, so he could truly celebrate living in the Keys and forgetting the past.

He picked up Fred from Key West International airport.

"How was your flight?" Nevlin said.

"The usual. But the bonus was the hour-long flight from Miami. It was fantastic! What a clear view of the ocean. I can really understand why you love it here so much."

"Sorry my truck is a little crowded," Nevlin said. "My Ford pickup wasn't made for two men *and* a dog. Good thing you don't have much luggage. That duffel bag will fit fine in the back bed."

Fred laughed. "No problem. I travel light. It's just the right size for me. Sandy can sit on my lap, if she wants."

"Oh, I forgot," Nevlin said. "Sandy, meet Fred. Fred, meet Sandy. No, girl." Nevlin addressed the dog. "No lap sittin' for you. Jump behind the seat."

After they rode back to the bungalow, Nevlin realized it was time for lunch.

"Hungry?" Nevlin said. "I know this neat little restaurant where we can go with Sandy. I know you've never been to Key West before, so take in the sights as we walk. Everything's super convenient and within walking distance."

They stopped at the house, and Nevlin introduced Fred to Mrs. Nielsen.

"He'll be staying for the long weekend," Nelvin said. "We're just dropping off his bag."

"Any friend of Wade's is a friend of mine," Mrs. Nielsen said. "Nice meeting you, and welcome to the Keys!"

Nevlin had made many friends in a short period of time. It felt good to have so many people greet him as he walked down the street.

"Well, aren't we the popular ones?" Fred said, referring to Nevlin and Sandy.

"I must say," Nevlin said, "Sandy had a big part in that. She's got to be the friendliest dog I've known. People are so attracted to her."

The two sat by the water near the wharf and watched the boats coming and going. Most of them left the harbor to scout out the perfect spot they'd return to the following day for the fireworks spectacular. The town's people had told Nevlin what a great traditional show they had. The town played patriotic music in coordination with the sky displays. It could be seen and heard by everyone in a boat with a ham radio.

"When I found out about their custom," Nevlin told Fred. "I made sure my boat got a ham radio too. I'd never heard of that idea before, but it's a marvelous one. I can't wait to see it."

"Sounds like I'm in for a treat," Fred said.

The parade started early the next morning right on time. People lined the streets, and vendors handed out free mini American flags. Fred, Nevlin, and Sandy joined the festivities. They watched, waved, and cheered as everyone marched or rode by. The military came with their army tanks, the Girl and Boy Scouts marched in lines, the vets rode in cars, and the local high school band played with their majorettes twirling their batons and throwing them into the air.

After the parade, the three of them had a light lunch at home before they had to meet the Elmore family at the marina. The fireworks wouldn't start until after eight o' clock, so the plan was to go fishing in the late afternoon. The boat would anchor somewhere offshore, have a light dinner, and then wait for the fireworks to begin.

Nevlin decided to leave Sandy at home. He didn't know how she would respond to the fireworks with all the people screaming and cheering. The arrest might scare her too, he thought, and the parade was enough excitement for one day.

The Elmores showed up right on time at four in the afternoon. The plainclothes men too, with their fishing garb on, came a few minutes afterward. They introduced themselves to everyone with first names, saying that they were only down for the Fourth. The Elmores said they were too and that they were excited Mr. Nevlin had invited them on this excursion.

"I normally only allow six people," Nevlin said. "But there is definitely room for eight. We can make it work. Hop aboard, ladies and gentlemen."

He drove out to his closest fishing spot, and everyone fished for a couple of hours.

Before Fred had flown down, Nevlin had gotten word from Brady Mason explaining more details that hadn't been previously known.

"I went through the files again," Brady said. "It appears no one ever asked Laura at the trial whether she had the combination for Bryce's office safe or the keys to the building. She had had access to both. She could have staged that break-in and locked up after she killed Michael. We questioned Bryce again. He was able give us more evidence and the motive we need to arrest her."

The day of the planned trip, Nevlin couldn't get those words out of the back of his mind. It did make him nervous this was finally happening. But he was satisfied the police had the requirements they needed to put Laura away for the death of his friend. He was also happy he didn't need her to confess.

After several hours of fishing, Nevlin announced, "You can put your fishing rods away and have a few bites to eat now," he announced. "Sandwiches and snacks are in the little cooler, and the cold drinks are in the big one."

The men and women ate their light dinners on the boat while watching the beautiful sunset.

"This is the best Fourth of July," Brittney said. "I've never experienced anything like it."

"Me neither," Steve said. "This is something I'll never forget. What a cool idea for the music to play in tandem to the fireworks."

"Yes, I can't wait for them to begin," Gregg said.

The fireworks displayed with the music were remarkable. Everyone seemed to enjoy it.

"How long will this go on?" Laura asked. "These are the longest fireworks I've ever seen."

"About thirty minutes," Nevlin said. "We've got about ten more minutes to go. I'm sure you'll remember this moment for the rest of your life."

"Really?" Laura asked.

As the fireworks were coming to a close, one of the police officers stood up in the boat.

"Laura Elmore, I'm placing you under arrest for the murder of Michael Briscoe," he said. "You have the right to remain silent." He finished reading her the Miranda rights as the other police officer flashed his badge and told her to put her hands behind her back. When she compiled, he placed the handcuffs on her.

"Oh, Mother!" Brittney cried out. "What the hell is going on?""

"Shut up, Brittney," Laura said and gave her a sneer. She wiggled once the handcuffs were locked as if trying to break free.

"Better sit down, missy," the officer said. "We're going back to town where some other officers will extradite you back to Jacksonville."

Laura's family gasped and looked perplexed. They wondered what was going on and who else had been in on the trap.

The other officer told Nevlin, "Get your motor going and make it snappy."

"Yes, sir," Nevlin told the officer. He nodded and signaled to Fred to pull up the anchor. When it was on board, Nevlin revved up the engines and drove the boat with a speed he'd never used before. He went as fast as he could while remaining safe. He couldn't hear a word being said by anyone in the seats behind him. Fred whispered in his ear that the family members were trying to get Laura's attention, but she refused to lift her head or talk to any of them.

When the marina was in sight and the sound of the motor became softer, he overheard Laura say, keeping her head down,

"I didn't do it. Y'all know it was your father."

"Now look who's turn it is to shut up," Brittney said to her mom. Fred told Nevlin later he thought Brittney looked pissed. Laura never responded or said another word to anyone as they docked.

When they got off the boat, Nevlin noticed Laura's fiancé, Gregg, stare at her like he'd never met the woman. He looked like he wanted to get as far away as possible. Brittney and Steve clung to each other like their world had just crumbled.

Police cars filled with Jacksonville officers were on the shore waiting. Everyone exited, except for Laura with the local police, so Nevlin and Fred could finish mooring the boat. The officers untied Laura from the starboard side railing and walked her down the platform to shore. They took her to the patrol car parked at the far end of the marina. She was ignored by her family and fiancé like Bryce had once been when he was hauled off to prison.

"Happy Fourth of July," Nevlin yelled to his passengers. "I know it's one I'll never forget."

Brittney, Steve, and Gregg ignored his remark. Laura twisted out of the grips of the officers. With her hands still in cuffs behind her back, she turned and pointed double middle fingers at Nevlin. The officers jerked her back around before she could say or do anything more and pushed her into the waiting squad car.

About the Author

Sue Andrews retired in 2010 after forty years in education. She taught elementary school for ten years before getting her first master's degree in Deaf education and then spent her last thirty years dedicating her life to working with deaf children as a teacher, program specialist, and principal.

When not writing or traveling, Andrews currently involves herself with volunteer programs. She primarily devotes her time between the Inland Empire California Writers Club, of which she is currently president, and the WomenHeart and American Heart Association, publicly speaking at events to share her heart episodes and teach women how to be more proactive about their heart health. She and her husband are both involved in their church, St. Mark's Episcopal of Upland.

Andrews lives in San Antonio Heights, California, with her husband, Ken, and their puggle, Wiley.